Dedication

For my parents, who filled our house with books and never limited our reading choices – I wish you were here to read mine, Mom.

Author's Note

This book is a work of fiction. The characters, incidents, dialogue, buildings and businesses are all drawn from the author's imagination and are not to be construed as real. Any similarity to actual events or persons is purely coincidental and unintended.

However, the White Mountain National Forest, Mount Washington, Mount Lafayette, Cannon Mountain, and Interstate 93 are actual places, as are the hiking trails and towns mentioned in this book. The New Hampshire Investigative Services Bureau exists and consists of dedicated professionals, however I have taken some liberties with their procedures where it suited the plot, and any inaccuracies are mine alone.

Acknowledgements

So many people have helped me bring this book from dream to reality. My husband John, who understood I needed to write and provided me with the space and time to do so (and overlooked the dust-bunnies on the floor when the writing was going too well to stop.) My daughter Jennifer, who edited my book for grammar and punctuation and gave valuable advice on tone. My son John, who shared his professional knowledge as a police officer regarding procedural questions. My sister Sharon, who took my headshots and made me look far more glamorous than my day to day self. My first readers, Lynne, Wendy and Nancy, who gave valuable input and priceless encouragement. My friend Cathy (TOC – the other Cathy) who supported me through the ups and downs of blogging and Jenny who gave advice on how to survive riding the roller coaster of self-promotion. And finally to my publisher, Oak Tree Press for all the anxious questions they answered and the wonderful support they provided.

CHAPTER ONE

The body of a fully clad young woman was found on Mt. Lafayette at eleven AM on Monday, May 30th. Its finding was due more to Kenny Brainerd's colossal ineptitude rather than any skilled search effort.

Kenny had arrived in Lincoln, New Hampshire, on Sunday afternoon to follow his new hobby of 'peak bagging'- climbing as many three thousand foot mountains as possible during his week's vacation. He'd targeted the Presidentials in Franconia Notch State Park for his initial assault.

To prepare for this trip, Kenny spent exhaustive hours researching proper hiking gear. He studied the REI, EMS, and LL Bean catalogues. He joined climbers' chat groups and posted questions. By the time he arrived in Lincoln, he was equipped with the most advanced state-of-the art gear available. He had a backpack with a built-in water bladder so he could hydrate as he hiked. He had a fleece-lined gore-tex jacket that was windproof, waterproof, and warm down to twenty degrees. He had custom made hiking boots and moisture wicking socks. He'd wavered between purchasing a walking stick or trekking poles but – after some surreptitious sessions in front of his bedroom mirror – he had decided on the polished, hand-carved, iron tipped walking stick favored by professional Himalayan Mountain

Guides.

"My goal is thirty peaks by my thirty-third birthday," Kenny told his skeptical co-workers. "If I do five during this vacation week and one a week for the rest of the summer, I should reach my goal, no sweat."

Kenny researched hotels to call 'home base' with equal care. The Mountain Glen Hotel wasn't the newest hotel in Lincoln, and it didn't have hot tubs, a four star restaurant, or a game room; but it did have something that trumped all these other amenities. It had Kurt Pelletier. Kurt, whose craggy face could have been a prototype for the famous "Old Man" of Franconia Notch, had led guide services in the White Mountains for over forty years before going into the hotel business. He'd headed the search and rescue team out of Lincoln for so long that it was simply known as Kurt's Crew. And he gave twice yearly, sold-out classes on survival in the wild.

Kenny thought his hotel had to be where all the serious 'baggers parked their packs, and the place to rub elbows with the best, so that's where he headed. Monday morning he sat in the dining room finishing his breakfast – a sustaining meal of pancakes, bacon, eggs, and home fries, suitable fare for a major hike – and trying to engage Kurt in conversation.

"I'm going to start with Mt. Lafayette today," he said, pushing wisps of brown hair off his forehead with pudgy fingers. "I figure that'll be a good warm-up. Next I'll do some of the smaller Presidentials and end up with the big one, Mt Washington, by the end of the week."

Kenny waited for a response, pushing his lower lip out when none came.

"I was thinking I'd go up the Falling Waters trail. The Old Bridle Path sounds like it might be clogged with amateurs," he tried. This time he got an answer.

Kurt turned away from his reservation book and finally looked in Kenny's direction. "Mmm. The Falling Waters goes straight up, with very few switchbacks. If you're really looking for a warm-up, the Bridle Path might be a better idea. And you won't see too much traffic up there on a Monday."

Kenny nodded, considering. "You might be right. If that's your recommendation then that's where I'll go."

"At least you'll have a chance of reaching the summit on that trail. How about the weather?"

Missing the sarcasm in the older man's voice, Kenny glanced out the window at the bright sunshine. "What do you mean? It's gorgeous out."

"Yeah, down here. But that trail is up in the Notch, and the weather there is very unpredictable. And it's been an unusually cold spring this year with frost a couple of nights a week. You might even find patches of snow in the higher elevations. Make sure you bring warm clothing: pants, jacket, a hat, and gloves."

Kenny glanced down at his Cool-max T-shirt and fast drying shorts. He was sweating slightly in the sun coming through the window. "I'm trying to travel light. It's going to be hot enough with my pack on."

Kurt frowned. "I've been up on that mountain when its seventy-five degrees at the base, but above the tree-line it's a sleet storm. A little extra weight can make the difference between safety and hypothermia."

Nodding thoughtfully, Kenny speared the last of his home fries. "Good point." Privately, he decided Kurt sounded more like a mother hen than a seasoned adventurer. Talking about sleet at the end of May! It seemed that the old man was past it, and spent his energy imagining disasters that would never happen. "Well, I'm wasting the best part of the day. Time to strap on my pack and get moving." Giving Kurt a forced smile, Kenny moved toward the door.

He missed Kurt's comment to a passing waitress. "That fool has no idea what he's getting into. Hopefully he'll make it through this week without needing a rescue."

****

By ten thirty, Kenny was furious. His boots hurt like hell (so much for their custom fit), he was out of breath (so much for the easy trail), and he was freezing. The warmth and sunshine had disappeared about an hour ago and what seemed like a gentle breeze at the trailhead had become a brisk wind with dropping temperatures. His T-shirt and shorts offered little protection and – as he thought longingly of the gore-tex jacket thrown carelessly on the bed back in his warm hotel room – it started to rain.

Peering up the trail, Kenny glimpsed darker clouds on the way. His survival book had a chapter on this. It told how to construct a temporary shelter out of branches and leaves. Pulling his brand-new multi-tool out of its case, Kenny moved off the trail to look for a likely place to build. Five minutes later, when the rain intensified to a downpour, Kenny abandoned the multi-tool and started searching for a low-growing bush or a pile of branches to crawl under. Twenty feet off the trail he found what seemed like a promising spot.

A number of pine branches were heaped together under the overhang of a boulder. Without stopping to speculate on what this unnatural arrangement was doing in the middle of a national forest, Kenny lifted up the nearest branches and crawled under.

The smell hit him immediately. Something rotten. Like stale garbage left out in the sun. Maybe the nearby remains of some animal's dinner. Assuming the odor to be outside his shelter, Kenny burrowed deeper into the branches. Instead, the smell got worse. As he shifted around under the branches, he touched something soft and slightly yielding. Wiggling his fingers, he realized that he was touching cloth. All thoughts of smell fled. Someone had discarded a blanket or sweater. Warmth! If he could just get the material around his shoulders....

Lifting the branches, he tugged at the fabric. The stench became unbearable, and Kenny saw flesh and hair and maggots and bone and black seeping fluid. He threw himself backwards out of the branches and promptly deposited the remnants of pancakes, eggs, bacon, and home fries on the ground to add its smell to the general reek coming from whatever hid under those branches. Scrambling to his feet, he started a headlong slipping, sliding, falling, crawling descent down the trail to the parking lot where he'd left his car.

Fumbling with his cell phone, he called 9-1-1 and finally got through to someone inclined to believe his story. She instructed Kenny to stay put and be prepared to lead the arriving officers to whatever it was he'd found. Kenny agreed and sat shivering in his car, looking at the leaves and dirt that were stuck to his expensive Cool-max shirt, the splashes of vomit on his custom hiking boots, and realizing he'd left his hand-carved Himalayan hiking stick somewhere up on the mountain.

CHAPTER TWO

Sergeant Cliff Codey, of the Investigative Services Bureau for the NH State Troopers, was looking over fire reports when he got the call. There had been five fires in the last four months in the town of Littleton, and that many accidental fires that close together in that small a town were statistically improbable, if not impossible. The ringing of the phone was a welcome diversion.

"Codey here."

"Hi, Cliff. Got a wild one for you. A hiker just down from the Bridle Path Trail out in the Notch claims he found a body up there."

Cliff pushed the pile of fire reports out of the way. "A body? Out on the trail? C'mon, Deidre, that's one of the most hiked trails in the Notch."

"Look, I just pass on the messages. This guy said it was a body and it sounded partially decomposed from his description."

A quick pat down of the desk's surface turned up a pencil and a fresh pad of paper. "How did this hiker find it?"

"He tried to crawl under some branches to escape the rain, and there it was."

"Uh-huh." Cliff considered this for a minute. "How did this guy sound? Was he high or drunk or anything?"

"He seemed scared and shook up. It took a while to get his story straight, but I think he really found something up there."

"Okay, I'll check it out. Would you call the park and ask someone to block off the Trailhead so no one else goes trampling over the alleged site? And give them instructions not to talk to the hiker until I get there. Thanks, Deidre."

Glancing at his watch, Cliff decided to eat lunch; it didn't sound like he'd have much free time for the rest of the afternoon. Unwrapping his ham and cheese sandwich, he carefully added mustard and mayonnaise, opened his drink, and demolished almost a third of the sandwich in one bite. A big man with thinning hair and over twenty years of experience, Cliff had learned power eating early in his career. Polishing off the rest of the sandwich in three bites, he headed out to his car. He could make it into the Notch in less than ten minutes with his lights on and foot to the floor, but a decomposed body wasn't going to move much if he stayed within the speed limit and got there in twenty.

Cruising down the interstate toward the towering granite outcrops that marked the entrance to the Franconia Notch, Cliff fought off the intrusive vision of another body on a different hiking trail in a different year.

'Ancient history', he told himself, 'nothing to do with this.'

Slowing to enter the Notch, he automatically looked right to scan the slopes of Cannon Mountain. The ski area had that sad, soggy end of the season look. Most of the snow was gone from except for a few small piles at the edges of the trails and under the trees that bordered each run. At the base of the slope, Echo Lake had also shed its winter coat and the ice had retreated to the far shore, blown across by the stiff breeze that formed intermittent white caps on the water.

It was not a great day for a hike. Adding that fact to the list of potential questions to pose to the hiker waiting for him, he put his mind back on the case at hand and the possible body. Mentally he reviewed the latest missing person's bulletins. No recent reports on a missing human, although there had been several posters in local stores describing a variety of missing pets.

A prime vacation area, Franconia and Lincoln – the two towns on either side of the Notch – had their share of transient residents. Lured by the promise of seasonal work in local tourist attractions, people came from all over the country. But the summer workers were just starting to arrive. These temporary workers usually didn't go missing until the height of the season when boredom or simple lack of money drove them away. The ski season had ended in March with everyone accounted for, so this body probably wouldn't turn out to be anyone local.

That also was typical. Interstate 93 runs from Boston to nearly Canada, and the Notch was just a couple of hours of travel from either place. The park was large, undeveloped, and easily accessible by highway.

A painless place to dispose of a body.

Cliff's radio crackled into life.

"Cliff? Mike here."

"Hey, Mike. You got the gen on this case?"

"Yeah. I should be there by about thirteen hundred hours."

Listening to the stress level in Mike's voice, Cliff knew his partner was less than happy with this assignment. The last body they had been called in to investigate had been someone Mike recognized. Had gone to school with. Knew the family. That was the down side of working in a small town. Cliff had known the victim too, but not as a contemporary. And, after twenty years on the job, he had grown a thick shell. Mike, in his first year as a trooper, would grow one too, but it would take a while.

Cliff didn't envy him. It was not a process he wanted to repeat.

The fact that this body was female made it both worse and better. Worse because it made him think of his daughters, and better because it upped the distance from that other, older, silent and broken body. Shifting in his seat to bring himself back to the present, Cliff clicked the send button. "I'll be there about ten minutes before you, Mike and start interviewing the witness. We'll probably have to hike up there, so be ready."

"Great. Just what I feel like doing."

Cliff didn't try to hide the chuckle in his voice. "Look at the bright side; at least it stopped raining."

"Bloyer and out."

'Bloyer' was Mike's short-hand for 'blow it out your ass'. He used it whenever the full phrase was inappropriate, like now. Too many people in the area owned scanners tuned in to this frequency, and Mike had been burned twice by the public broadcast of an injudicious expression.

Cliff drove south past the Old Bridle Path Trailhead, performed a U-turn at the next exit, and drove north again to the parking lot for the Trailhead. Accessibility to the myriad trails off I-93 could be confusing. It would be interesting to see why the hiker picked this particular trail. Pulling into the parking lot, Cliff surveyed of the scene.

Steel grey clouds hung over the top of Mount Lafayette, obscuring the peak and blending with the darker evergreens near the tree line. The lower slopes gradually lightened as the new green of the deciduous leaves mixed with the pines, and wisps from a few straggling clouds curled among them. The trail entrance was taped off, and a Park employee stood nearby, trying to look casual about the probable presence of a body on the mountain. Cliff relaxed as he spotted her. He knew Jeanette. She was level headed and no worse a gossip than anyone else living in a small town. She wouldn't have called all her friends to come and see the show. Cliff nodded hello as he parked his car.

Across from Jeanette Cliff spotted the lone car in the parking lot. Making note of the Massachusetts plates as he walked toward the car, he focused on the driver, a wet, miserable looking white male of about thirty to thirty-five years of age. Cliff's experienced eye immediately moved drunk and/or stoned to a spot low down on the list of possible explanations. This guy looked scared sick.

Cliff found out his interpretation was true, literally, when he opened the hiker's car door. The smell of stale vomit hit immediately, forcing him to take an involuntary step back. Masking that reaction by pulling out his notebook, Cliff bent down slightly and asked, "Are you the hiker that called in the report of the body?"

"Yes, Officer and it was horrible. I was just trying to find shelter from the rain and there it was. And the smell was just awful, it made me sick, and..."

Holding up a hand to try to interrupt the flow of words, Cliff diagnosed shock aggravated by cold and immobility. At least the guy had the brains to turn on his car to keep himself warm. Unfortunately this intensified the smell.

"Hold on, hold on. We'll get to the part about the body. I'd like to start by seeing some ID."

Cliff accepted the wallet that the man handed him, and took a cursory look at the interior of the car as he did so. It was clean, except for the driver's seat, and the car itself looked well maintained. The driver's license photo matched the man in the car and gave his name as Kenneth Brainerd. "All right Mr. Brainerd ..."

"Kenny. People call me Kenny."

"Okay then Kenny, I'm going to check on this and then I'll take your statement. Why don't you close your door to keep warm."

Cliff took the license and radioed in to check on Kenny. While he was listening to the reply, Mike pulled in and parked next to Cliff's car. Brushing a few stray raindrops from his stiff black crew cut, Mike folded his tall frame into the seat beside Cliff and asked, "What've we got?"

"Cold, flabby hiker by the name of Kenneth Brainerd says he found a body and it smells. Seems he lost his lunch or breakfast over it. Guy's got no record or outstanding warrants and doesn't seem intoxicated."

"So we've got to hike up there and see what he found."

"Looks like it."

Mike squinted up at the clouds. "Damn. How far up is this body?"

"He didn't say. Let's ask him."

They approached Kenny together, and he rolled down his window. Cliff handed back the wallet, and began. "I'm Trooper Codey, and this is Trooper Eldrich of the New Hampshire Bureau of Criminal Investigation. Can you please tell us exactly what happened this morning, starting with where you are staying?"

"I'm staying at the Mountain Glen Lodge in Lincoln and I was discussing my hiking itinerary with the owner, Kurt, over breakfast and he recommended this trail...."

Both Cliff and Mike took notes as Kenny talked. "...and so I called 9-1-1."

"Did you see anyone else on the trail?"

"No."

"And did anyone go up the trail after you got back to your car?"

Kenny shook his head. "No, the parking lot was empty when I got to my car and then that woman came and put the barricade up."

"Good. Now, how far up were you when you found the body?"

"Almost to the top, I think. It was hard to tell because of the rain."

Mike swept his eyes top to bottom over Kenny and came up skeptical. "Can you guide us to where you found the body?"

Kenny gazed up at Mount Lafayette, still partially obscured by layers of clouds, and shivered. "I guess so."

"We need your help, Mr. Brainerd," Mike began sternly and watched Kenny visibly wilt back into his seat. Cliff stepped forward and leaned down to window.

"I have a blanket and some raingear you can use on the way up," he told the drooping hiker, "and you'll warm up once you're moving."

Kenny brightened and nodded, seeming comforted by the offer of extra clothing. Collecting a 'better you than me' look from Mike, Cliff went to get his raingear.

****

It took the three men over an hour to reach the body. Sporadic gusts of rain and low lying clouds made the hiking slippery and the visibility lousy. If it hadn't been for Cliff's outdoor skills and knowledge of the trail, they would have walked right past their goal. By the time they reached the body's location, both troopers were very tired of Kenny Brainerd. The hike up the mountain had been one long grumble about his shoes, his feet, and how cold he was. The last complaint was particularly galling, since Cliff had surrendered his raingear to keep Kenny warm and comfortable. The blanket he insisted on bringing along slowed things down even further.

"So this is where you went off the trail?" Mike asked for the second time.

"I think so, but it was raining so hard, I was just looking for some kind of shelter, so I didn't pay too much attention to where I was going..." Kenny's voice trailed away under Mike's look.

Cliff stepped between the two men again, as he had several times on the hike up. "I see a large rock outcrop with pine trees around it that matches your description. You stay here on the trail while Mike and I go take a look."

Kenny seated himself quickly on a fallen tree, looking relieved. Cliff and Mike – glad the intermittent rain had stopped and the cloud cover had lifted enough to improve visibility – walked cautiously in toward the rock formation. It was large, about twenty feet high, Cliff estimated, and covered with moss. A birch tree grew out of a small side fissure, its roots wrapping around the boulder. As they moved closer, both men noticed the pile of pine branches at the same time, and signs that someone or something large had moved through the area recently. Keeping to the brush on either side of this faint trail, Cliff motioned Mike to approach the pile from the downhill side while he went in close to the rocks.

The branches showed signs of recent disturbance. Cliff took out his pocket tape recorder and switched it on. "We are approaching a pile of pine branches, obviously man made, at the base of a large rock formation. The pile is about six feet in diameter and about four feet tall at the center." Pausing, he nodded to Mike, who bent down to start pulling branches away. "There is an area of the pile that looks as though it's been disturbed recently, with branches pulled part-way out of the pile. As we pull these branches out..."

Mike suited his actions to Cliff's words, looking up to make a face as he did so. Five seconds later, Cliff knew why. "...there is a foul odor is emanating from the pile, growing stronger the more we disturb it."

With a final heave, Mike pulled a large clump of intertwined branches out of the way. There, covered with pine needles from her improvised blanket, lay what used to be a young woman.

Cliff turned the tape recorder off. "Oh, shit."

"You got that right," Mike scowled and pulled his hat down more firmly on his head. "This is gonna be a very long day." He bent down and gently pushed the remainder of the branches out of the way. Both men stood silently looking at the body.

Decomposition had begun, along with what looked like help from some of the local insect and/or wildlife. The clothes were basically intact, proclaiming the body as female, as did a long braid of dirty blonde hair. Most of the face and exposed extremities were missing, but the center of the body seemed, at first glance, undamaged.

"See anything you recognize?" Mike asked, finally.

Cliff shook his head. "You?"

"Nope." Cliff heard the relief in Mike's voice and had to admit that he shared it. Taking a deep breath, Cliff restarted the tape machine.

"Under the branches, is the body of what appears to be a woman in a state of partial decomposition. She is laying on her back, with her arms at her side and legs extended, wearing thick stockings, a long multi-patterned skirt, a bulky tunic sweater embroidered with yarn, and a red turtleneck shirt underneath." Cliff paused and nodded to Mike, who leaned in closer over the branches. Gingerly, he stretched and peered at the body, then shook his head. "There is no visible identification on the victim, and no jewelry. There is no obvious cause of death visible and no weapon of any kind easily visible in the surrounding area." Cliff clicked the stop button with an air of finality.

"All right, let's radio this in and get the CSI team up here to gather whatever they can find and take pictures, and get the medical examiner in to move the body."

Mike nodded. "K-9 team for a thorough search of the area?"

"We'll let CSI make that call. Looks like she's been here too long for any scent markers to have survived."

Both men heard Cliff refer to the body as 'she' and moved quickly away, trying to convert physical distance into professional detachment.

The two troopers made their way back to the trail, grimfaced, to be confronted by a very woebegone Kenny Brainerd. "Did you find it? Is this the place?"

Mike pulled a little ahead and stood with his back to Kenny. "What about him? Is he a suspect or just a jerk in the wrong place at the wrong time?"

"I agree he's an idiot, but I hate coincidences. And finding the exact place that the body was hidden seems like a big one to me. So, until further notice, he's suspect number one."

CHAPTER THREE

Four hours later, Cliff looked across the parking lot toward Kenny and sighed. After a quick clean-up and a semi-permanent appropriation of Cliff's blanket, Kenny had seemingly recovered from 'the horror he'd never get over' and was enjoying the attention and notoriety of having discovered the body. He chattered on to anyone who would listen about his experience on the mountain.

Cliff had been spared most of this performance, having stayed up on the mountain until the body was moved. The follow-up search and examination hadn't turned up anything helpful; the only excitement had been the finding of a new-looking, garishly carved hiking stick. Kenny had eagerly claimed ownership and then surrendered it to the BCI officers for examination with reluctance, asking worriedly how soon he would get it back. Cliff was still undecided about Kenny. Either the guy was a true jackass or one of the best actors he'd come across in a while. He strolled over to where Kenny was holding forth to an audience of park workers manning the barricades around the parking area.

"...and when I reached that part of the trail, it started to rain harder, so I decided to use my survival skills to make a temporary shelter and wait out the storm. I found a place off the trail..."

One of the park workers suppressed a yawn, having heard this story from Kenny at least twice before. With each telling, Kenny's bravery and backwoods savvy had grown. Cliff decided it was time for a more in depth interview with Kenny. He stepped up behind Kenny and asked him to come over to his patrol car, and several covert smiles and rolling eyes from the park workers expressed relief. Signaling to Mike, Cliff steered Kenny – blanket and all – into the back seat. Mike took the seat next to him, while Cliff remained standing by the open door. He rested a forearm on the doorframe and leaned forward to make eye contact with Kenny.

"We need to ask you a few questions, Mr. Brainerd, and I am bound to tell you that you have the right to remain silent or have an attorney present because anything you say here can be used in court. We could go back to my office but I'd like to save time and do it here. That all right with you?"

Kenny shifted in the seat to pull the blanket more closely around his legs, and beamed up at Cliff. "Sure, anything to help. What happens next? Where do they take the body? Will you need me to testify?"

Cliff decided it was time to dig past the chirpy tourist façade. He squared his hat more firmly onto his head and leaned down until the brim was almost touching Kenny's forehead. "Is this some kind of pilgrimage for you?"

"Pilgrimage?" Kenny repeated blankly, looking from Cliff to Mike and back again. "What do you mean?"

"I mean, did you come back to visit the body, then decide the time was right for someone to find her?" Cliff deliberately lowered and roughened his tone of voice.

Kenny's eyes stretched as his chin receded. "No, of course not, I told you what happened, I was hiking and..."

"That's what happened today, but I'm talking about a while back when you killed her. How'd you get her up there, Kenny? Did you carry her, or did you walk up together and then kill her there? And how did you kill her? Did she struggle?"

Watching Kenny's face flush and then whiten, Cliff stepped up the pressure. "Was it a lover's quarrel? Did you do it for money? Or maybe she had something on you that you didn't want anyone to know. What was it, Kenny? Why did you kill her?" Cliff ended up nose to nose with Kenny, close enough to see his eyes dilate and hear how rapid his breathing had become.

"I didn't!" Kenny panted, shrinking back against the seat. "I don't know her. I had no idea she was there. I was just trying to get..."

"...out of the rain." Cliff finished for him. "We've heard that story before, Kenny, but now it's time to tell the truth. You went up on the mountain today to check on her, and then brought us up there because you wanted someone to find her. Why'd you do it, Kenny? What happened between you two?"

"N...nothing," Kenny stammered as his chin started to tremble. "I just came out for a hike and ..."

"Sure, sure." Cliff turned away in disgust, crossed his arms and leaned against the side of the cruiser, scowling across the parking lot.

Kenny turned to Mike, wiping the sweat off his upper lip. "You've got to believe me! I had nothing to do with this! I've never been up in this part of the state before in my life!"

"We'll check all that out, Kenny. If you're telling the truth, there'll be no problem. But if you're not...well, it's not going to look good for you." Mike narrowed his eyes, keeping up the pressure.

"I'd tell you if I knew something, honest, I would." Kenny was now babbling. "But I don't know anything. I've never been here before. I needed directions from Kurt at the hotel to even find this trail, and this is my first time on it. It's my first time hiking, period! I ...."

"Okay, Okay," Mike said, backing off. "We'll check all that out. I just hope you're telling us the truth."

"I am. I swear I am..."

"That's fine then. You just go on back to your hotel and stay put while we check out your story." Mike told him, easing him out of the car.

Cliff repeated the instruction as they escorted Kenny back to his own car. "Make sure you stay put at that hotel. We'll be talking to you again."

The two men watched as Kenny shakily started his car and drove off.

"So what do you think?" Mike asked. "Is he our killer?"

"My gut says no. I don't think the guy could set a mousetrap, let alone murder a young woman. But right now, he's the only suspect we've got."

****

Back at the Station, Cliff gestured toward two empty desks. "Take your pick, looks like we're not going to wrap this up today."

Mike circled the desks, then chose the less battered one near the door. "I must be moving up in the world, having my own desk."

"And no extra charge for the chair, either. So pull one up and let's look at what we've got."

Mike grabbed the sturdiest looking one and flopped down into it. "I'd say we don't have much at this point. A decomposing body and a blithering idiot."

"And that's where we should start. We need to look a little more deeply into Brainerd's story and see if it holds up. I'll send an inquiry to the local PD down where Brainerd lives and ask them if they have any info on him. Have them talk to his co-workers, see if they can dig anything up. In the meantime, let's head down to Lincoln tomorrow and talk to people at his hotel."

"You mean the legendary Kurt Pelletier? I've heard he's a tough guy to get to know."

Cliff kept his face and voice neutral. "He's cooperated in other search and rescue cases. I don't think he'll give us any problem." Taking a deep breath he turned to his computer. "There are no local missing person's reports matching the superficial description of our victim. Once we have a better idea of the timeline for her death we can expand our search".

"Sounds like a plan." Mike stretched and stood up. "Meet here tomorrow and travel down to the Mountain Glen?"

"Meet you here at eight."

Mike sketched a one finger salute and headed for the door. Cliff kept his eyes on his computer until he heard the outer door slam, then leaned back in his chair with a sigh. He'd managed to avoid any contact with Kurt in an official capacity for years, but there was no way out of this one. And Mike's presence would complicate things even further. The only way to play it would be to keep it business-like and hope the old man would go along with it. After all, Kurt shouldn't want to bring up the past any more than he did.

CHAPTER FOUR

Cliff sniffed appreciatively as he and Mike sat down in the front office of the Mountain Glen Hotel on Tuesday morning. The scent of freshly brewed coffee mingled with the smell of bacon and drifted in through the doorway from the dining room. The hotel's owner, Kurt Pelletier, noticed. "Can I offer you gentlemen a cup of coffee?"

"Sure," Cliff answered, and Mike nodded. "Cream and sugar for me, just sugar for him."

Kurt called the order out the door, and resumed his seat behind the desk. "Now, Officers, what can I do for you?"

Cliff ignored the sardonic emphasis on the word 'officers' in Kurt's voice. "We'd like any information you have about one of your guests, Kenny Brainerd."

Leaning his chair back on two legs, Kurt laced his fingers behind his head, and addressed the ceiling in a bored voice. "He checked in at two o'clock on Sunday afternoon and spent the rest of that day sight-seeing here in Lincoln. He ate dinner somewhere in town and was back in his room by nine. He wanted a seven AM wake-up call yesterday and came down to the dining room by eight. He ate a huge breakfast and told me about his hiking plans for the week." Kurt paused and brought his gaze back down to his guests. When he resumed, his voice had lost its undertone of irony.

"His plans were pretty ambitious for someone who was obviously a newbie – brand new gear and boots without a scuff mark on 'em. He was talking about doing the Falling Waters Trail as his first hike. Ever."

Cliff raised his eyebrows while Mike shook his head and muttered "Idiot."

Kurt nodded. "Exactly. Instead, I steered him toward the Old Bridle Path Trail, thinking that was his best chance of making the top of Lafayette. I tried to give him some advice about the weather he might be heading into, but it seemed he didn't want to listen. He left here just after nine."

"How was his mood? Nervous? Keyed up?"

Kurt shook his head. "No, he was just like most greenie flatlanders out for their first hike – convinced he'd set new records as soon as he hit the trails."

A quiet knock on the door signaled the arrival of the coffee. A tall stoop-shouldered young man with hands and feet that looked like they should belong to a much larger man brought in a tray loaded with three mugs, handed them around and slipped out again. Cliff took a sip, and then leaned back in his chair. "OK, those are the facts. Now tell us what you think of him."

"All right, Cliffy, anything to oblige the authorities," Kurt answered with a big grin. Mike looked from one man to the other, startled.

Cliff sighed. "C'mon, Kurt, you know I've got a job to do, and I know there's a lot more you can tell us about this joker Brainerd."

With a final grin, Kurt took a mouthful of coffee and turned serious. "Sure, I know what you want. Brainerd is exactly the kind of guy I used to tell you kids about, someone with more money than smarts. He showed up here with all the latest equipment and not a single ounce of common sense."

"And?"

"And, as far as I can tell, he paid for it by getting stuck halfway up Lafayette in a cold rainstorm wearing just shorts and a tee-shirt. The fool is lucky to have made it back down in one piece."

"So you think he's just a jerk who's never been up in the mountains before."

Kurt nodded and reached for his cup, clearly finished with the subject.

Cliff took the hint, putting his cup down and motioning for Mike to do the same. "Thanks for your time, Kurt. I appreciate it."

"You could show your appreciation."

Cliff stopped with a hand on the doorframe. "How?"

Kurt studied the cup in his hand. "Come by some night on your own time. There's usually a couple of the boys from the Crew here Sundays."

Hesitating in the doorway, Cliff studied the older man. The last thing he wanted to do was renew his association with any of that group. He suppressed a shudder, thinking of the circumstances surrounding the last time they'd been together. He'd worked hard to get that picture out of his mind. Still, there was no sense in antagonizing a witness. And he maybe he did owe the old man something for all the knowledge he'd shared. "I'll keep that in mind, Kurt. Sundays."

Mike waited until they were inside the cruiser. "You want to tell me what the hell was going on in there? Or do I need to know the secret handshake?"

Cliff started the engine and turned to face the younger man. "When I was a kid, I hung out with Kurt, did a bunch of hiking with him, and learned a hell of a lot. He wasn't thrilled when I went to the academy, thought I was wasting my time and talent. We had a few arguments about it, and I quit hanging out with him and his little gang. But Kurt knows the mountains and he knows people, and I trust his assessment of Brainerd. We'll wait and see what the cops in Massachusetts turn up about him, but he's moving down on my list of suspects."

After a few minutes of silence, Mike ventured a further comment. "I hear Kurt's Crew was a wild bunch, back in the day."

"I wasn't one of the official members – I didn't have that kind of time. Like I said, I just hung out with them for a bit." He headed out of town and turned up the ramp onto I-93. The looming cliffs of Cannon Mountain and Mount Lafayette seemed to close in around the cruiser as they traveled north and Cliff struggled to push the bad memories back where they belonged. He accelerated up to highway speed and decisively changed the subject. "Let's go back and dig through the last six months of missing person reports for the Northeast and see what we come up with."

Mike nodded, accepting the subject as closed. "Maybe we should check across the border too into Canada. You never know."

"Good idea. Let's grab some lunch on the way back. Smelling that bacon made me hungry."

****

Cliff leaned back, closed the window on his computer, rubbed his tired eyes and started to gather up his lunch remnants. He'd searched the files of missing persons for all of New Hampshire and Vermont without finding anything that looked promising. There had been a missing college student in Vermont that made him sit up briefly, but the student was male and the time frame was wrong. He looked over toward Mike. "No luck over here. You?"

Mike turned to Cliff who could read the answer on his face before he spoke. "Zip, zero, zilch. Couple of deadbeat dads in Maine and one confused Grandma that wandered off but was located a couple of towns over, but no young women."

"Guess we better expand the search south and west..." Cliff began but Mike's groan in response was interrupted by the ringing telephone.

Scooping up the receiver, Cliff turned away from Mike's silent cheer. "Codey here...Great, we'll be right over." He put the phone down and stood up. "Reprieve from files. That was the Medical Examiner's office saying they're ready for us."

****

Cliff and Mike stood in the office of the Medical Examiner for Coos, Grafton, and Carroll counties, waiting for her report. Her name was Brenda Harris, and the unit generally agreed that they were lucky to have someone of her caliber this far north. She was short, stocky, and very quiet. Cliff knew almost nothing about her, an unusual occurrence in a division this small. His contacts with her were totally business-like and devoid of the usual chit-chat so common in most local departments. The only personal thing Cliff had heard from her was a chance remark Brenda had let slip last year when she mentioned that being a doctor was great, except for the patients. The M.E.'s office seemed a perfect match.

"Gentlemen." The door opened and Brenda's blonde head, the hair scraped back into a tight ponytail and hairnet, popped into the room. "Sorry to keep you waiting."

Cliff walked over to the door with Mike shuffling along behind him. Mike hated cadavers. This surprising admission had come out late one night, early in their last case. An avid hunter, Mike felt it was a sign of weakness to be bothered by a corpse. After all, he had taken down and gutted his share of deer, turkeys, and one memorable moose. Cliff had tried to point out that people and animals were two entirely different things, but Mike had just reddened and asked him not to talk about it. Leaving Mike by the door, Cliff followed Brenda over to the table where Jane Doe #1, 2013, was partially covered with a white sheet.

"What can you tell us about her?" Cliff came to a stop about six feet from the table. The examining room was cool, but the smell emanating from the table was still powerful.

"I'll start with the cause of death. Strangulation."

"What was used? A rope, a wire, or what?"

"Someone's hands." Brenda pulled the sheet down a little lower. "You can see the trachea was crushed right here," she pointed with a pencil, "while the first, fourth and fifth fingers left indents on the lateral aspects of the neck."

"Any idea how large the hands were?"

"Pretty large and very strong. It's not easy to kill someone this way."

Cliff thought that one over, looking broodingly at what was left of the victim's face. "Was she pretty?"

Brenda raised an eyebrow at the question.

"It's a possible motive, pretty girl, crime of passion. Any sign of a struggle?"

"The state of decomposition was too advanced to determine if there was any tissue under the fingernails and the decomposition was too widespread to reliably determine any additional bruising."

"How about unreliably?"

Brenda shot a puzzled look at Cliff. "What do you mean?"

"I'm asking for your opinion. Given the state of the tissue, is it possible there was bruising on other parts of the body or not?"

"I'd have to say no. But I couldn't testify to that."

"I won't ask you to," Cliff said. "That brings us to the big question. When did she die?"

"This is a very interesting case," Brenda began, settling her hip against the side of the gurney, seemingly oblivious to the smell. "Because we've had such a cold spring, this body didn't decompose in the normal way."

"There's a normal way?"

"Sure. Normal decomposition happens from the inside out. The bacteria that are in the digestive tract multiply and basically eat the body away from the inside with the side effect of gaseous excretions. In most cases, this then spreads outward, concluding with the extremities."

Cliff nodded, trying to keep his face expressionless. Behind him, he heard a small distressed noise from Mike, but ignored it. "But in this case...?"

"In this case, the body was left outside in cold weather. Initially, I'd say it was frozen for a period of time, preventing any decomposition. Then, as the weather slowly warmed up, the body went through an extended cycle of freezing and thawing. Because we've had such a cool spring, only the extremities thawed most days. The core of the body, the thickest part containing the internal organs, remained frozen, retarding normal decomposition."

Cliff had the distinct feeling that Brenda was enjoying herself. He tried to get her to come to the point. "So that means...?"

"That I can't use any of the usual methods to determine the time of death. I did contact the Mount Washington Observatory for a summary of weather conditions in the area for the last three months. Of course, Mount Washington is a thousand feet higher than Mount Lafayette where she was found, so I had to calculate a ten to fifteen degree difference in temperature for the area where she was found. With that information, I estimated that the earliest the body could have started its freeze/thaw cycle was mid-April."

Brenda drew the sheet further down from the body, exposing an arm now devoid of clothing. "The other factor to consider is the local wild-life. I had to determine what type of animals live that far up on the mountain, their diets, hibernation patterns, and feeding territory. If you look closely here, and here," the pencil was out again, circling several places on the hand, "you will see several sets of small tooth marks, where the flesh has been nibbled away. After talking to the Fish and Game Department, it seems likely that these would be from a rodent. A weasel, bobcat or fisher cat would have made much larger bites using a tearing type of motion and leaving a more ragged edge than we see here."

Cliff heard another, louder sound from Mike behind him, and tried not to echo it. "And your conclusion is?"

"Not less than six weeks, not more than six to seven months."

"That's the best you can do?"

She shrugged, but didn't look apologetic. "This is a very unusual case. I actually thought I did pretty well in narrowing it down that much!"

Cliff nodded and suppressed a sigh. "All right, we've got a time frame, even if it's a hefty one. What can you give us as far as identification?"

"I can match DNA, hair, and dental patterns if you give me some info on possible suspects from a missing persons file." Brenda pulled the sheet further down below the waist. "And I have some information that might help you narrow your search. For starters, she came from a fairly high socio-economic bracket."

This announcement finally brought Mike a few cautious steps away from his post at the door. "How can you tell?"

"Welcome back," Cliff said, trying to suppress a smile.

"Up yours." Mike muttered out of the side of his mouth, then refocused his attention on Brenda.

"She's had bonding done on all her teeth, which costs a pretty penny, and she's had breast reduction surgery." Brenda continued, ignoring the interplay between the two men. "Both of those are cosmetic procedures, not generally covered by insurance plans. And both are pretty pricey."

"Can you give us an estimate on her age?"

"Between seventeen and twenty-five." Brenda pulled the sheet back up over the face and turned back to the troopers. "And yes, looking at her bone structure, I'd say she was pretty."

****

Cliff and Mike followed Brenda into her office. "I'll have a formal report for you in a few days," she said. "If I come up with anything else that will help with identification, I'll call."

"It's going to be tough getting an ID on her without a photo to go along with it."

"Actually, I think I can get you one in a day or so." Brenda said, raising an eyebrow and waiting for their reactions.

Cliff decided to play. "OK, I'll bite. How are you going to do that?"

"I have a colleague with a computer program that reconstructs what a face might look like from photos of victims like this. I took a bunch of pictures and e-mailed them off to him yesterday. I should hear back tonight or tomorrow."

"Brenda, you're brilliant."

"Just make sure you spread that around." Brenda finally smiled, then looking down at the forms on her desk; she became all business once again. "Her clothing is down in the evidence locker. Forensics has finished their preliminary with it, but it doesn't sound like they came up with much. Handle it carefully; it's in pretty rough shape. I'll let you know as soon as those pictures come in." She started back toward the examination room, her mind clearly refocused on Jane Doe.

The two men took the hint and went over to the evidence locker to examine the clothing. They were quick but thorough, to minimize any complaints from the clerk about air pollution. Brenda had been right, the material threatened to fall apart in their hands. The black tights seemed generic, thick and without any label. The long, floral patterned skirt had an elastic waistband that crinkled as they un-folded it and collar of the red turtleneck did the same, but each garment still had an intact but faded label.

"Both from LL Bean. That stuff's not cheap. How about the sweater?"

"Woolrich. Also pretty pricey. It supports Brenda's theory that the girl had some bucks. Let's get some pictures of these spread out on the table. Even if we don't have a mug shot, someone might recognize the clothes."

They arranged the clothes as if there was a body inside them and took a few pictures. When they finished, Cliff stood looking at the display in silence.

Mike lowered the camera. "What are you seeing?"

"What I'm *not* seeing are shoes or boots of any kind. And if Brenda's right and she died after the weather turned cold, how did she get that far up the mountain without shoes?"

"She was carried?"

"That would have been tough – she's wasn't that small. And it would be difficult to do without anyone noticing."

"Could have been done at night."

"Again, tricky job. Dark slippery trail, big package, not an easy task." Cliff studied the clothes again. "Could be she hiked up, but someone took the shoes away with them after they killed her."

Mike thought about that one. "To avoid identification by distinctive footwear?"

"Or as a trophy. And as far as distinctive, what do these clothes remind you of?"

This time Mike came up blank. Cliff smiled slightly. "You're too young. To me, they say crunchy-granola hippie-type clothes. All that's missing is the Birkenstocks."

"I thought all that went out in the sixties."

"It lingered on a little longer up here. There were a couple of progressive schools in this area attracting that kind of crowd. The word spread, and for a while it seemed that all the back-to-the-land enthusiasts were moving up here."

"I've heard about those schools," Mike said. "And some of the kids I grew up with had parents that were a little to the left of the norm. But I thought that was all mainly in the older generation."

"That's the other thing that doesn't add up. Brenda says this girl is exactly that, a girl, just out of her teens. So her age is all wrong for these clothes. You're single, you watch girls. How many have you seen dressed like this?"

"I can't think of any, off-hand. But I have to confess; if I did see one, I'd look away."

Cliff nodded. "Exactly. Occasionally you see a whole family where the women dress like this at the some of the local farmers markets. And I know there are still a few groups of people around here that like to fly just below the radar. Maybe we should look into some of those places."

"The missing person's reports for this area didn't turn up anything."

"Like I said, these groups keep a low profile. If one of their own went missing, I bet they'd keep it quiet." In answer to Mike's doubtful look, Cliff continued, "Look, we don't have much else to go on. Kenny Brainerd seems to be washing out as a possibility, local missing persons came up negative and we both agree that our vic was not dressed right for her age. Let's take the picture of these clothes and whatever simulated picture Brenda comes up with and take it around and see if we stir up any reactions."

"Okay, just let me dig out my peace symbol necklace," Mike said with a grin.

"Oh yeah; that will go great with the uniform." Cliff quickly but carefully packed the clothes back into their bag and returned it to the clerk. "Just don't start quoting Jack Kerouac."

Mike's blank look kept him smiling all the way to the cruiser.

CHAPTER FIVE

Nelson Simon sat scowling in front of his hotel window at the view of the White Mountains. They were beautiful, he had to admit that. The early morning sun caught the remnants of snow on Mount Washington and turned it a soft rose against a pale sky, which slowly deepened to a brilliant blue while the snow paled to peach and finally into a clear crisp white. And the hotel in Franconia was elegant, with Victorian wallpaper and dark walnut wainscoting throughout the building. All dripping with old world charm, just as the guidebook said it would be.

The problem was that no one, not the guidebooks, not the hotel clerk, not even the attractive young woman who had brought him here, had told him about the bugs. Black flies, they called them. Nelson called them a season in hell. The instant you stepped outside, the beasts swarmed around you, crawling into your ears and nose, getting inside your clothing and into your hair, and biting! For such a small bug, they packed one hell of a bite.

Nelson had one on the side of his neck that swelled almost to the size of a grapefruit. Alluring Alyssa told him he was exaggerating, that it wasn't that big, and that if he stopped picking at it, it would go away sooner. Alyssa was becoming less alluring as the week went on.

This was supposed to be the next step for them as a couple, a week alone together at a quaint old inn out in the country. Nelson had envisioned long soaks in the outdoor hot tub the hotel advertised as 'situated under the stars', long evenings on the couch in front of the massive stone fireplace in the bedroom, and long leisurely mornings in the king-sized bed.

Unfortunately, Alyssa's mental pictures turned out to be completely different. Her ideas included long drives to remote places for lengthy hikes through scenic trails that all went either straight up or straight down. Nelson had been willing to try it – she really was very appealing - but one session with the black flies drove him right back inside, ceding victory to the bugs. Alyssa had been remarkably unsympathetic and very resistant to his view of the ideal week together.

"For God's sake Nelson, we could have stayed in New York to do all that. The whole point of coming up here was to get away and do something different."

Nelson had tried to persuade her that there were other goals possible for a week away together, centering around the large, premium priced room he'd paid for.

She remained unconvinced. "You can choose to skulk inside for the entire week, but I for one am not going to waste the beautiful weather, fresh air, and gorgeous scenery because of a few bugs."

And off she went each day, leaving Nelson bored and irritated, thinking of all the things they could be doing and unable to find a substitute. Today was Tuesday. They still had four days to go, and he was starting to wonder if Alyssa's fast fading charms were worth sticking this through to the end.

Unfolding himself from his chair, he glanced down at his watch. Just about five o'clock, Alyssa's usual return time. Nelson checked himself in the window's reflection. Dark wavy hair touching an Armani shirt collar, a jutting nose and chin, and dark eyes looked back. He hoped Alyssa would have a little more pep tonight. Last night she had fallen asleep almost as soon as her head contacted the pillow, leaving him more than a little testy this morning. If tonight was a repeat, he was hiring a car and getting the hell out of here. There were several unfinished news features he'd left waiting in his 'in' box. Jerry, his editor, had grumbled about his taking the entire week; if he came back early he'd earn bonus points with someone, at least.

Leaning forward, he could see Alyssa's small red car pulling into the parking lot. As she unfolded herself from the driver's seat, Nelson marveled again at the distance from thigh to ankle that regularly folded itself into such a small opening. That, added to her long cinnamon-red hair and peacock-blue eyes, made up for a lot of differences in opinion. Watching her cross the parking lot, there seemed to be a bounce to her step that hadn't been there the previous evening. This could be a decided improvement.

Entering the room, Alyssa threw her handbag at the bed and bounced across the room. "Nelson! I have great news!"

"They're blanketing the entire state of New Hampshire with DDT tomorrow to kill all the bugs."

"Try not to be such an obvious New Yorker and go for a little of the 'when in Rome...' frame of mind, won't you?" She kissed his cheek. "Anyway, I have an idea that should be right up your urban avenue."

"We pack up and spend the rest of the week in Boston?" Nelson tried for dry humor over annoyed irritation.

"You are impossible." She sounded more amused more than exasperated; evidently his irritation was successfully hidden. "I met a very nice couple from Connecticut on the trail today, and they recommended this bar. All the locals hang out there. They said it is positively a hoot. All flannel shirts and work boots, practically right out of Deliverance."

Nelson grimaced. "You do remember how that movie ends, don't you?"

"Not that bad, just totally authentic country-style. This couple, Dave and Suzanne, stopped there on Monday, and say we haven't really experienced rural until we've tried it."

"Do we really need to get the total pastoral experience?" Nelson said, weakening. Alyssa aglow with enthusiasm was hard to resist.

"Don't tell me you're afraid to go. Not Nelson Simon, award-winning investigative reporter, nervous about a country bar in the back of beyond?"

That got him. She knew him too well, dammit. "All right, all right, I'll go. But what should we wear? All our flannel is at the cleaners and our work boots are being re-soled."

"We'll just have to fall back on jeans and casual shoes. I'm going to shower. Would you like to come and be my wardrobe consultant?"

Nelson didn't need a second invitation. Things were definitely looking up.

****

"Dave and Suzanne said they'd meet us here around nine," Alyssa said as they stood at the bar's doorway. "Why don't we just get a table near the door and keep an eye out for them."

"Good idea." That would make a fast getaway easier. If the Dewdrop Inn looked unprepossessing from the outside, the interior trod the fine line between shabby and well used. The unfinished pine floor bore the scars from several generations of boots. A few small tables were ranged along the walls and a pool table dominated the center of the room with the bar behind it. Alyssa's new friends, wherever the hell they were, had been right about the standard attire. Nelson felt as out of place in his black jeans and western boots as if he were wearing black tie and tails. He followed Alyssa to a table, checking the seat carefully before settling gingerly onto it. After the earlier conversation about *Deliverance*, he was relieved to see that no deer heads or other animal trophies hung on the walls.

"Isn't this great?" Alyssa slid her chair closer to his. "This is authentic."

Nelson scanned the room once again, seeing nothing that special.

"This is the part of the country that Grace Metallious wrote about in 'Peyton Place'." She giggled. "What do you think; are we looking at any alcoholic child-molesters?"

"C'mon Alyssa, you know as well as I do that behavior like that isn't limited to rural communities. You read my piece on Internet stalkers. They were more urban than rural by a ratio of more than two to one."

Alyssa wasn't listening. She straightened in her chair and waved furiously toward the doorway. "Suzanne! Dave! Over here!"

Nelson turned to see a couple making their way over to the table. They were obviously products of the suburban New York area. Normally, he and Alyssa, as ardent Manhattan-ites who disdained anyone outside of that borough, wouldn't associate with the 'McMansion' crowd. Yet here was Alyssa, greeting them like long lost friends. Were they really so far from home that anyone living within fifty miles of Manhattan seemed like a soul mate? Nelson had observed this phenomenon abroad, but never within the continental U.S.

They exchanged introductions and occupations. Dave worked in banking and Suzanne was a teacher. They responded neutrally to the news that Nelson was a reporter. In his eyes, that eliminated the possibility that Dave was an embezzler or Suzanne a closet pedophile and he felt his interest in them wane. It dropped a notch or two further when the conversation turned exclusively to hiking.

Nelson let his eyes rove around the bar once more. It was filling up, mainly with men, most wearing flannel shirts or sweat shirts, worn jeans, and the thick work boots. Scruffy haircuts matched sporadic contact with a razor. A newcomer in a green shirt caught Nelson's attention. Green Shirt was dressed much like the others, but his dark hair was cut almost militarily short, and something about his posture screamed 'cop' to Nelson. He waited for the bar to clear, the typical scenario in New York where the bars were either blue or not, and was surprised to see Green Shirt welcomed and greeted by name. Mumbling to Alyssa about getting a refill, Nelson moved up to the bar, working his way unobtrusively to where the newcomer was standing.

Nelson heard a few people greet the man as Mike.

A man in a Red Sox baseball cap propped his elbows on the bar. "Any further word on that body up on Lafayette?"

Nelson's interest sharpened. A body?

"Nothing yet," Mike said. "We're checking out missing person reports from around the northeast, but no bites so far."

Trying to remain inconspicuous, Nelson turned his head slightly so he could see Mike Green Shirt with his peripheral vision. Red Sox was talking again.

"I heard it was up there awhile, with mainly just clothes left."

Mike shrugged and grunted an indistinct response. It seemed to Nelson that he wanted to avoid talking about it.

"Blonde and young, right? And weird, kinda hippie looking clothes." Red Sox wouldn't quit.

Mike took a swig of beer and finally gave Red Sox his full attention. "It sounds like you know just as much as I do about this case. You coming up to the barracks tomorrow to do my job for me?"

Nelson turned his head just enough to see Red Sox grinning unabashedly. "Naw, I wouldn't look as pretty as you in that uniform."

Mike snorted. "Let me prove there's brains over here as well as beauty by beating you at pool. Again."

That resulted in a chorus of jeers toward Red Sox, as well as a sputtering protest, "What do you mean – again? That game was a draw and everyone knows it."

The crowd moved toward the pool table, still arguing the point, leaving Nelson deep in thought at the bar. The decomposed body of a young blonde woman, dressed in hippie clothes? Nelson often had started on a story with less information than this. And this was a bona fide, basically confirmed by some type of local cop. Now, to find out who Mike was. Leaning forward, he signaled to the bartender.

"That guy, Mike, looks familiar. I think he gave me a ticket the other day."

The bartender stared without expression at Nelson for ten seconds, then answered just this side of rudeness. "I doubt it. Mike works ISB. He doesn't waste his time with traffic tickets."

"ISB?" Nelson tried to look harmless and befuddled. "What's that?"

"Investigative Services Bureau. Why?"

"Just wondering. I thought I heard him say something about a body." Nelson knew he was pushing his luck, but he wouldn't be in here again and wanted to milk the situation for whatever information he could get.

"You'd have to ask him about that." The finality in the bartender's tone warned Nelson the conversation was finished. He nodded and ordered two beers he didn't want just to allay suspicion. The bartender delivered them with a hard look and Nelson paid without further comment, returning to the table with his prizes. Alyssa welcomed him back.

"We thought we'd lost you," Alyssa said. "And what are you doing with those? You hate beer."

"Camouflage."

Alyssa frowned slightly, but dropped it. "We were just discussing what we might do tomorrow. Would you like to join us if we stay closer to civilization and pavement?"

Nelson shook his head. "I don't think so. I do need a car, though. Do you think there's a rental place anywhere near here?"

Alyssa blinked at the sudden change of subject but obligingly turned to consult with Dave and Suzanne. They had vacationed in the area before and discussed a few possibilities but all involved driving a distance to get to pick-up the rental pick-up. Further questioning came up empty and finished with everyone shaking their heads. That figured. But additional discussion resulted in an offer from the Connecticut couple to pick Alyssa up at the hotel tomorrow, leaving her car available for Nelson. He smiled his thanks while the other three firmed up plans and said their good-byes.

Once Nelson settled into Alyssa's car, she skewered him immediately. "All right, what's going on? What do you need a car for?"

"To identify a body."

"Come again?"

Nelson filled her in on the conversation he had overheard, watching Alyssa's skepticism change to interest and then enthusiasm. "It sounds bizarre; a decomposed body dressed in thirty-year-old clothes. Where will you start?"

He could see the request to accompany him quivering on her lips. As a second year reporter, she was usually relegated to the soft news assignments. They had met when Alyssa requested an interview. The interview, and the evening following, had been a great success, but Nelson suspected that his by-line more than his biceps fueled their relationship. So far, he'd been able to keep Alyssa happy on the fringes of his work, but until now all the stories had been in progress when they met. This new story might change things.

"I'm going to do some preliminary research tomorrow. If I find I need your help I'll ask, but the story comes first."

"Of course it does." Alyssa smiled at him. "I'm just interested to see how you approach it."

"Don't worry; I'll fill you in on whatever I find."

She leaned forward to fit the key into the ignition, then turned back to him. Looking into her shining eyes, Nelson felt an answering adrenalin rush. This was familiar ground for them and a welcome return to their pre-vacation rapport. Nelson was eager to pursue both.

****

He watched the couple leave the bar and climb in to a car with

New York plates. Leaning back in his chair, he peered out the window and followed the car with his eyes as it pulled out of the parking lot and turned off toward the Easton Valley. There was only one hotel and two bed-and-breakfast places out that way; it wouldn't be too hard to spot a red TT Hardtop with out of state plates again if necessary. Snooping flatlanders weren't too much of a threat anyway. What concerned him more was hearing they'd found her body.

He lowered his head and studied the table in front of him, pushing his bottle around and following the trail the condensation made. What had seemed almost impossibly far off the trail in the deep snow of December was obviously more accessible in May. So someone had found her, and now the troopers were in on it. He shot a quick look over toward the pool table. He didn't know this young guy Mike like he knew most of the other Troopers. Know your enemy, that's what he'd always been told, and he'd kept up pretty well with it. But this changed things. He needed more information and he had to get it without giving himself away. He needed a plan.

Leaving his bottle on the table, he waited until a particularly difficult shot sunk home over at the pool table. Under the cover of the ensuing sympathetic groans and congratulatory whoops, he slipped out of the bar and slipped around the back of the building.

No one noticed him leave.

CHAPTER SIX

Wednesday morning, watching the back of Dave and Suzanne's car convey its owners and Alyssa off to yet another scenic vista, Nelson considered what would be the best method of gathering information about this body. Being a reporter by trade, he decided to capitalize on what he knew best, newspapers and how they worked. Returning to the hotel lobby, he asked the desk clerk for a copy of the most popular local paper.

"That would be the *Dispatch*. It comes out every Wednesday and has all the local events."

Nelson could remember picking up that paper yesterday but discarding it quickly for its lack of hard news. Now he went back to it with rekindled attention. The front page consisted of a story about a local business award, news about the possibility of a highway rerouting, litigation about a proposed zoning change, and a large picture of some kind of local flower as filler. The remainder of the paper was equally innocuous, with the most in-depth stories centering on the local sports teams. Should be easy pickings.

The address was on the masthead, and another conversation with the desk clerk elicited directions. Twenty minutes later Nelson pulling into the town of Littleton. The main street had obviously had some recent care and renovation and seemed to be living up to the guidebooks description of 'authentic New England charm'. Nelson decided he might bring Alyssa here in an effort to pry her away from the damn mountains.

The newspaper building sat on the outside of town where the trendy boutiques gave way to auto parts stores and welding garages. Parking the car in a small weedy asphalt lot, Nelson walked up to a large square granite building that proclaimed "Home of the *Dispatch*" in etching on the glass of the outer front door. The inner door sported a more prosaic sign with removable letters giving office hours and telephone number. Stepping through the doorway, Nelson found himself in a small, well-worn lobby furnished with a saggy brown couch of uncertain age and a low table spread with past copies of the Dispatch. A receptionist behind a glass partition asked, "Can I help you?"

Smiling, Nelson walked up to her and extended his press card. "Is there any way I can get an appointment to speak with your editor?"

****

Philip Morton, editor of the *Dispatch*, was a blunt, square built man. A flat-topped head connected without any sign of a neck to a chunky body and short thick legs. Within a very few minutes, Nelson learned that Philip, (call me Phil), had been the center on his high school football team, had done 'his stint' in the service, and had moved up to this area for the quality of outdoor recreation it offered. His office walls were lined with pictures of Phil sampling different parts of that quality in a variety of outdoor locations with an assortment of outdoor props, including skis, snow shoes, fishing rods and ATVs. It took all of Nelson's control to keep the interested look on his face throughout Phil's explanation of each part of his photo gallery.

"...but you didn't come up here just to hear about my escapades in the wilderness." Phil's eyes showed a sudden shrewdness that made Nelson revise his opinion of the older man up a notch. "So what can I do you for?"

Trying to cover his wince at Phil's phrasing, Nelson decided to tell the truth as far as he could. If that didn't get him what he wanted, he could always invent an additional question or two. "I have to be honest with you, Phil. I've been up in this area since Sunday, and I'm just not the outdoorsman you are. I don't like walking on uneven ground, scenery doesn't do much for me, and those damn flies you have up here are eating me alive every time I step outside. So that leaves me at loose ends, and I decided to stop in and see how the small town newspaper world looks."

"If you don't like the country, what made you choose to spend a week up here?"

Ratcheting his estimation of Phil's intelligence upward once again, Nelson spread his hands and tried for a rueful grin. "Following my girlfriend."

Phil threw back his head and laughed. "I should have known. When there's a woman in the mix, all common sense goes right out the window. Tell you what. Why don't I take you around and introduce you to my staff and we can have a quick cup of coffee together. I'd invite you to lunch, but this is the day the local Chamber of Commerce meets. I'm on it, so I can't miss it."

"That sounds great, Phil. I appreciate your time."

"Not a problem. We'll start out in the front office with our receptionist. She's a very important part of our team because she's our first contact with the public and sets the tone for everything that follows...."

An hour later, Nelson knew more about the *Dispatch* than he could ever hope or care to remember, including circulation, delivery routes, rivals, and future plans. Phil turned out to be an enthusiastic speaker even to an audience of one.

"...and I'm afraid we're out of time, Nelson. I really wish I didn't have this lunch meeting. I could probably finagle a seat for you if you'd like to come."

Suppressing a shudder, Nelson declined as graciously as he could then beat a hasty retreat to Alyssa's car. Having drawn a blank look when he asked Phil the location of the nearest deli, Nelson looked again at the directions to a local market that Phil promised would make a sandwich to order. He'd grab a bite there and organize his next move.

Sandwich in hand, Nelson sat in the car considering what he had learned from his hour plus in Phil's company. It wasn't promising. Phil seemed to view his paper as a community service operation, with an emphasis on keeping the public informed of the various activities of the local town and business leaders. There was little in the way of investigative reporting. In fact, Phil had flat out admitted that they took their police report copy directly from the hand of that same department. Basically, it was a bare recital of facts, often toned down so it wouldn't upset the families of the arrestees. When Nelson had cautiously questioned Phil about the amount of space dedicated to crime in each edition, Phil had laughed.

"This isn't like your big city papers. We don't have all that much crime and scandal up here and frankly, we like it that way. This is still a small enough town that most of us know each other and try to pull together. It wouldn't help anyone to go in for public muckraking and besides, when everyone knows everyone else's business, it's not really news anyway!"

Nelson sighed as he bit into his very thin turkey sandwich. The woman who made it didn't seem to understand his request for a full inch of meat between the slices of bread. Maybe he should have followed her suggestion to get two sandwiches and combine them. It was a far cry from his usual pastrami on rye. Bringing his mind back to the present, Nelson decided to try the library next. Research through the back issues of the *Dispatch* might yield a different starting point.

****

Nelson's initial suspicion that library was another dead end was a useful reminder not to judge any situation by first impressions alone. And the library's first impression had been bleak. A cavernous, two hundred year old building without a research department or microfilm, and containing only two aging desktop computers seemed at first glance to be a complete waste of time.

But what the library lacked in modern technology, it made up for in the person of Muriel Wheelock, librarian and town clerk for the past thirty-two years. Muriel, as she proudly informed Nelson, knew everything there was to know about the town, the people in it, and what they had all been up to. A small woman with severely crimped dark gray hair, Muriel told Nelson that she had lived in the North Country her entire life, keeping in close contact with myriad friends, cousins, nieces, nephews and grandchildren in the area. On this sunny Wednesday afternoon, they were the only two people in the entire building, and she was happy to talk.

Again, following the path of truth as far as possible to avoid trip-ping over his own inventions, Nelson admitted up front that he was a metropolitan reporter, vacationing in the area, and curious about the town. That opened the floodgates. After listening politely to some ancient history dealing with the founding of the town, Nelson was able to steer Muriel to the meat of the visit, local law enforcement. Muriel had a couple of friends and at least one relative spread through the various departments in the surrounding towns. Since she thought they were all doing a bang up job, she was happy to brag about them and their accomplishments.

In a short span of time, Nelson was able to nail down the process of investigation that a stray body would go through and had a pretty good idea of who to contact next. That safely accomplished, he de-cided to try for more recent, specific information.

"It sounds like you've got things pretty well under control up here, Muriel."

"Well, we have an advantage that the big city cops don't."

"Really?" Nelson tried hard to hide his skepticism. Nothing he had seen in the area had impressed him as cutting edge. "What's that?"

"The community. There aren't that many people around here and we all know each other pretty well, so it's hard to hide if you've done something wrong. And it's the same thing with strangers. Someone new sticks out and gets noticed."

Nelson pursed his lips. With all the open space around, it seemed easy to disappear, but he wasn't going to argue with his information hotline. He decided to move in on his target.

"I was in one of the local bars the other night, and I heard some guys talking about a body that had just recently been found. Does that kind of stuff happen often around here?"

Muriel lifted an eyebrow. "Where'd you hear that?"

Nelson couldn't see the harm in telling her. "The Dewdrop Inn."

"Mmm. You have sharp ears. To answer your question, no, it doesn't happen often. As a matter of fact, this is the first one in al-most ten years. The last one was an older gent from down south who took it in his head to go hiking alone and without leaving anyone in-formation on what trail he was using." Muriel shook her head at such foolishness. "You should always let someone know where you're hik-ing if you head out alone. Young couple found his body a year later. Completely spoiled their weekend."

"I heard this body was a young woman and she was wearing old-fashioned, sixties-style clothing."

Muriel's eyes narrowed and Nelson was afraid he had pushed too far. He decided to drop the frontal assault in favor of a flanking movement. "That interested me because I had a cousin that was into that whole living off the land thing. I was too young to be in on it, but I remember thinking it seemed to make a lot of sense, provide most of your own food, and leave no footprints. I thought all that died out by now. Are there people like that still around up here?" The lies came easily, and Nelson watched closely to see their effect.

It seemed to be working. Muriel relaxed slightly. "Oh yes, we had a lot of that around here. There was a local college that was run along that philosophy; lots of open classrooms, self-sufficiency, and equality between staff and students. The college is long gone, but a lot of the people it brought to the area liked it here and stayed on. There are still a few pockets of them, trying to raise everything they eat. It makes me laugh. There they are, doing all the things my grandparents did, but planning it out on computers."

Nelson smiled politely, and moved in for the kill. "Would you happen to know where any of these 'pockets' are? I'd love to go out and see one, rather than just hear about it second hand."

"Sure, there are a couple of places north of here. Let me get a map and I'll give you directions."

Bending over the map, Nelson following Muriel's finger. It looked relatively easy to find since there didn't seem to be that many roads in the area. Bundling up the map, he thanked her again for her time and information and stepped out into the late afternoon sunshine. He could feel the tingling rush that always accompanied the start of a new story. And this one had the potential to go national.

Nelson paused at the bottom of the steps, trying to identify a slight prickle of unease. Had there been something off kilter in Muriel's face when she was giving directions? He shook himself mentally. He must have mingled too often with the dregs of the city if he started imagining something sinister in Muriel's grandmotherly smile. It was too late to go anywhere today he decided, but now he had a plan for tomorrow. First thing would be to check in with the local Investigative Services Bureau to see if he could draw any more information from official sources. After that he'd drive north to do some interviews.

CHAPTER SEVEN

Cliff sat at his desk, staring moodily out the window at the late afternoon sun. Since the discovery of the body two days ago, he and Mike had been working on that case exclusively. Now here it was, Wednesday afternoon, and they had little to show for all their efforts. The morning had started hopefully enough. Brenda's ME friend had come through with a composite picture of what their body looked like before being left exposed to the elements for the six to eight weeks Brenda told them was the minimum.

The face was unremarkable; pleasant-looking even features topped by dark blond hair. The picture helped some but it was disappointingly bland, obviously computer generated and lacking any spark of individuality. Not that a corpse generally had much personality, but it was surprising how often the uniqueness of the living person left an impression in a picture even after death. Cliff thought it had something to do with laugh lines, or skin texture. He couldn't put a finger on it, but he knew it was there.

He and Mike had taken the victim's picture and the one of her clothing around to a few of the likely communities in the area that morning.

Mike had shaken off his discomfort from the day before and appeared to be enjoying himself thoroughly, smiling at the irregular pattern of fields and wooded areas as they drove north. "I could see living like this. Out in the fresh air every day, enjoying the sun and the breeze. No deadlines to meet or alarm clocks to listen to."

Cliff raised an eyebrow. "Are you kidding? No alarm clocks? Have you ever heard the racket from a bunch of cows needing to be milked? They're louder than twenty alarm clocks and don't have a snooze button."

"All right, so you do have to get up, but you are your own man; you make your own schedule for the day."

This time Cliff snorted. "Shows how much time you've spent on an actual working farm. When a fence breaks, you fix it right then and there, rain or shine, or your stock gets out. And you muck out and clean up every day, no matter how you feel, if you want that stock to stay healthy."

Mike's reply was lost in the bumps of the driveway at the first farm they visited. The house was a rambling affair that looked as if a number of additions had been tacked on over the years. Several small pens held goats, cows, a couple of ponies and a pig while chickens contentedly scratched around the yard and garden. Setting his hat firmly on his head, Mike followed Cliff's lead by getting out of the patrol car and waiting to be acknowledged. A small head peered around the door of a barn shed and disappeared, soon replaced by an older head attached to a middle-age body dressed in jeans and a sweatshirt.

The greeting was cautious. "What can I do for you, Officers?"

Cliff didn't move from beside the car. "Mr. Peter Tappling?"

A swift dip of the chin was the only reply.

"We're looking into a missing person case. We have a picture of a girl and some of her clothes we'd like you to look at and see if you recognize either."

The shoulders inside the sweatshirt moved slowly down while the chin came up and Mr. Tappling approached the Troopers. "I'd be happy to help if I can, but I haven't heard of anyone missing from around here."

"I understand. But if you could just look at the pictures..." Cliff let the sentence hang as he held out the photographs of the clothes and reconstructed face of the victim. Tappling wiped his hands quickly on the back of his sweatshirt and then took the pictures. Focusing on

Tappling's face, Cliff watched curiosity fade to disinterest.

"Nope. Never seen her before."

Cliff tapped the picture with his knuckle. "Any word of a young blonde woman in the area? We think she was interested in your type of self-reliant lifestyle."

Mike shot a swift look over at Cliff, but Tappling took the question at face value. "Haven't heard of anyone. We just had a potluck for our home-school group, and no one mentioned any new faces in the area."

"Can I leave a copy of this picture here with you? Show it around, see if any friends or neighbors know her?"

Tappling accepted the picture with a nod, and stowed it away in a back pocket. "I'll do what I can, but don't hold your breath."

Cliff held out a hand which the other man shook firmly. "Thanks for your time. Here's my card if you hear anything more."

Tappling tucked the card into the same spot as the picture, then waved a casual good-bye as he headed back toward his shed. Three small heads peeked out from around the door, but vanished quickly at Cliff's friendly smile.

"No luck there," Mike said as they reversed their way carefully down the driveway.

Cliff shrugged. "It was a long shot."

"How many more long shots are on the schedule?"

"Three. That should set the word out. Then we wait to see what turns up."

****

No one at the three other farms where they stopped recognized or had ever heard of the dead girl. All accepted pictures and promised earnestly to ask around for any information, and one family volunteered to pray for her soul. Both offers were received with polite acceptance by Cliff and covert amusement from Mike, until the final interview. That family tried to simultaneously bestow a scripture quote and extract a promise to attend their next meeting. Mike declined firmly, then muttered a comment about waiting until the cows came home which brought out a sharp look of reprimand from Cliff.

"Right now, these people are the only local leads we have," he said to Mike once they were back in the car. "Let's not alienate them right off the bat, OK?"

Mike nodded stiffly. "My religion is my own business and being coerced into someone else's sends a hair up my ass."

"So squeeze it until we're out of earshot," Cliff said, "and then you can extract it anyway you like."

****

It was after two when they got back to the office and found a report waiting. It had been emailed up from the Massachusetts P.D. describing the search of Kenny Brainerd's apartment. Kenny had eagerly authorized the search by his local law enforcement. "Anything that clears my good name is fine with me. I've got nothing to hide. I've never even gotten a parking ticket, much less murdered someone."

There was a lot more along that line, but Cliff and Mike had quickly learned to develop selective deafness in Kenny's company.

Cliff looked at the printout of the report, then held it at arm's length and tilted his head back, trying to make the print more legible. It didn't help. He knew he should look into getting a pair of glasses, but was finding it hard to admit it. Only old guys need glasses, and he was only forty-five. A long way to go until old.

"Damn printer, it's low on ink and practically illegible."

"Pass it over; let me see if I can get anything out of it." Mike said as diplomatically as possible.

The feeling of being humored was worse. "Sure, take a look at it. I'm going to call the guy – what's his name, Murphy? – who sent it over. I'll always choose talking to someone over reading a report. There are some things you notice that you don't want to put into an official document."

Prudently, Mike just nodded and buried his nose into the report.

It didn't take Cliff long to get Detective Brian Murphy on the phone. Cliff introduced himself, got through the obligatory comments on the weather ('you still got snow up there?') and the rural character of their community ('I heard there's no take-out up there after nine PM, how can you stand it?') and moved on to the purpose of the call. "Kenny Brainerd? Yeah, I tossed his crib. What a weirdo."

Cliff's attention sharpened. This was exactly what never got into a report. "What did you find; porn?"

"Nah, nothing like that. I don't think he's a perv, just a nutcase. He's got a two bedroom apartment, right? One of the bedrooms is just that, a bedroom. But the other, it could be some kind of outdoor equipment showroom. He's got all kinds of gear, scuba stuff, climbing rope, cameras and tripods; all neatly arranged in different corners. Then there's his bookcase. It's full of books and how-to manuals on diving and photography and something called spelunking. You ever heard of that?"

"It's exploring caves."

"Exactly. Who'd want to do that?"

"So that's what was weird? His hobbies?" Cliff relaxed back in his chair, disappointed.

"No, it's that most of the stuff looks brand new, like it's never been used." Murphy blew into the phone in exasperation. "Hundreds of dollars worth of stuff and it's never been used."

"Anything else about him? Job?"

"He's a number cruncher for an insurance company, gets paid pretty well, good credit, no outstanding debt other than a car loan. His office speaks highly of his work but I get the impression that he's not the life of the corporate party, if you know what I mean."

"After meeting him, I do. Any pictures in his apartment of a young blonde woman?"

"Hardly. A couple of family pictures and lots of outdoor, spectacular scenery type prints. You know, low budget, stock kind of things."

Cliff sighed. "So no trophies; like women's panties or date books or anything?"

"Nothing. This guy looks clean. My impression? He's one of those 'legend in his own mind' kind of guys. Goes out, buys all the fancy equipment, but doesn't have the guts to use it."

"That matches what I've seen. It just would have been a lot easier if he'd been the murderer."

Murphy laughed. "I've been there, pal. But when it comes to homicides, nothing is easy."

Cliff thanked him again for the information and hung up. He looked over at Mike who had been simultaneously reading, listening in on the conversation, and eating a bag of chips. "Anything else in that report, or is the orange from your chips covering up all the pertinent information?"

"Bloyer" Mike said indistinctly through his last mouthful. He swallowed and dusted off his hands, chest and a six inch radius of his desk. "Nope, nothing in here. I guess Kenny is pretty much in the clear. So what's next?"

"Nothing more today. Tomorrow we'll go back to Missing Person reports for the last six months but expand the search to be nation-wide." Cliff looked down, rubbed the back of his neck, and then moved his hand around across his mouth and chin. "We'll start with the Northeast, then spread out through the rest of the country."

Mike nodded glumly. "And if that doesn't give us anything?"

"We hope some kind of lead walks through our front door.

CHAPTER EIGHT

Nelson dressed carefully Thursday morning for his trip to the New Hampshire Investigative Services Bureau. He had decided on an initial frontal assault, followed up with a flanking movement with Alyssa's help if needed. Therefore, he wanted to power dress to impress the small town cops that Muriel Wheelock, librarian extraordinaire, had described. He hadn't brought many muscle clothes along for his week in the country, but judging by what he had seen so far, his sports jacket, tailored linen slacks, and Italian loafers would provide enough dazzle. Luckily, he had recently gotten a trim from his favorite barber, and with a little extra attention now from his razor and aftershave, he felt equipped for battle.

The muffled exclamation from the waitress in the hotel dining room reinforced Nelson's feeling of having dressed for success, as did the open stare from the desk clerk. With directions to the Trooper's office and barracks written in on his map, he headed toward Franconia and then up and over Mount Agassiz to hit Route 302. 'Up' turned out to be the operant word as the road climbed in a series of twisting steadily steepening curves that required repeated downshifting on Nelson's part. The scenery was nothing special – any mountain views were obscured by trees - and that, combined with a rising temperature in the transmission, made him happy to reach Route 302.

This was one of the main roads on his map, marked by a solid blue line rather than the smaller red lines of the secondary roads so Nelson expected to see a fairly major thoroughfare. However, once he had driven a few miles out of Bethlehem, styling itself as the 'Poetry Capital of the World', he was sure he had fallen off the map. Worse, there wasn't a gas station or convenience store in sight to ask directions. Just miles of pine trees with an occasional dirt track heading off into them. Every so often he saw a brook or a field, but nothing that looked remotely like human habitation. He took out his cell phone for an emergency navigational check with the hotel, but found he had no service.

Finally, signs of civilization appeared on the right. Maybe there was a town around here after all. A campground, a convenience store, a garage cum gas station that needed more than just a coat of paint, and at last, a sign for the ISB. Nelson pulled into the parking lot with a flourish and a secret sigh of relief, collected his notebook, double-checked his press card, and approached the front door.

The front office was small and clean, with a counter protected by the ubiquitous plastic bandit barrier, a row of four blue plastic chairs that promised ease of cleaning rather than comfort, and a wall of informational pamphlets on both the requirements for registering and licensing a vehicle and the dire consequences of driving while intoxicated. The outer office was empty except for a tall, weedy looking young man and an older woman – his grandmother? – struggling with a stack of forms while the receptionist/clerk, a pleasant looking woman in her mid-forties, sat behind a plastic partition at a computer. With memories of chatty Muriel Wheelock fresh in his mind, Nelson approached the front desk confidently.

"Good morning, Patti," he said, reading her name tag and flashing his most engaging smile. "I wonder if you could help me."

"I hope so. What do you need?" Patti returned his smile and Nelson relaxed. This was going to be easier than he'd thought.

"Information." Nelson leaned forward and dropped his voice. "I understand the body of a young woman was recently found in the area and I'd like to know a little more about her, such as her age, how she was dressed, what kind of state she was in when found."

"Why?"

Nelson blinked in surprise, but rallied quickly. "I've done some

investigative work in the past into similar situations with good results and I'd like to do the same here."

"What type of work and where?" Patti's smile had vanished.

This was not going as smoothly as he had anticipated. Time to
bring out the big guns. He slid his press card under the plastic shielding the desk. "I'm a journalist and I've done several stories similar to
this which have led the police to facts they might not have uncovered
on their own."

She made no move to pick up or even look at his card. "Where?"

"New York City. Specifically the Bronx, the Hell's Kitchen area,
and along the East River docks." Nelson waited, sure that would get
her.

"Oh, New York." Patti flicked her eyes from his head to his waist.
"Things are a little different up here. The ISB handles everything,"
she said, "without any help from the press." Nodding to Nelson, she
turned back to the paperwork on her desk.

It was a setback, but Nelson had slain far bigger dragons. Pasting
a pleasant expression on to his face, he stood at the desk, rocking
slightly back on his heels. The dragon-lady did a good job of ignoring
him for about five minutes before she began darting unsettled looks
in his direction. Nelson continued to stand and rock for another five
minutes, half listening to the low voiced conversation about license
renewals from the counter behind him.

"There's no sense in hanging around. I told you the ISB doesn't
involve the newspapers in their work." Patti threw at him over her
shoulder.

Nelson smiled pleasantly and nodded, showing no sign of leaving.

The dragon-lady shrugged and worked doggedly on for another
fifteen minutes. Finally, caving under the pressure, she lifted the
phone and, turning her back on Nelson, spoke softly into the receiver. The narrow eyed glower she directed at Nelson told him he
had won. Reinforcements were obviously on their way.

****

Cliff looked up from his twelfth missing persons file in irritation
as the intercom on his desk buzzed. He blinked sharply, trying to
bring the telephone into focus, then realized the magnifying glasses
he wore made that impossible. Whipping them off in disgust, he

hoped the call wasn't his wife, wondering where her spare glasses had gone. He lunged for the telephone. "Yes?"

"Sorry to bother you Cliff, but there's some reporter out here asking about the body up on Lafayette."

"Tell him we don't speak to the press in the middle of an investigation and send him on his way."

"I tried, but he won't leave. He's been standing here in front of my desk for almost half an hour now."

Cliff exhaled sharply. "I'll be right there," he said and slammed the phone down.

Mike looked up. "What's going on?"

"Some fool reporter is out front bothering Patti for details about our body. She says he won't leave, so I need to go bounce him out of here. As if I don't have enough to do."

"Want some company? It's always a pleasure to watch the master disembowel an unsuspecting victim."

Cliff dropped his head, then lifted it with a faint, wry grin. "Why not? Let's grab our hats for good measure."

The two men walked to the lobby door, squaring their shoulders and donning their 'work faces' as they went. Mike opened the door and made an 'after you' gesture.

Cliff surveyed the figure waiting in the lobby and suppressed a groan. He could see why Patti had asked for help. This was no local reporter looking for some extra details to flesh out a slow news week. This guy's clothes and manner pegged him as some big city shark bent on throwing his weight around. The satisfied smirk on the man's face showed he thought he'd scored some kind of victory by getting to see them. It was time to put him firmly back into his place.

"Good afternoon. I'm Trooper Codey and this is Trooper Eldrich."

The stranger's smile broadened. "Nice to meet you. My name is Nelson Simon, freelance investigative reporter. How do you do?"

Cliff looked down at the hand extended out to him and pointedly crossed his own arms. "I'm a busy man, Mr. Simon, and I don't appreciate being called out here because you won't take no for an answer. You've been told we don't give out information to the press on cases currently under investigation. Waiting around won't change our policy, and it might result in a loitering ticket."

The other man's expression went from smirk, to surprise, to

sneer. "Are you threatening me?"

Cliff shook his head. "Informing you. Now everyone here in this office is very busy, so we'll thank you to leave and let us do our jobs."

"Are you denying the public their right..."

"The public has a right to see that this department doesn't squander their tax dollars by wasting our time." Cliff overrode the other man's voice calmly. "Which is what you are doing now. Good day, Mr. Simon, I trust Patti won't be calling me out here again."

Turning sharply, Cliff strode back through the door that Mike held open for him. Hearing it latch firmly, he answered Mike's grin. "I don't think we have to worry about any more interruptions from *him*."

"That was wicked smart. Sent him off with his tail between his legs."

With a satisfied smile, Cliff settled back at his desk. "Let's see if we can get through the rest of these by lunch time." Good humor restored, he turned back to the reports, picking up his wife's glasses without a second thought.

Mike glanced over, lips twitching. "I do think the blue frame goes well with our uniforms."

Cliff continued to focus on the computer screen. "A word to the wise. Don't start a fight you know you're going to lose. Got it?"

"Sure boss."

Cliff stifled a sigh. From Mike's tone he knew the battle was delayed, not abandoned.

****

He sat quietly in his car, working on breathing regularly so he didn't spook the woman beside him. He'd kept his head down through the entire altercation starting with the flatlander's entrance. That had been a nasty shock, seeing that nosy bigmouth from the bar walk through the door and hearing he was a reporter. It was all he could do not to choke, or run, or yell. But he had been taught to be stoic, and now he could see that those lessons, difficult as they were at the time, were valuable. At least now he had a name, Nelson Simon. He'd written it down on one of his extra forms, so he wouldn't forget. As if he could. But that was another lesson, be thorough and keep good records. So far, the lessons were helping.

And he could see the guy was an obnoxious bigmouth. The way he wouldn't leave when asked, just stood there. He noted that as well – it could be a useful technique in the future.

Then the two troopers from Investigative Services came out of their office. He wrote those names down too, Codey and Eldrich. Mike from the bar looked a lot more impressive in his uniform, but now he had a full name. Codey looked familiar somehow. But there was no time to think of that now.

Even more valuable, he'd learned the talk in the bar was true. Someone had found her. He'd have to figure out how to get away and hike up there tomorrow to make doubly sure. It was risky, they might have a watch on the place, but he knew enough backwoods tricks to get in and out again without anyone knowing he'd been there. It shouldn't be too hard to find the place – after all, he'd brought her there. Then he'd decide what to do about all these busy-bodies, butting in where they didn't belong. First step; get home and collect his gear. Then he needed to get away, far from people, to be able to think it through. He'd make sure to do that tomorrow.

CHAPTER NINE

Nelson squinted unseeingly at Alyssa's car from the front steps of the barracks. Conceding the first round to the troopers, he nonetheless felt the trip had been worthwhile. The younger man who came out of the back office, 'Trooper Eldrich', was definitely the 'Mike' that Nelson had seen at the Dew Drop Inn Tuesday evening. Now Nelson knew he was on the right track. He flipped open his notebook and wrote down the names Eldrich and Codey. He knew about the body and the names of the investigation team. Now it was time to look into some of the alternative lifestyle communities Muriel Wheelock had told him about. Knowing the Troopers' names might give him extra cachet to extract information.

The first place Muriel mentioned was fairly close to the library, so Nelson jumped back onto 302 and headed into Littleton then turned the car north on Route 16 through Whitefield and then off on to Route 135. He quickly ran out of town and after ten minutes he was traveling along yet another narrow two-lane road with little sign of civilization. Muriel's directions, which had seemed comfortably clear within the security of the library's granite walls, now seemed woefully vague and haphazard. The sight of a tractor mowing down tall grass in a field off to the right - to be turned into hay? – brought the phrase needle in a haystack to mind.

Finally Nelson spotted the landmark he sought, a large barn that had once been red, with a burned out foundation next to it. Turning up the road, which rapidly ran out of pavement, he slowed to a crawl, hoping the car's suspension was equal to the task in front of it. Muriel's next direction said there would be a sign at a driveway advertising fresh eggs, venison, and manure for sale. He tried not to imagine how those three things were inter-related. The sign appeared, obviously hand-lettered, and Nelson nosed his car up the steep, rutted driveway, offering a brief prayer to the god of mufflers that his would remain intact.

There was no sign of human life in the yard, but there were enough animals to get through several rousing choruses of 'Old Mac-Donald'. Nelson stepped out of the car and surveyed the scene. A number of chickens, much larger in real life than they looked packaged in plastic, minced purposefully toward him. Nelson stepped back, looking carefully behind him to avoid anything that might squish unpleasantly under his boot, but the chickens kept on coming. Finally, to deter the birds as much as to bring out the humans, he sounded the horn.

Instantaneous chaos resulted. The chickens scattered, squawking wildly, while several species of large four-legged animals jumped, squealed, brayed and mooed. The cacophony brought a woman to the front door of a long low building that Nelson had dismissed as too small to house a family, with a dishtowel in one hand and a spoon in the other. She stared at Nelson, then turned and called over her shoulder.

The man that approached Nelson looked like a holdover from the musical "Hair'. Jeans, tie-dye shirt, pony-tail; all that was missing was a medallion hanging around his neck. Struggling to keep a straight face, Nelson took the initiative.

"Mr. Tappling?"

A cautious nod was the only reply.

"Muriel Wheelock from the Littleton Library gave me your name. She said you're doing some wonderful things here on your farm."

Another nod and no noticeable thaw.

"I'm a reporter from New York and I was hoping you'd show me around a little. We might feature you in an article about life in New

Hampshire."

By now, three small heads were peering around the tie-dyed waist, and what Nelson could only assume was Mrs. Tappling peered over his shoulder. A whispered consultation ensued.

Evidently, the outcome was positive, because the entire Tappling family tramped down to give the tour. Nelson held onto his smile as they pointed out several garden areas with lengthy explanations of plant identification and while they led the way through unidentified piles of organic matter. When they reached the barn, he told himself repeatedly that it smelled no worse than some of New York's back alleys. Then they reached the pig pen and things got a whole lot worse.

"And this is our sow, Daisy, and those are her piglets." Mr. Tappling spoke with obvious pride, apparently unaffected by the odor.

Nelson, manfully trying not to gag at the stench, stared at the enormous animal and six smaller mud covered versions that were a far cry from his dim memory of the cover of Charlotte's Web. He tried for a question to distract himself. "Do the piglets have names, too?"

"Oh yes," piped up one of the smaller heads still firmly fastened to their father's waist. "That one's Bacon, that's Pork Chop, over there is Sausage..."

This was too much for Nelson. The smell, combined with the thought of what produced it ending up on his breakfast table, caused a sudden forceful exhalation and a rapid exit from the pen.

Luckily, the Tapplings interpreted his sound as laughter and joined in. This seemed to melt the ice further, and Mr. Tappling even forgot himself far enough to slap Nelson on the back. "You like that, don't you? We do that every year. It reminds us where they're headed and keeps us from getting too attached to them."

Nelson quickly capitalized on the change in attitude. "That's very clever. I'll make sure I include that in my article." He moved a few more cautious steps away from the source of the smell. "You know, I had a friend that moved up here, a young woman, who was very interested in this type of farming and animal husbandry. I lost touch with her during the last year or so, you haven't heard of anyone new in the area, have you? Young, blonde...?"

Mr. Tappling started to shake his head, but Mrs. Tappling over-rode him. "Do you think it could have anything to do with the picture the troopers left with us? That girl was blonde."

Swallowing his excitement, Nelson cleared his throat and tried to keep his expression blandly interested. "Picture?" If those two stiff-hatted yahoos from yesterday at the barracks had left a picture, so much the better.

Mr. Tappling scowled at his wife, but she had already turned away and was hurrying up the path to their house. She popped back out minutes later, gingerly holding a four-by-six photo by the edges. "Is this anything like the girl you're looking for?"

"May I?" Nelson asked, taking the picture from her outstretched hand before she could answer. He thought quickly. He needed an ex-cuse to take the picture with him that wouldn't send Ma and Pa Ket-tle running in to telephone or send smoke signals or whatever they did to contact those two boorish troopers. "It does look like her, but you know, I haven't seen her since high school and I'm not quite sure. Could I take this with me and show it to my wife? She knew her much better."

The mention of a wife seemed to reassure both of the Tapplings. "Of course," Mrs. Tappling said, while Mr. Tappling nodded, gazing back toward his barn and seeming suddenly bored with the whole proceeding. "I've got to get back to my stock," he told Nelson, and turned away abruptly.

Nelson thanked his rapidly retreating back, repeated the same to Mrs. Tappling's anxiously smiling front, and withdrew to his car, treasure in hand. He backed cautiously out of the driveway, trying not to imagine what a squashed chicken would do to the underside of the car, and drove away with a final triumphant sounding of his horn.

Back at his hotel, Nelson sat down to examine his find a little more closely. The picture showed a young woman, Nelson guessed to be in her early twenties, with dirty blonde hair. There was something odd about the picture, though. The face looked both too perfect and fuzzily unreal. It was hard to put a finger on. Maybe Alyssa would have some ideas. Photography had drawn her into journalism in the first place, and she still had a good eye for it and contacts in that end of the business.

Nelson flopped down into a chair and kicked his shoes off. Thursday night and they finally had something he thought worth celebrating. This trip hadn't been such a waste of time after all.

CHAPTER TEN

A crumpled chip bag sailed past Cliff's desk, banked off a wall marked with a faint orange sheen, and landed in the gunmetal grey garbage can with a muffled clank.

"Yes! Ten points!" Mike exclaimed, holding up both hands in a victory salute.

"Is that all you've got left from your high school career?" Cliff asked dryly. "The ability to hit the damn can nine times out of ten?"

"Jealous?"

Cliff turned away from Mike's cheesy grin, a literal thing, since the chip bag was another in the long line of orange-dusted snacks that Mike favored, and glanced at the clock. Four thirty on a Thursday. No wonder. The time of day together with the size of the stack of missing person files in the 'completed' pile directly correlated to the upswing of Mike's juvenile antics. Combining all that with having to go back to paper files for the older cases made a tough chore even worse. And paper files were harder to read because he couldn't increase the font size to make it easier on his eyes. His wife's glasses – which he'd borrowed again to try to help his eyes – had given him a headache that simultaneously slowed him down and soured his temper so that his own pile was a quite a bit smaller than Mike's. He really had to get a pair of his own glasses and soon.

"'Bout ready to call it quits?" Cliff asked, throwing the offending glasses onto his desk and massaging the bridge of his nose.

"Twenty minutes past. I've got three possibles from my stack of reports. Two blonde sisters from Massachusetts who haven't phoned home in awhile, and one case of a blonde teenager snatched by a non-custodial parent in Virginia five years ago."

Cliff held out his hand for the files. Neither sounded promising, but he wanted to cover every base. "We'll start with these two first thing tomorrow. I'll take the rest of my pile home and look through them over tonight." With the help of a magnifying glass and spotlight, he added silently. He thought he had something like that out in his garage. Right now he needed aspirin and a break from the anemic lighting in the squad room. Once the sun went behind the hills, the wattage in the room dropped by half. Maybe it really was time to pick up that desk lamp he'd been promising himself. And he might just take a look at an over-the-counter pair of glasses. Only to use when the light was bad, of course.

Suppressing a sigh, Cliff squared up the pile of folders on the corner of the desk. He knew that the chances of finding anything useful in that stack were slim to none, but he was running out of options. Their only possible suspect, Kenny, had dropped even further down on the list of possible suspects after today's visit.

****

They'd stopped to see Kenny again that morning after receiving the mocked up photograph from the M.E.'s office on Wednesday. He was still at Kurt's hotel, but seemed to have shelved any thought of hiking in exchange for milking his minor celebrity status.

Kurt had greeted them at the door of the Mountain Glen. "Tell me you've come to lock this bozo up."

Mike had taken the older man at face value. "Do you have any new information for us?"

"Besides this guy being a jerk who's full of hot air? No. I'd just like to see him gracing some other place with his presence. He's getting on my nerves."

"Join the club," Cliff told him. "Has he said or done anything unusual?"

"Other than drive paying customers away with his boring story?"

Kurt shook his head. "Good thing he's leaving tomorrow, otherwise you might have another dead body to deal with."

Cliff nodded in sympathy. "Where is he?"

"Hanging out in the dining room. Our breakfast attendance has gone down by fifty percent every day since he's been here. Can you at least get him out of the room for a while?"

"Sure, we need to take him some place private to talk to him anyway." Cliff motioned to Mike and they both walked toward the dining room.

Kenny saw them coming and his eyes widened with excitement. "...and here are the troopers that I showed the body to! What are the latest developments in the case, boys?"

Cliff looked expressionlessly down at Kenny's excited face. His audience had melted away in happy gratitude after being given a polite excuse to leave. "Will you step up to your room with us please, Mr. Brainerd?"

"Sure, and its Kenny. Remember I asked you to call me Kenny?"

"Yes Mr. Brainerd, I do remember."

"It's great to see you guys again," Kenny chattered on over his shoulder as he walked up the narrow staircase to his room. "I've been thinking hard about the case all week and trying to figure out a possible motive for why someone would do such a horrible thing...."

Once in his room Kenny proved equally unsquelchable, snatching the photograph eagerly from Cliff's hand. "Is this the girl? Oh, yeah, now I recognize her. She looks a lot better in this picture than she did on the mountain."

Over Kenny's head, Cliff exchanged a raised eyebrow with Mike. Kenny had refused to look at the corpse on Monday, both before and after she was brought down from the mountain, practically crying that he would never be able to sleep again if forced to look.

"What do you mean, Mr. Brainerd? You declined to look at the body on Monday."

"Oh. Yeah, well, I must have just had a quick peek at her, you know, just a glimpse."

"And you can make positive identification between that glimpse and this photograph?"

"Sure, I know that's the girl."

Cliff closed his eyes and clenched his jaw. Kenny was turning out to be the worst type of witness, one who convinced himself he had seen things he couldn't have.

"Have you seen this girl anywhere else?" Mike asked.

"No, of course not. How could I have? She was dead."

Both troopers jumped on that immediately.

"What do you mean?"

"How did you know she's dead?"

Kenny quailed before the onslaught. "C'mon guys, you were there with me when we found her. With that smell there wasn't any doubt she was dead."

Cliff ran his thumb and fore-finger down his nose. "Look, Kenny," he said, spacing each word with care. "Let's start again. Have you seen the woman in this picture anywhere other than on Lafayette on Monday?"

The use of Kenny's first name seemed to have cheered him. "No, but you guys know that. I told you that on Monday."

"No Kenny, on Monday you told us you didn't kill her and that you had never been up on Lafayette before. Now we're asking a different question. Have you ever seen the woman in the photo before this week, anywhere?"

Kenny's expression didn't change. "No. Like I told you when you first came in, I didn't. But if you guys give me that picture I'll bet I could help you find out about her – you know, show it around and question people. I could be your civilian liaison!" He stopped and gazed up hopefully at them.

Cliff signaled to Mike and they both stepped out of the room, telling Kenny, "Wait here" and closing the door on his cheerful reply of "Sure".

"What do you think?"

"I think you got it right on Monday. Either he's one of the most brainless morons I've ever met, or he should have a shelf full of Oscars."

"I just wish I could be sure which one it was."

They wrapped up the interview by asking Kenny when he planned to leave. He told them his original reservation ended Friday. He'd wanted to extend it but Kurt told him the hotel was too full. Remembering Kurt's comments on the way in, Cliff wasn't surprised at the sudden lack of vacancies.

****

The mountain welcomed him back, as it always did. Up here, away from all the people with their sneers and their stares, he could relax and think. And he had a lot to think about. He had returned to this hallowed spot, hiking up the Falling Waters Trail and traversing across the Franconia Ridge Trail to the peak of Mount Lafayette then bushwhacking down the mountain to where he'd left her in March. He'd been careful, using all his outdoor skill and knowledge not to leave a trail. It hadn't been easy – the brush was thick off the beaten path – but he took the challenge to be another test of his skills.

He found that her resting place had been desecrated with footprints and destruction and remnants of yellow tape. He retreated to the top of the boulder he'd chosen to mark her place and act as her protector, to consider what needed to be done. The original plan had been to give her back to the mountain so the weather and the wild life could cleanse her and heal his memories. But that natural cycle had been broken so now he needed to decide what he could do to rebuild it again and restore his peace. He'd brought his overnight gear – a nylon bivvy sack, tinder and matches, a folding saw, and some twine – and planned to stay at the site until he was shown what his next step should be.

Fading back into the brush, he climbed up to the spot he had noted earlier for his campsite. It gave him a clear view of both the peak and the valley below him, and the moon would provide any light he might need. He had some serious thinking to do. The people who had violated her grave must be made to pay. Now he needed to decide how and when would be best to do it.

CHAPTER ELEVEN

Friday morning, Cliff slipped in to work early, trying to get his new desk lamp and drug-store glasses firmly established on his desk before Mike arrived in the hope of forestalling any smart comments.

He should have known that was a non-starter.

Mike sailed in at eight, full of Friday cheer and bonhomie, and the whoop he let out at the sight of the new additions to Cliff's desk had curious heads peering around doors in all directions.

"Well, what do we have here?" Mike stopped and gave an exaggerated stagger back, shielding his eyes. "Some fancy new lighting for our old tired desks? Oh wait, it's not for *our* tired desks, it's just for your tired desk! Is this discrimination I see? Or maybe it's a touch of favoritism from on high?"

Cliff let him run on for a bit longer, then put his hands on his desk and slowly rose to his feet.

"Okay, okay, I'm done." Mike flapped both his hands in a tamping down motion. "I'm sitting down now and I promise I won't say another word." He suited his actions to his words, but his toothy grin remained intact as he opened drawers and laid out materials on his desk.

Cliff remained standing just long enough to make his point then sat back down. He punched the 'on' button of his new desk light, placed his new glasses firmly on his nose and glanced over at Mike, who was now biting his lips in an attempt not to let any sounds escape. Cliff glowered a minute. "I'm only going to say this once. Wait till you're my age." He grabbed a folder from his stack, snapped it open and added, "Weren't you going to run down those missing person reports?"

Mike nodded and ducked his head, still apparently unable to speak without breaking his promise. Cliff sighed and rustled his papers while looking pointedly at Mike's desk. Taking the hint, Mike took out his files and a temporary peace settled over the office.

Over lunch, Mike filled Cliff in on his three possible leads from the day before. Hefting his lunchbox – which looked more like a small suitcase – onto his desk, Mike unloaded while he talked. "I started with the girl from Virginia, the one snatched by the non-custodial parent." Two sandwiches, a bag of cheez crunchies, and a Danish were piled on the desk. "The girl gave her Dad the slip and ended up back home, so happy ending for them." A sleeve of chocolate chip cookies and a quart of chocolate milk joined the pile on the desk. "The two sisters from Massachusetts were seen briefly in California then vanished again. The prevailing theory seems to be that they went out west to break into business in the movie world and probably found their way into the oldest business in the world." A packet of beef jerky and a granola bar completed the pile that now teetered precariously close to the edge of the desk. "So basically I got nothing from my pile."

Cliff brought out his sandwich, his apple, and his water bottle and tried not to make any comparisons with the feast laid out on Mike's desk. After Cliff's last physical, his wife Anna had gently insisted that he should start watching what he ate. Cliff agreed in principle but the practice wasn't easy. "I checked missing persons for the last six months from eastern Canada, but nothing popped out at me." He opened his sandwich and spread a squeeze packet of mustard and mayo between the layers. "So now we widen our search parameters to go back two years and cover all fifty states and Canada and see if that brings us anything."

Mike nodded and mumbled around bites of cookie. The sandwiches and the Danish were already history. The cheez crunchies seemed to be next on the hit list.

Cliff sighed, pushed aside his apple and brushed the crumbs off his desk. "I can read basic French, so I'll take Canada. You get started locally going back two years and I'll join you as soon as I get through what our northern neighbors have to offer."

Mike finished chugging the last of the chocolate milk, grabbed a trash can and started brushing the mixture of empty wrappers, crumbs, and bags off his desk. "Works for me. I took Spanish in high school and after four years all I can do is ask how to find the library."

Cliff rolled his eyes. "I'll keep that skill in mind if we get lost in Mexico."

"Yeah, like that's going to happen!"

****

By late afternoon, both men had worked through their respective piles with negative results and were more than ready to talk about something – anything – else.

"Any plans for the weekend?" Cliff asked idly, watching Mike tidy his desk by sweeping everything into a top drawer.

"Yeah, some big family shindig on Sunday. My cousin graduated from college this year, so we're all getting together to celebrate." Mike's disgusted expression showed exactly what he thought of the idea. "I think it's just a power exercise by my Aunt Muriel. She likes to be able to say 'you must come' to all of us, and then watch us jump through her hoops. I'd blow it off except it would upset my Mom."

Cliff nodded in understanding. "How's she been?"

"A little better. This round of chemo seems to be working. It's making her sicker, and she thinks that's a sign that it's doing its job."

"What do the doctors say?"

Mike shrugged one shoulder. "That anything she believes is helping her actually is." He bent down and rummaged aimlessly in a bottom drawer. "Whatever."

Recognizing the warning signs, Cliff changed the subject. "Will you be roasting a pig?"

Mike straightened up and happily retreated onto safer ground. "I think so. That's one thing about Aunt Muriel. She makes our presence mandatory, but she feeds us well when we get there. How about you?"

"Softball tournament."

Mike grinned. "Wanna switch?"

"No, I like watching the kids play..."

"...but six hours in a row is torture for everyone." Mike finished for him.

Cliff opened his mouth to deny it and then shook his head. "By the end of the day we're all sunburned, bug-bitten, and grouchy. Why they can't spread it out over two or three days...." It was an old argument, and Mike barely looked up as he slammed his drawer shut.

"Not enough ball fields."

"Right. If we build a few more someone will have the bright idea to get a baby-bambino league of two year olds going."

"Not so loud! If someone hears you they might just do it!" His good humor restored, Mike headed for the door. "See you Monday, unless Kenny finds another body."

Waving Mike out the door, Cliff picked up the phone. Kenny was another loose end he could tie up before he left for the day.

****

Now that Friday had arrived, Cliff dialed Kurt's number to double check that Kenny's departure had gone according to schedule, and was surprised and thrown when the man himself answered the phone.

"Hi Kurt, Cliff here. Didn't know you were on phone duty these days."

"I'm not." Kurt's growled. "One of my staff took some unexpected time off so I'm a bit short today. You want to come down and help out?"

Cliff tried to keep it light. "Can't today. Actually just checking that Kenny Brainerd left on schedule."

"Finally. Our check-out time is two o'clock, and he stayed parked on my front porch nattering on for another hour after that. I have never met such a bagful of flatulence in my life."

"Did he say anything that might remotely be considered significant before he left?"

Kurt's snort of disgust carried clearly over the phone line. "Are you kidding? Other than those same tired boasts about his backwoods skills that led to the body, it was just a lot of speculation about the 'poor dear girl left lonely in the woods'."

"That's the only thing Kenny seems to do well; talk." Cliff noted the time of his departure in the file. "Thanks, Kurt. I appreciate your help with this one. We've got his home address if we need to ask him anything else." Cliff hesitated, looking for a graceful way to end the conversation, but Kurt took the initiative away from him.

"Will we see you on Sunday?"

"I'll see what I can do, Kurt. My girls have a softball tournament, and..."

Another snort from Kurt cut short the excuses and showed plainly what he thought of them. Cliff pressed his lips together and bit them from the inside. It had been this way as long as Cliff had known Kurt. Any deviation from the older man's value scale was greeted with derision.

"I have to see how the day goes, Kurt. I can't make any promises."

"You never could."

The conversation ended with the sharp click of Kurt's disconnection. Cliff put his phone gently back on the cradle, wondering how long past obligations carry over into the future. When would his debt to Kurt be considered paid in full? He'd spent five years on 'the Crew', and Kurt seemed to feel that entitled him to a priority in Cliff's life for the rest of it.

Cliff slid open the bottom drawer of his desk and dug around in the back, finally pulling out a picture with a diagonal crease across the center. He'd stashed it away in a miscellaneous work file early in his marriage. A boozy Friday night reunion with the Kurt and company had resulted in harsh words from his wife Anna, an invitation to sleep on the couch, and a question about what kind of advancement there'd be for a trooper who was known to get regularly shit-faced on the weekends. The morning-after hangover had underlined the truth in his wife's comments, and that had been his last evening with the Crew.

Looking over the picture, Cliff could name those who found local jobs that kept them in Kurt's group, and more significantly, what they had done with their lives. Duane had stayed closest to Kurt, and was now guiding hiking trips for him from his hotel. Jake and Zack were next in line. They owned a small building firm running on the principle that rescue work for Kurt trumped any current company project and could be found hanging around the Mountain Glen most weekends.

The rest of the guys in the photo had drifted away from the Crew the same time Cliff did. Two had moved away, living over an hour south of Lincoln – too far for rescue work or easy stopovers. Another former member became a teacher, and the last three of the originals were in retail, all positions that prevented them from closing shop at the whim of a rescue. But there always seemed to be new blood ready to fill in any gaps, as long as they were willing to adopt Kurt's code of Crew first, everything else second. The younger ones used the hotel as a home base, often working there to spend as much time with their leader as possible.

There was, of course, one face missing from his picture, one that could never return. Kurt had told them never to mention his name again, and, to the best of Cliff's knowledge, no one had. He pushed the picture back into the recesses of his drawer, pulling a batch of old notebooks out to cover it, wondering about the real question. If Kurt told them not to talk, they didn't. But did any of the others have the nightmares he did? Had they done the right thing? And did their obligation to Kurt, their ringleader, still hold?

Cliff pushed the drawer closed, the question of obligation still unanswered. He'd had no trouble avoiding Kurt in all but a professional capacity for the last twenty years, Kurt's scornful attitude made it easy. But the pull was still there and now that Kurt had asked nicely, at least what passed as nicely for him, it was harder to resist. He'd see how the weekend went. Maybe the time had finally come to get some answers.

CHAPTER TWELVE

Nelson also spent Friday night analyzing hid plans for the next few days. He and Alyssa had originally thought of spending the weekend in Boston before continuing on to New York. But with the lure of a new story tugging at him, Nelson was reluctant to leave. They discussed it in low voices after dinner on the porch; screened in, of course – it was Nelson's favorite seat. He enjoyed watching the bugs buzz impotently against the screen, knowing fresh meat was in there, but unable to reach it. He'd felt the same way taunting a corrupt city official he'd exposed in his newspaper, once the man was safely incarcerated as a twenty year guest of the same state he'd hoped one day to run.

"I asked at the front desk, and they said our suite was already booked for the weekend, but they did have a very nice room further down the hall if we wanted it." Alyssa said.

"We wouldn't have to share a bathroom, would we?"

"No, this has its own private bath."

Nelson nodded, satisfied. There was only so much he was willing to do for his job. He pulled the picture of the murdered girl out of his pocket again. "So you think this is some kind of composite?" he asked, continuing the conversation started at dinner. It had been interrupted by the obvious fascination of an eavesdropping family whose attention had been caught by Nelson's persistent references to 'the body'.

Alyssa squinted at the picture in the dim light. "Yes, I do, although it's hard to tell for certain from this picture. I think it's a copy of the original, so some of the details have been lost."

"Why would they send out copies of a picture that has been altered?"

"My college roommate, Tracey, now works for a mortuary. She's started a whole new line of 'mourning portraits'. She takes pictures of the bodies and computer enhances them to look life-like. She said she got the idea from her own grandmother. They realized after she died that they didn't have a nice, recent picture of her. So Patty went down to the funeral home, snapped the finished product, tweaked it on her computer, and viola! A portrait that looked better than real life, ready to be eulogized."

"And your point is?"

"Something about this picture reminds me of her portfolio."

"So that means this," he flapped the picture at Alyssa, "is not something that the family provided to help find the killer. So..." he let the sentence hang and waited for Alyssa's response.

"So this is an actual picture of the dead girl! They enhanced it to make it look better."

"They enhanced it to make identification possible. The guys in the bar said she'd been out in the woods for a while. There may not have been much left to take a picture of, and nothing that you'd want to show around without making people lose their lunch over it."

Alyssa appeared slightly green herself at the thought of it.

"It also means that since the authorities don't have a real picture of her from her family..." He leaned toward Alyssa and dropped his voice. "They don't know who this girl is. They're working blind from *both* ends, trying to find the killer and the girl's identity. If I could find either first, what a story that would make! And even if I don't, I could still use the human interest side of it. 'Who could solve this mystery' type of thing."

Nelson sat back and studied the picture once more. "What do you think? Ready to stay another day or two?"

"Of course. You need to keep going on this. What's your next step?"

"I want to go up to where the body was found and look around."

Alyssa looked doubtful. "Nelson, you told me it was halfway up a mountain. You've spent the entire week avoiding the outdoors by going from building to car and back again. And now you want to climb a mountain?"

"For a story. Not just to look at a view. I've been uncomfortable for other stories. Have you ever seen the mosquitoes in the Pine Barrens in southern Jersey? This can't be any worse."

"But what do you hope to see up there? I'm sure the police have searched the area thoroughly and picked up any clues that might have been left."

Nelson sighed. "I know that," he said, enunciating carefully. "What I want is to open a window into the killer's head and get a feel for his psyche. Why would he pick such a desolate spot to dump a body? Did he think it was so far off the beaten path that no one would ever find her or did he secretly want her to be found and planted her next to a popular trail for that reason? And I want the atmosphere. What kind of place hid this young woman and her secrets for all this time? I want the mood to add to the story."

Alyssa nodded, and then shifted forward to the edge of her seat. "You know, I've been doing a lot of hiking this week, and I've picked up a lot of good tips. If you wanted me to come along, I could help you find the spot, or take notes, or just be an extra pair of eyes on the scene."

Listening to the eagerness leaking through Alyssa's attempt at a low-key request, Nelson felt an answering frisson of excitement. Given the right fuel, their chemistry worked. "Of course I want you with me, that's what this week has been all about."

There was no mistaking the flash of anticipation on Alyssa's face. That could be put to good use right now.

"Let's go upstairs," Nelson murmured, leaning closer and smiling into her eyes. "And you can help me get in the right frame of mind."

CHAPTER THIRTEEN

"Ball four! Take the walk!"

Cliff leaned forward and yelled to the pitcher. "Don't worry about that, Debra! Play your game! Think about the next one, not the one you just finished!"

His oldest daughter's eyes cut briefly over to him and she nodded slightly, and then refocused on the next batter. Cliff straightened up and stepped back to stand next to Bruce, the catcher's father. "Is there anything worse than having your kid as pitcher?" he muttered, half to himself.

"Yeah," Bruce answered; his eyes tight on the game. "Having the bases loaded and seeing someone hit a foul straight up."

Cliff nodded in sympathy. He was proud of Debra's pitching, but in pressure situations like this, he sometimes wished she played left field. It was the same for Bruce. The two men tended to stand together and support one another at all the games Cliff's duty schedule let him attend. "C'mon, honey, one more! Then you get a break!"

Debra's next three pitches were high, but the batter found them irresistible, swinging wildly despite shouted admonitions from her coach and screams of dismay from her teammates.

"Strike three! Retire the side!"

Cliff straightened up and resettled his hat on his head, smiling at

Bruce. "One more inning to go. If they can just hold them off..."

Bruce nodded. "Should be able to. We're at the top of our line-up and they're at the bottom of theirs. That will give Debra and Katie a good long break. After two games, they need it." He settled into his camp chair, looking as tired as the players.

Cliff sat down next to him, watching the opposing team's pitcher warm-up. "What's new in the Selectman's Office?" Bruce was one of three Selectmen for his town. Each town elected Selectmen as a governing committee, and Bruce was in his second term. In the past, he'd given Cliff the heads up for a couple of problem situations, so Cliff made a point of asking each time he saw him.

"So you heard about the latest Bonner Felton blow-up?"

"Not the details," Cliff evaded, not having heard anything but not wanting to admit it. "And it's probably gotten garbled. Why don't you fill me in on the real facts?"

"It's a typical Bonner thing. Claimed someone came onto his property and made off with some of his stuff. As far as we're concerned, we wish someone would steal every damn thing he's got. Place is an eyesore."

"What does he say is missing?"

"Some weaving or rugs or something. He had a girl living there with him for a while last year who did that kind of thing. She's gone – what a surprise – but he claims she left a bunch of her work and now someone's swiped it."

"A girl?" Cliff asked, trying to keep his voice casual.

"Young enough to be his daughter," Bruce said, not bothering to keep the disgust out of his voice. "She bought Bonner's whole paranoid 'government is Big Brother' line."

"What'd she look like?"

"I only saw her from a distance. Long blonde hair, wore a woven poncho instead of a winter coat, very back to nature."

"When did she leave?"

"Sometime over the winter. I guess she found an outhouse a lot less romantic in the winter."

"Any one catch her name or where she was from?" Cliff asked, but their first batter came up and Bruce moved up to the edge of the field to cheer.

"No," he threw over his shoulder as Cliff joined him. "Like I said, she bought into Bonner's whole paranoid thing and didn't mix much. She wasn't anyone local, I know that." Turning back to the game, he called, "C'mon girls, sew this one up!"

Cliff echoed his cheer, but his mind was only half there. The rest was out with Bonner Felton, reviewing what he knew and wondering where his young blonde houseguest had gone.

****

Bonner Felton was an anti-government fanatic who took the state's 'Live Free or Die' motto literally, having threatened the town property tax assessors at gunpoint so often that they now sent an armed escort at revaluation time. Not that there was much to assess. Bonner lived in a tumble down assortment of discarded trailers and self-built sheds. He retained a fully functional outhouse in defiance of state and town ordinances. His property was littered with rusting pick-ups, stacks of lumber covered with scraps of tin, collections of barrels, old bathtubs, and lengths of drainpipe, six goats, three rabbit hutches, and an old ice cream van hand-painted with his own personal philosophy of life.

Understandably, his neighbors weren't pleased.

At one time, they decided to be proactive about Bonner's property and organized their own clean up, enticing Bonner away with the promise of a barn demolition project. While Bonner paced and measured, estimated and examined, the rest of the group descended on his property and hurriedly relocated the worst of his eyesores to a spot invisible from the public road. Bonner's response, when he got back, was to paint a large fluorescent sign on several moldy sheets of plywood, giving details of his 'persecution' and inquiring where the rights of individual property owners had gone.

The sign was worse than the junk.

Repeated complaints to the Board of Selectman, the Zoning Board, Planning Board, Police Department, and even the Sheriff's Department brought little response. It was a civil matter, and no one was completely sure how to proceed. So Bonner persevered, happy in his squalor, and boasting he could and did live on less than five thousand dollars a year, not counting the iniquitous and – in his opinion – possibly illegal property tax the town persecuted him with each year.

He earned his money the old-fashioned way; odd jobs paid in cash, unrecorded with any institution or government agency. Bonner was the man you called to dismantle and cart away things you no longer needed. These things included outbuildings, old, and usually non-running cars or trucks, livestock, leftover building supplies, unwanted trees, and the contents of any basement or attic. He would then turn around and sell whatever seemed of value from his haul. He had dozens of contacts in the antiques business around the state, and was surprisingly knowledgeable about values. No one was sure exactly how much Bonner did make, but it was obviously enough to get by.

Cliff knew of Bonner in the way he knew of all the unusual characters in the area he covered. The stories of his clashes with the tax assessors had become something of a local legend, and Cliff had driven by Bonner's property a time or two, just to see what all the fuss was about. The mess made him wince in sympathy for the sensibilities of the neighbors, but he had seen the whole issue as more of a joke than a serious problem. Perhaps that view needed revising.

The first thing to do would be to call the local police department and get their take on the situation. Abel Woodson was chief over in that area. Cliff knew him fairly well and didn't anticipate any interdepartmental territoriality. First thing Monday, he'd put a call in to his office. Now it was time to concentrate on his daughter's tournament. The win they were about to pull off would ensure her team a place in tomorrow's play-off's.

"Go Leopards!" he yelled, clapping his hands loudly. There were worse ways to spend a Saturday afternoon.

CHAPTER FOURTEEN

"Nelson, would you take that thing off your head? I can't see your eyes and it's hard to hear what you're saying."

Nelson, uphill, turned to face Alyssa. "This *thing* as you put it is all that stands between me and insanity. It stays on." For good measure, he tucked the screening more securely into his collar. "I said we must be getting close. We've been climbing for hours." He looked back over Alyssa's head, noting he could finally see over the trees to the top of some other mountain out that way, and a get a view of the valley to the right with a ribbon of highway winding south, bordered on one side by a small, almost perfectly oval lake. The mountainside opposite had an alternating pattern of trees and mown grass and Nelson wondered briefly about the strange arrangement before refocusing on Alyssa as she responded to his comment.

"Hours? Try forty-five minutes. And how are we going to know when we do reach the spot?" Alyssa squinted up at him. "Are you expecting a sign and an arrow saying 'body found here'?"

"I expect to see the remnants of crime scene tape, or a bunch of ground up bushes to show that a large number of local lawmen were messing around."

Nelson stopped to take a breath, placing his foot on a hefty log and leaning forward to rest a forearm on his thigh. For all his talk about tough situations, this afternoon's exertions were taking their toll. Getting up this damn mountain was like climbing stairs for almost an hour straight. Steep stairs. While he'd scaled a large portion of the stairway in the Empire State Building, it was on a dare and almost twenty years ago. Not to mention the influence the crowd of fellow students and several pitchers of beer had on the entire proceeding.

He turned his face up hill and started to climb again, hoping to catch a bit of a breeze. While he appreciated his new head-gear, it did cut down on air circulation, making this whole exercise uncomfortably warm. He considered lifting the screening to wipe his forehead, but seeing the bugs swarming just outside the mesh, he decided to sweat in safety.

The 'hunter's friend' on his head, a soft hat in camouflage colors with screening attached to the brim and extending down to his shirt collar, was a suggestion from the hotel clerk. It was a cross between a beekeeper's headgear and the hokey costumes seen in old space-invader movies from the fifties.

Nelson knew he looked ridiculous in it. He suspected that the clerk had recommended the 'friend' not to help Nelson, but to get a good laugh, a notion supported by the crowd of sniggering employees who miraculously materialized to watch him try it on. Nelson didn't care. It was keeping the bugs at bay, and that was all that mattered.

"Hey Nelson, what do you think of this?"

The note of excitement in Alyssa's voice brought him quickly up the trail. She was standing about ten feet off the main trail, on a small side path.

"Don't you think all this looks recent?"

The surrounding bushes were bowed, some splintered and broken. The ground was muddier here, with trampled vegetation mixed in.

"You might have something," Nelson said. "Let's see where this goes."

The side trail was wide enough for them to walk shoulder to shoulder. The pattern of crushed bushes continued then dead-ended at a large boulder. In front of the boulder, the flattened area expanded to encompass a circle of about twenty feet in diameter. There were large pine branches strewn around at the base of the rock, and individual footprints could be seen at intervals on the ground.

"This must be where they found the body," Nelson said, bending to pick up a small piece of fluorescent plastic. "And I'd say this confirms it." He moved back to the center of the open area and took out a small notebook. "Let me just jot down a few impressions, and then we'll search around to see if there's anything else here the local law enforcement missed."

Standing with his back to the boulder, he gazed around the clearing. A clump of trees blocked the view below, giving the flat area a curiously cut-off feeling. The top of the mountain opposite was barely visible to the right of the clearing, while a solid wall of vegetation blocked all vision to the left and above the wall of rock behind him. Alyssa was standing respectfully off to one side, and the silence was something you could almost touch. Nelson jotted down a brief physical description, and then paused; looking for the mood. A sudden gust of wind set the pine branches sighing and Alyssa's voice came suddenly from just behind him.

"Nelson, are you almost finished? This place is creeping me out."

Turning to scold her for interrupting, Nelson changed course after a glimpse of her face. She was pale and sweating, her eyes were slightly dilated and her breathing was audible. "What do you mean? How does it creep you out?"

"It's too quiet here, and the wind is eerie. It's so lonely, you feel like the nearest person is a million miles away."

Nelson was scribbling rapidly. This was great, an unsolicited woman's viewpoint. It could have been the victim herself talking. "What else?"

"That big rock bugs me, I feel like it's bearing down on me."

"Anything else?"

"I know you're going to say I'm crazy, but standing out here in the middle of nowhere, I feel like someone's watching me."

"That's good, really good. Can you tell me more?"

Alyssa grabbed his elbow. "Nelson, are you listening to me? I'm telling you I want to get out of here and all you've got to say is 'good'?"

"No baby, that's not it," Nelson said, shoving his notebook into his back pocket. "I meant you have a great grasp of atmosphere. No wonder you do such an excellent job of getting the feelings across in all your pieces."

Alyssa shot him a suspicious look and Nelson changed tactics. "You're right, this is a creepy place. Let's get out of here, there's nothing more to see." He cradled her arm and steered her back toward the main path, aware she was still watching him warily.

"I wish you'd take that stupid thing off. It's hard to see your expression through that screening," she said, finally taking his words at face value.

"As soon as we get to the car, baby, off it comes. I bet we get back down a lot quicker than we came up," Nelson was glad the 'hunter's friend' hid his expression of gleeful impatience. He needed to get to his computer. He had the ideal opening for his article and wanted to get it down on the screen. He just hoped he could sufficiently distract Alyssa so that she wouldn't recognize a verbatim quote.

****

There they went, crashing off through the bushes; oblivious to their obscene sacrilege of a holy site. He'd wanted to spend the day up here in solitude, remembering what had come before and thinking of how it all had ended. Lord Byron said it best:

When we two parted
In silence and tears,
Half broken-hearted,
To sever for years,
Pale grew thy cheek and cold,
Colder thy kiss;
Truly that hour foretold
Sorrow to this.

It had been exactly like that. Her cheeks had grown pale and her lips cold, and he had drawn comfort from that. No one else would know her warmth after him.

Now it was ruined, first by the troopers who took her away, and then by these sensation seeking journalists who would strip away her privacy. He couldn't do anything about the troopers yet, he knew that, but this crass talking reporter and his hard polished girlfriend were another story. The girlfriend had an inkling of what it was really all about. She was the opposite of his Missy, but she had felt her presence, she was aware...

He needed to consider this further. Missy had been about sorrow and betrayal. But this new one? She seemed hard where Missy had been soft. Could it happen again and be about anger and betrayal? Would it feel the same? And could he manage it? Setting up for Missy had been easy. Was he up to the challenge this new one would bring?

It could be an experiment. A new experience. Those were supposed to make him stronger, better. It might be time to find out.

CHAPTER FIFTEEN

Nelson hit 'save' and closed his laptop. Alyssa was still in the shower, washing away the sweat and grime from their hike. Nelson had practically pushed her into the shower once they returned to the hotel, declining her coy invitation to join him. It would take some sweet talking to get her over that, but the extra time she spent sulking in the shower allowed him to complete the first two paragraphs of his article. Stretching, he walked to the window and stared up at the mountain they had just climbed. It was damn high, but it had been worth it.

The bathroom door flew open, and Alyssa entered the bedroom in a cloud of steam. Ignoring Nelson completely, she grabbed some clothes and marched over to the far side of the bed to dress. Carefully keeping his expression neutral, Nelson moved to take possession of the shower. He closed the door and stood for a minute, listening. As expected, he heard slamming drawers. Turning on the shower, he leered at his steamy reflection in the mirror. "You've got your work cut out for you tonight, calming her down enough to be decent company for the evening." Snapping the shower curtain across the rod, he reached contentedly for the soap. He always did like a challenge.

****

"I can't believe you wanted to come back to this place. I thought you hated it."

Nelson tried to keep his smile of satisfaction from sliding into a smirk as Alyssa lolled against him. It hadn't taken much to bring her around after all. A split of champagne sent to the room before dinner, a nice bottle of wine with dinner, and a brandy afterward had provided the initial thaw. A constant stream of compliments, ascending in ardor while descending in veracity, had hastened the process. The final touch, suggesting they return to the Dew Drop Inn, resulted in her present position. Maybe he'd gone a little too far.

"Can I get you something from the bar?" Privately he thought coffee might be the best idea.

"All that wine made me thirsty. Could you just get me a soda?"

Even better. A speedy drink of something cold would get the caffeine in to her system that much faster, which should enable her to leave the bar at least semi-upright. "Sure, honey. You sit right there and I'll be back with something as soon as I can."

Walking up to the bar, Nelson gave the room a quick survey. He'd come here hoping to see that trooper Mike Eldrich again, but there was no sign of him. This place's Saturday night crowd was larger and rowdier than Wednesday's. The jukebox wailed county western, the TV blared engine rebuilds, and everyone in the place was doing their best to drown them out.

"A beer and a Diet Coke."

The bartender was different tonight too. With no sign of Eldrich, that might work in his favor. He paid for the drinks with a twenty. "Keep the change."

Smiling, the bartender nodded and swept the money into his pocket, his expression hovering between amiability and scorn. Nelson took another five out and laid it on the bar. "Here's one for you. Bet its thirsty work back there with a crowd like this."

The bartender took the five and grabbed a beer for himself, his expression sliding into a smile. Nodding toward Nelson, he raised his bottle and took a swallow. Nelson mimicked the action, keeping his tongue across the top as a stopper. God, he hated the taste of beer. He put his bottle down and smiled. "Slides down just right."

"Sure does," the bartender said, then turned as someone shouted "Hey Steve! Three more over here."

While Steve filled that order, Nelson glanced over at Alyssa. See-ing her deep in conversation with a local wall-leaner, Nelson turned back to the bar. "Crowded tonight," he threw out as Steve passed by.

"Always is on a Saturday."

Nelson practiced another fake beer swig. "I heard there was some excitement in town this week. Everyone was talking about some girl's body found up on a mountain."

Steve, remembering the size of Nelson's tip, stopped to talk. "Yeah. First one that's been up there a while. Usually when people go missing, we know about it. They think as long as they have a cell phone, they can pull any kind of crazy stunt and help is just a phone call away."

Nelson leaned across the bar. "I understand this one was long past any ability to call for help. Any idea who she was?"

"Nah. She wasn't a local."

"Will they be able to find out who she is?"

Steve shrugged, clearly not interested. "Eventually, I guess." He moved away down the bar in response to another bellow.

Chalking the money up to his expense account, Nelson took his un-tasted beer and Alyssa's soda back to their table. Alyssa's new friend had moved on by the time Nelson reached their table, but her flushed face and glittering eyes told him the conversation hadn't been dull.

"Well?" he said, handing over the can. "What did Grizzly Adams have to say?"

"I think he was trying to put the moves on me."

"He's setting his sights high. Did he succeed?"

"You're impossible." Alyssa took a long swallow, put the can down and fussed with it, turning it until the logo faced her and running her fingers over the design.

Raising his eyebrows, Nelson leaned closer. "Alyssa?"

"What?" She wouldn't meet his eye.

"Don't tell me you let this guy get to you!" He'd obviously fed her way too much booze.

"Not really."

"But...?" Nelson prompted.

Alyssa gave a half shrug and tossed her hair back from her face. "It's hard for a guy to understand."

"I understand he was scruffy and unkempt and probably had an IQ that matched his shoe size."

"All true, but he also had this odd kind of draw, a living-on-the-edge, desperate outlaw kind of thing. It's hard to explain."

"Insanity usually is." Nelson lifted his head to scan the bar, trying to locate this Svengali of the boondocks.

"Stop it." Alyssa clutched his arm. "I don't want him to see you're looking."

Nelson decided the evening's early promise was washing out on every front. No one willing to talk about the body and Alyssa suffering some bizarre attraction to what passed for local talent. Time to cut his losses before it got any worse.

"Shall we go?"

Nodding, Alyssa gathered up her purse. "Are you angry?"

"No. Puzzled, mystified, and confused, but not angry." Nelson took her arm to steer her toward the door. Once there, he reached around her to open it, his eyes connecting with... was that the same man who'd been talking to Alyssa? He wasn't sure. The man's pale blue eyes burned into his, and then cut away. Nelson paused, ready to go over and confront the challenger.

"Nelson! Are you coming?"

Alyssa's voice distracted him. He turned to ask her to come back to identify the stranger, then quickly glanced back over his shoulder to keep the man in sight. But he'd vanished. Holding the door, Nelson leaned further back into the bar, searching the crowd.

"Nelson!"

The escalating shrillness in Alyssa's voice warned him the evening was fast moving beyond repair. The weirdo would have to wait.

"I'm here, sweetie. I just wanted to check for the rural Romeo once more."

Alyssa pulled her sweater closer and shivered. "I'd be happy never to see him again. Let's get back to the hotel. We can pack tonight and make an early start tomorrow."

Nelson helped her into her car and slammed the door. Packing. It seemed all that liquor was wasted after all. Going around to the driver's side he straightened his jacket and smoothed down his hair, trying to readjust his thinking along with his clothes. Today wasn't a total loss. He'd gotten a good start on his story and tomorrow they'd be back in civilization where they could hit that new fusion restaurant. Monday he'd see his editor and pitch the story, and any further research needed up here, he'd do on his own. Squaring his shoulders, he slid into the driver's seat. No need to visit or even think about this hole in the wall again.

Through the window, he watched them climb into that little red car. He'd gotten closer tonight. The woman felt it, she could sense his power. She was older, stronger and more polished than his Missy, but the same things drew her in. The elemental power of the wild. It echoed in both their blood, and only he could call it out. Make their eyes glitter. Make their faces flush. Make them breathe through their mouth. A little more time alone with her, and he'd have her. The bar wasn't the right place. He needed somewhere quiet without distractions to cement the attraction and compel her to accept the invitation.

That big-mouthed reporter came back too soon. He had gotten in the way again. He might have to do something about him. He'd gotten that message across as he was leaving. The reporter felt the threat and realized his control. But the time hadn't been right to confront him. Not yet. He needed time to make a plan and prepare.

He knew where they were staying. He might have to go out there for a few hours. His power was growing. He might be able to pull the woman outside with it. He needed her. He was ready for the challenge. He knew that now. It was time to start again.

CHAPTER SIXTEEN

"Did they win?"

Cliff turned to face Mike. "Happy Monday to you too. And no, they didn't win. But they came damn close. Extra innings in the last game, we didn't get out of there till after eight last night. It was exhausting."

"You look beat. Too much fun in the sun, eh?"

Turning back to his desk, Cliff suppressed a sigh. He was tired and seeing Mike bounce in, brimming with energy, made it worse. "How was the party?" he said, trying to change the subject.

"The usual." Mike flopped down in his chair and tilted it back on two legs. "My family just keeps getting nuttier. I look around at these shindigs and wonder how I managed to turn out so normal."

Cliff looked over and raised an eyebrow.

Mike interpreted his expression correctly. "Comparatively speaking, of course."

"Of course. You ready to get to work? I'd like to get an identity for our Jane Doe."

"So would I. She was on my mind all weekend. It seemed like half the family wanted to give me their thoughts and opinions on who she could be or where she might have come from. She was the major topic of barbeque conversation."

"Anyone say anything useful?"

"Nah, just a lot of hot air blowing around. At least no one mentioned alien abductions!"

Cliff snorted in sympathy. "I did get one useful lead over the weekend that I'd like to follow up on today."

The front legs of Mike's chair hit the ground with a thump. "Great, what've you got?"

"I was talking to Bruce Mansfield, one of the Selectmen from Dalton, and he mentioned that Bonner Felton had a young blonde house guest last year but she disappeared some time during the winter or spring."

"Bonner Felton! That kook? The mystery is not that she's gone, but how'd he get her there in the first place."

"Either way, it's worth looking into. I put a call in to Abel Woodson to tell him we'd be stopping by this morning for the latest on Bonner. You ready to roll?"

Mike stood up and grabbed his hat. "Let's do it."

****

Route 135 to Dalton took them past some of the older farms in the area. The bright sun and warm temperatures of the past few days had brought the lilac bushes into full bloom. Two or three bushes fronted most farmhouses, in some cases towering over the roof in a large woody hedge. The outsized purple flowers made a nice contrast with the houses' white siding, and their perfume came drifting through the open windows of the cruiser.

The Dalton Police Department was a one-room office behind the Fire Department's garage. Abel Woodson was the Chief and only full time officer. He had the high complexion and substantial gut of someone who'd lived and played hard. Light on his feet despite his size, he came swiftly out from behind his desk with his hand outstretched in greeting.

"Cliff, you old SOB, how are you. Haven't seen you around here in a while."

"That's because you keep things so well in hand, Abel." Cliff grabbed the hand thrust in his direction, pushing his palm deeply into the large meaty one.

Abel grinned, holding his grip somewhat longer than customary.

Cliff stood his ground, faintly smiling. "You can't catch me on that one, Abel. You know that." He turned to Mike. "Watch out when you shake hands with this bastard. He'll try to break your fingers. Make sure you jam your hand as far as possible into his palm so all he can do is squeeze muscle, not grind bone."

Mike nodded and followed instructions when Abel offered his hand. The older man looked him in the eye as he applied pressure, and then nodded. "You'll do. You've got yourself a good partner there," he threw over his shoulder as he moved back toward his desk. "C'mon over and take a seat and we'll get down to business."

Answering Mike's look, Cliff explained. "I swear that's how Abel keeps things in line around here. If anyone gets out of hand, Abel grabs theirs and squeezes until they beg for mercy. Unorthodox, but it gets results."

The two men took seats across the desk from Abel, who had settled into a swivel chair that creaked in protest as he leaned back. "All right then, Bonner Felton. He came in here about a month ago, breathing fire about his rights being violated as usual, but this time he sounded like he might actually have something."

"Bruce said something about weavings being stolen?"

"Yeah, though how you could tell if anything went missing in that jumble of his is a mystery to me."

"Bruce also mentioned some girl that was living with him? You know anything about her?"

Abel pursed his lips. "So that's what you boys are here about. I didn't think Bonner's robbery claims warranted the trip." He leaned forward and put his arms on the desk. "This have anything to do with that body up in the Notch I heard about?"

Cliff crossed his arms. "We're following up leads. We found the body of a young blonde girl. Then we hear a report of a young blonde girl living in the area for a while and now she's gone. So what can you tell us?"

Abel straightened up and nodded once. "I'll tell you all I know, but I'm afraid it's not much. I heard reports late last summer that Bonner had found a live-in girlfriend. That didn't surprise me, he's had women up there from time to time, and they don't usually last too long. Then I heard that this one was young and kind of pretty. That did surprise me. I mean, why would someone like that hook up with Bonner?"

"That's what we were wondering," Cliff said, while Mike nodded in agreement.

"Now you know Bonner doesn't always see eye to eye with the local authorities around here..."

"You mean like threatening them with a gun?" Mike interjected.

"That was only a couple of times," Abel said, relaxing back into his chair again. "And we don't send that particular assessor out there anymore. The problem most people have dealing with Bonner is that they don't realize he's a very intelligent man. And if you get into an argument with him, you're probably going to lose."

"Intelligent? Bonner? Isn't that some kind of oxymoron?"

"He's a very well-read man, Mike. Don't underestimate him." Abel swiveled his chair from side to side, ignoring the squeaks. "As I was saying, Bonner doesn't like most forms of authority, but he and I have an understanding. I don't hassle him about the stupid stuff, but when I do come around, I expect a courteous reception. So once I heard about this girl, I stopped out there for a look-see."

"I bet he loved that," Cliff murmured.

"You better believe it. 'What the hell does my private life have to do with anyone but me?' was the way I he put it, though there may have been some more colorful language in there." Abel grinned at the memory. "I told him it was just common courtesy to introduce myself to any new residents in town, one of the benefits of living in a small community. He didn't seem too impressed."

Mike shifted in his chair. "Did you actually meet the girl?"

"Sort of. Bonner yelled 'Melissa' over his shoulder, and she poked her head out of one of his sheds. He explained who I was and why I was there. She waved once and disappeared."

"Were you close enough to get a good look?" Cliff asked.

Abel tilted his head. "I'd call it a fair look."

Cliff took out the composite picture. "Was this the girl?"

Abel leaned forward to take the picture. He studied it for several minutes, then sighed. "I can't say for certain. It looks something like her, but I couldn't make a positive ID. I was too far away and she kept most of her face hidden behind the door." He shrugged. "I didn't think much of it at the time, just wanted to make sure she knew there was someone official to come to if she needed help."

Cliff nodded, trying to keep his face expressionless. Out of the corner of his eye, he watched Mike sag back into his chair. "Keep the picture," he told Abel. "Is there anyone else we could show it to that might be able to tell us who she is?"

"Can't think of anyone. She didn't leave Bonner's place much. My impression? She was a run-away, using old Bonner as a hiding place. I checked all the reports for missing girls at that time, but nothing came up that matched her general description."

"Yeah, we've been down that road too," Mike said.

"Can you tell us anything about when she went missing?" Cliff asked.

"Again, not much to tell, and most of it speculation and rumor. One of the Road Crew mentioned that Bonner was on his own again. At the time, we all treated it as common sense. I mean, what woman or girl in their right mind would choose to stay there for an extended period of time?"

"How did the Road Crew know she was gone?"

"Well, they're the only people that have a good relationship with Bonner in this town. They let him know when they've cut up a downed tree on the side of the road, and Bonner will usually go along and collect the wood. Or they'll let him know about any abandoned furniture or appliances left on the side of the road and he'll go haul it away. It's a good system, Bonner gets free wood or more stuff to sell or barter, and it's one less thing for our guys to deal with."

"And the girl?"

"The guys had been kidding Bonner about the girl and he turned around and said she'd gone so they needed to jump start their brains to find a new topic of conversation, if they could manage it."

"Ouch!" Mike said. "Real sweetheart, isn't he?"

"Doesn't really care who he pisses off."

"When did this conversation take place and could we have the names of the guys who were in on it?"

"I can give you the guys' names, or you could stop back around noon when they come in for lunch and talk to them yourselves."

Cliff checked his watch. "Ten o'clock now, that'll give us plenty of time to go talk to Bonner first."

"Tread lightly. Remember he's not fond of uniforms."

Standing up, Cliff looked down at Abel's mocking grin. "This is a murder investigation. I don't give a damn what he likes. We need information and we'll get it from him, one way or the other."

Mike was silent on the way out to the cruiser. Once they were settled inside, he turned toward Cliff. "You came down pretty hard on old Abel in there. I don't like him much either, but if he's one of the few people Bonner will talk to, it might be useful to have his help."

Cliff turned the key in the ignition and put the cruiser in gear. "I did that specifically to prevent Abel from coming along. I know he claims to be the only one who can talk to Bonner, and to a certain extent that's true. But I also have a hunch that Bonner doesn't take Abel very seriously because he overplays the 'most of authority is stupid' routine with Bonner."

He pulled out of the parking lot and headed north. "I don't want Bonner trying to pull anything over on us. I think he's more likely to try it with someone he's hoodwinked before."

"Like Abel?"

"Exactly. Bonner gets away with a lot up here because he barks loudly. I'm ready to muzzle him if I need to and don't want any interference from Abel." He slowed to turn off the main road onto a narrow side road. "And I wouldn't put it past Abel to stick a hand in and try to twist things to his advantage to preserve his 'I'm the good guy' status at our expense."

"All right then. Let's go in and get some answers."

****

Cliff nosed the cruiser cautiously over the ruts and dips in Bonner's driveway while Mike put a hand on the dashboard to brace himself. "Jeesum," he said. "Hope we don't rip the damn exhaust pipe off."

It had been easy to determine where Bonner's property began. A large piece of particleboard propped against a tree proclaimed "Tyranny, like hell, is not easily conquered". Further on, another stated "Except our own thoughts, there is nothing absolutely in our power". Flanking the driveway were twin pieces of plywood. The one on the right stated "The condition of man...is a condition of war against everyone," while the left board warned "In this world a man must either be anvil or hammer".

Mike twisted from side to side. "Where does he get these kooky sayings?"

"They're quotations of some kind. He used to have the ones about absolute power corrupting absolutely and man being nasty brutish and short out here too. I looked them up once, but I forget who wrote them."

The driveway, an overgrown double track curving off between a rusting pick-up truck that might once have been green and a trailer with two flat tires, curled off around some trees toward a cluster of buildings.

"I'm looking for a clear place we can back into," Cliff said, slowing down even further. "That way if we need to leave ..." He broke off and pointed to a small clear spot. "What do you think?"

Mike stretched forward. "Looks good to me. Just so long as it isn't booby trapped with buried tacks or anything."

Cliff grunted in reply, twisting and hooking an arm over the seat as he backed into the spot. Grabbing his hat from the back seat, he nodded to Mike. "It's show time."

The two men moved cautiously down the driveway, scanning the vegetation on either side. "This is worse than up on Lafayette," Mike muttered, peering through some bushes at a small side building. "He could be anywhere."

They came to a small clearing in front of an old trailer sporting a weathered plywood addition. Cliff stopped about ten feet away from it and planted his feet. "Bonner?" His voice set a distant dog barking, off to the left of the trailer. Cliff turned in that direction and tried again. "Bonner?"

The dog's barking changed pitch and grew louder as it approached. Mike placed his hand next to his weapon and spread his legs slightly. The dog, a large furry animal with at least some German Shepherd in its ancestry, burst into the clearing from the right, circling the men and barking continuously. Mike turned to keep the dog within eyesight, while Cliff faced the direction the animal had come from.

"You gentlemen are trespassing." The voice came from the left, and Cliff spun to face the owner. A man in his late forties stared back. He was tall and thin, with a prominent nose and eyebrows, and a bushy black beard threaded with grey. He wore a knitted cap that looked handmade, as did the sweater that topped a pair of worn jeans.

"Call off your dog."

The dog's bark had ratcheted up several notches in pitch and intensity as it ran frantically back and forth between its owner and the troopers.

"I said you're trespassing," the man said, raising his voice to be heard over the dog.

"Call off your dog," Cliff repeated, returning the other's stare without flinching.

The silence between the two men stretched out, while the dog, sensing the tension, bared its teeth and feinted toward them in a snarling rush. Cliff didn't move, but Mike's weapon flew out of the holster and centered on the dog's head.

"Sam! Heel!"

The dog broke off in mid-stride and retreated behind the man, standing tensely, obviously ready to rush out again on command. Mike's weapon returned to its holster, but his hand rested on it, ready. The man ignored Mike completely.

"Now why don't you two just turn around, get back in your car, and get the hell off my land."

"Are you Bonwit Felton, more commonly known as Bonner?"

The man pursed his lips as though considering the question. "Who wants to know?"

"I'm Trooper Codey and this is Trooper Eldrich. Are you Bonner Felton?"

"Yeah, and this is my property and I'm telling you to leave. My taxes are paid up, there are no outstanding warrants on me, and you have no right to be here. So why don't you both get back in your car and get the hell out of here."

"As soon as you answer a few questions."

"And if I don't?"

"Then you'll accompany us to the barracks and remain there as our guest until you do."

Bonner stared in silence a few minutes, then spit toward, but not quite reaching, Cliff's shoes. Cliff heard Mike shift restlessly behind him, and twitched his head slightly to the side. Mike settled back into immobility and Cliff waited for a reply from Bonner. The three men stood in silence, except for a faint growing from the dog.

"We need to ask you a few questions about a young woman who

was staying with you this past winter." Cliff waited, but Bonner remained mute. "I understand some materials the young woman made were stolen from you." This produced a response.

"Three woven blankets and two felted wall hangings. Do you have any word on them?"

"Do you have anything else she made? A comparison could be helpful."

Bonner shook his head. "No, everything was taken."

"When was that?"

Bonner's eyes narrowed. "How come you don't know that? I made a full report to Abel Woodson just after it happened. He should have given you all that information. Didn't you talk to him?"

"We'd like to hear the story straight from you," Cliff said.

Bonner's eyes chin came up slowly. "What are you really here about?"

Cliff decided it was time to change tactics. The verbal jousting was going nowhere. "We're looking for this girl." Taking two rapid steps forward he removed the reconstructed picture from his shirt pocket. Keeping his eyes tight on Bonner's face, he thrust the picture forward. "Have you seen her before?"

Bonner's eyes flickered toward the picture and came back to Cliff's face. "Nope."

"We heard you had a young blonde girl staying here part of the winter. We think this is her, and we want to know what happened to her." Cliff leaned closer, and the dog's rumbling growl intensified.

"Can't help you," Bonner said. "Never saw her. Now if that's all you're here for, you can leave."

"Are you denying there was a young woman living here?"

"I'm telling you my private life is none of your business. Who I have living with me and how long they stay is none of your concern."

"Unless they end up dead."

Silence stretched out once more between them. Cliff finally broke it with a sigh. "It's a simple question, Bonner. Have you seen this woman before?"

"I've answered everything I need to. Now you can leave. I've got work to do."

"We've been asking around. If we find that this is the woman that was here and you're lying to us, it'll make things harder for you."

Bonner stared wordlessly.

Cliff shook his head and replaced the picture in his pocket. "We'll be asking around. If someone recognizes this girl as the one that was living here, we'll be back." Turning away, he nodded to Mike and both men walked back to the cruiser.

"That went well," Mike said, slamming the car door.

Cliff grunted a reply and concentrated on negotiating the driveway as quickly as possible without leaving pieces of the cruiser's undercarriage behind.

Once they reached the relative safety of the dirt road, Mike continued. "Do you think he recognized her?"

"Yeah. He didn't look at the picture long enough for it to be a stranger."

"Do you think he killed her?"

"I don't know. There was something about his expression when he looked at her picture. Did you see it?"

Mike shook his head. "I was too busy watching that damn dog."

"It wasn't there long, but there was definitely a reaction. Let's interview the road crew. If Jane Doe was living there, we'll go back and talk a little more seriously."

They reached the paved road and Cliff accelerated sharply. "I don't like playing games. Bonner's going to find that out fast."

CHAPTER SEVENTEEN

By eleven thirty, Jane Doe's picture had made the rounds in the town garage twice. The general consensus seemed to be that she was Bonner's girl.

"Couldn't swear to it in court, though," was the road agent's final word. A chuckle of agreement swept around the crew at the picnic table in appreciation of their boss's wit.

Cliff suppressed a sigh. There were far too many cop shows on TV. "No one's asking you to. We just want to be sure this is the woman who was staying with Bonner last fall and winter."

"Jimmy'd be the one who could say for certain. He was the one making eyes at her whenever we were up there."

Jimmy, a young man with thick red hair and an even thicker collection of freckles, faked a smile while his skin tone slowly changed to match his hair.

"Mike, why don't you take down everyone's name and address, while I ask Jimmy a few questions in private." Cliff ignored the chorus of catcalls and advice about lawyers and signaled Jimmy to follow him outside. Jimmy followed without protest.

Leading the way around to the side of the garage, Cliff leaned a shoulder against the warm cinder block wall. Jimmy propped himself up by his back and studied his work boots.

"They get on your case like that often?"

Jimmy shrugged. "They're all right."

"They're a great bunch of guys, I agree, but they're not ready to do stand up, no matter what they think."

That got a chuckle and a nod.

"And maybe they saw a couple of conversations and made a big deal out of something that wasn't like that at all."

Jimmy's head came up and he turned to face Cliff. "That's just it, it wasn't anything but 'hi, how're you doing' and they practically had us married and our kids named."

"So what did she say?" Cliff tried to keep his voice casual.

"Not much. Just how pretty it was up here, and empty, and where did I go to meet people." Jimmy smiled slightly at the memory. "I think she was getting tired of all Bonner's lectures."

"So she was getting a little fed up with old Bonner?"

"Well, you know how he is, always going off about something. I think she was just looking for a beer and a little casual conversation."

"And what did Bonner think of that idea?"

Jimmy shrugged again. "How should I know? I just talked to her twice, and not for very long. I didn't even know her last name."

Don't push the boy, Cliff told himself. He's the closest thing you have to a lead. "So did you mention any good place for a beer?"

Jimmy looked away. "I might have named a few places."

"Such as?"

"What difference does it make? She's dead, isn't she?" Turning his back on Cliff, Jimmy walked a few paces and savagely kicked an old stump.

Cliff raised an eyebrow. So that's the way it was. The guys inside weren't that far off after all. He stepped up next to Jimmy. "That's right, she's dead. And I want to get the bastard who did it. And you can help by telling me her name, exactly what you said to her and what she said to you."

"Like I told you, it wasn't much." Jimmy's voice had dropped back into sullenness. "She was out near the road one day when we were ditching. She said hi and I said hi, my name is Jimmy. She said hers was Melissa. I asked her how she liked it up here; she said it was okay but quiet. She wanted to know where everyone hung out and I told her either the Dew Drop Inn or the Mooseland Grill. She said maybe she'd see me there sometime, and that was it."

"And did you ever see her at either of those places?"

Jimmy shook his head and gave the stump another kick.

And that accounts for the attitude. Cliff pursed his lips. "When did you have this conversation?"

"End of October. Early November. Something like that."

"Was that the last time you talked to her?"

"Yeah. A couple of weeks later I asked Bonner where she was. He just stared at me and didn't answer." Jimmy looked up, his mouth twisted. "Was that when he killed her?"

Cliff leaned forward. "Do you think he did?"

"I don't know. I guess so. What else could have happened?" Jimmy stopped abruptly. His next words were so low Cliff had to step closer to hear. "Did he kill her because I talked to her?"

That was Cliff's theory, but he wasn't about to add to this young man's misery by saying so. "We're trying to find out. How did he treat her? Did she mention any problems or did you see anything?"

Jimmy shook his head. "I never asked. Like I said, we barely talked."

"Did you see any signs of abuse? Bruises?"

"No. I would have said something if I did."

"I'm sure you would." Cliff laid a hand on Jimmy's shoulder. "Thanks for the help. We'll get to the bottom of this." Giving Jimmy's shoulder a final pat, he moved off toward the front of the garage. "Give Mike your full name and address so we can contact you if we need to."

Moving off to the car, Cliff looked over aT Mike, and then nodded pointedly toward Jimmy. Mike got the message and intercepted Jimmy on his way to the garage. Cliff waved good-bye to the group around the picnic table, climbed into the driver's seat and waited until Mike joined him.

"Well?"

"I think we hit the jackpot. That kid Jimmy not only ID'd the picture, but talked to the girl." Cliff quickly summarized his conversation. "The kid thinks Bonner did the girl in because she was talking to him, looking for a place to spread her wings a bit, end of last October or early November."

"Late fall?"

"It makes sense. The days were getting colder and darker, just the time a young woman would start looking around for a change in scenery."

Mike smoothed his fingers around the brim of his hat. "Will that fit with the probable timeline from the M.E.? It's right at the outside limit of what she gave us."

"I know. I want to call Brenda and make sure the earliest date is truly possible."

Putting his hat in the back seat, Mike turned toward Cliff. "Or else Bonner kept her out of sight from November on, making sure she had no chance of getting away or talking to anyone."

Cliff shook his head. "Couple of things wrong with that. First, holding a person inside like a virtual prisoner is not that easy to do. And we know Bonner is out and about all the time. We'd have heard about it from Abel if Bonner had dropped out of sight of a while. Second, we're looking at this as a crime of passion. He's furious that she might leave him for another guy, and bang, he chokes her. I don't see him waiting six months and then doing it."

"So you don't think he did it?"

"I think he had a good motive, but I'm not sure about some of the details. Either way, we have a witness that says Jane Doe was living with him and gives her a name, Melissa." Cliff leaned forward and started the car. "That's enough to bring him in for questioning. It's time to get some answers."

CHAPTER EIGHTEEN

Nelson stared at his editor and told himself to count to ten. The man was always in a pissy mood first thing Monday morning. "C'mon Jerry, you don't mean that. This is exactly the kind of story you like. Beautiful young girl found dead on mountain. It's got everything; sex, violence, mystery, and me to write it. What's not to like?" Nelson relaxed in his chair, pleased to be back in New York.

Jerry looked back without any noticeable change in expression. "An unidentified dead girl is found out in the middle of nowhere. Give me one reason why my readers are going to care."

Looking into the bloodshot eyes across the desk, Nelson wondered again what Jerry did on weekends. That might be a great feature story itself, but as career-builders went, it was a definite non-starter. "I'll make them care. I can play up the hippie angle. I can give it lots of atmosphere, you know, sighing pines and isolated areas. I can do the 'help us identify this tragic girl' thing. I'll have people on the edge of their seats."

"Hippies are ancient history, no one cares anymore. No one in this city likes isolated woods and wouldn't recognize a sighing pine if it bit them in the ass. And the media has been so saturated with run-aways that a new one is just one big yawn." Jerry punched a button on his desk. "Linda! I said coffee ten minutes ago. Are you harvesting the beans out there or what?"

"I could take the story someplace else."

"You could take yourself someplace else."

Realizing the tactical error of trying to push Jerry before his third cup of coffee, Nelson decided to back pedal. Giving a rueful grin, he switched gears. "That's why I work for you, Jerry. You don't let me get away with any crap. I couldn't respect an editor I could push around."

"And that's why I let you stay, Nelson. You always recognize when you've gone too far. Keep it that way and you'll keep your paycheck."

The office door opened, and Linda edged in carrying two mugs of coffee. "I brought one for Nelson also. I hope that's all right..."

Jerry grunted and reached for his cup.

Nelson beamed at her. "Thanks, honey. Jerry's lucky to have you."

Linda ducked her head and sidled out of the room, closing the door softly behind her. Nelson raised his mug to Jerry and took a sip.

"Don't push your luck, Nelson."

Putting the coffee down, Nelson dropped the charade. "Okay. You don't like the story. Fine. I'll stop beating you over the head with it. But my gut tells me there's something there. And my gut is usually pretty accurate."

Jerry's brows lowered, and Nelson held up a hand.

"I'm going to keep looking into this on the side. If I find something, I'll bring it back to you and we'll talk again. Fair enough?"

"Why are my readers going to care, Nelson? That's the bottom line. If you can't answer that, don't waste my time." Jerry turned toward his computer and put his hand on the mouse, ending the interview.

Nelson stood up. "The awards hanging on my wall show how much of your time I've wasted over the past six years. I don't think you need to be too concerned about that."

Leaving his coffee mug and holding on to his temper, Nelson stalked out of the room. Waste his time. It was the other way around. Talking to Jerry was the real time waste around this office. Reaching his own office, Nelson revisited the urge to slam the door. He could be smarter and more subtle than that. He sat behind his desk, took a deep breath and leaned back; willing himself to be calm. He'd made a tactical error in thinking Jerry could wrap his head around this story on a Monday. He'd do a bit more research – look into missing person's reports and murder stats in New Hampshire, and then do a rough draft loaded with plenty of hand-wringing and where-did-this-young-life-go-wrong angst.

By the time he brought this story in, Jerry would be begging for it.

****

"In the mood for some lunch? Or have you forgotten about me already?"

Alyssa leaned against the door of his office, covering a smile with a pretend pout. After their trip north, office gossip had them firmly marked as a couple. Alyssa clearly enjoyed the connection. A week ago, Nelson had too. But this morning's sparring match with Jerry still rankled. "Whatever."

Alyssa's smile faded. "What's up?"

"Jerry the jerk."

"Uh oh, what now?"

"I pitched the New Hampshire story to him this morning. He turned it down."

"But why?"

"Because he has no real clue into what the public likes," Nelson said, slamming his desk drawer closed.

"No, I mean, why did you pitch it today? You've always told me never pitch on a Monday because it takes Jerry at least a day to recover from his weekend."

She was right, which didn't improve Nelson's mood. "Because I thought this story was such a total no-brainer that even Jerry on a Monday would see it." He picked up the Jane Doe picture he had gotten from the Tapplings. "I mean, look at that face. Who wouldn't want to know what happened to her?"

Alyssa leaned across the desk. "Or at least her name." She picked up the picture. "May I?"

Nelson waved his hand in consent.

Alyssa took the picture and walked over to the window. "I can't imagine anything worse than being buried without one. I mean, what would they put on the gravestone? 'Jane Doe'?" She shuddered. "It makes it almost like she never lived, you know?"

Shaking her head, she turned away from the window and caught sight of Nelson's face. "What is it?"

"You have just given me my headline and my hook." He moved away from his desk and started pacing. " 'Don't let this girl be buried without a name.' 'Give her life meaning.' It's perfect. I might even build this into a series of articles."

Nelson stopped and rubbed his hands together. "I'm going down to the archives to look for some suitably lonely graveyard scenes to start off with. You coming?"

Alyssa's shoulders sagged. "I wish I could. I've got to set-up this interview for tomorrow morning with the former head of a baby food company."

"Reschedule it."

"I can't. This woman is a bit of a recluse. It was hard enough to get her to agree to the interview in the first place."

Nelson crossed his arms. "Great. Some fruit loop who makes baby mush comes before our Jane Doe."

"Jerry really wants this one. You know what he's like if I don't come through with it." She walked over to Nelson, slipped a hand under his arm and pressed herself lightly against him. "Tell you what. Why don't you come with me? We can talk about Jane on the way to my interview, talk to this woman together, and have lunch on the way back." Her eyes moved over his face, pleading. "You can give me some pointers about my interview techniques. It's always best to learn from a pro."

Knowing he was being flattered but unable to resist, Nelson nodded. That would give him time to complete his research with the added promise of a reward tomorrow. And if they came home with something exceptional it might change Jerry's mind about his Jane Doe story.

Alyssa leaned in to kiss his cheek, and then danced across his office toward the door. "It's a date!"

Grunting his assent, Nelson picked up the simulated picture of the missing girl. Something big was going to come out of this article. He had a hunch which he'd ride to the end and shove the results under Jerry's red eyes. Their readers would be pleading for more. When Nelson Simon set out to make them care, they did. Big time.

CHAPTER NINTEEN

Bonner Felton sat in the small interrogation room, staring stonily at the wall. Sitting across from him, Cliff swirled the dregs of his coffee around in his Styrofoam cup, wondering what kind of chemical reaction between the two always made the office coffee taste gritty.

"You want a cup?" he said to Bonner, hoping for something close to a normal response. "It won't compromise your principles."

"The condition of man...is a condition of war of everyone against everyone."

Mike rolled his eyes and moved forward. He'd been standing behind Bonner through the first half of the questioning.

Cliff kept his face expressionless. Since they'd pulled back into Bonner's driveway, he'd spoken to them only in quotations. It was getting old fast. "Would you like to call your lawyer?"

"We fight not to enslave, but to set a country free, and to make room upon the earth for honest men to live in."

Cliff crumpled his coffee cup and stood up. "I need a refill." He nodded to Mike and walked over to the coffee pot at the far end of the room.

Mike slid into the seat Cliff had just vacated. Bonner's eyes stayed resolutely on a spot just over Mike's right shoulder.

"You know, Bonner, I can appreciate where you're coming from.

Here you are, a law-abiding citizen, minding your own business, and Cliff and I come in and roust you about some broad. I mean, who wants to talk about a chick that split, right?"

Cliff could see Bonner's face from his position at the coffee station. He thought there was a reaction to the words 'broad' and 'chick'. He moved closer to get a better view as Mike continued.

"I know how much it blows when a bitch turns on you. You gave her a place to stay, food, warmth, and how does she pay you back? She's coming on to every guy she meets down by the road."

Bonner's expression remained fixed, but he blinked several times in rapid succession, and swallowed.

Mike handled it well, Cliff noted. No trace of excitement.

"So you just do what any guy would do. You grab her and try to make her see reason. Except she won't listen. So you grab a little harder and before you know it, she's on the floor."

Bonner raised his chin and compressed his lips into a thin line.

"No one could blame you for that, Bonner. Hell, most of us have been there ourselves. You were just trying to explain to her how it works, and she wasn't getting it."

Cliff stepped up and placed his hands flat on the table, leaning in close to Bonner's face. "So you pressed harder. But, big guy like you, small girl like her, you didn't realize you were hurting her."

"It was quick, wasn't it?" Mike joined in. "One minute she was arguing, the next she was dead? And then you were stuck."

"So you took her off to where no one would find her. Was it hard to carry her up there? Or is that where you had the argument?"

"Did she make any noise when you did it? Or were you yelling so loud you couldn't hear it?" Mike leaned forward, bringing his face within inches of Bonner's.

"Tell us, Bonner. Where did you kill her? Was it up on the mountain or somewhere else? Where did she die?" Cliff bent down but didn't lower his voice. "WHERE?"

Sweat dribbled down Bonner's temple but he pressed his lips even more firmly together.

"Tell us, Bonner. Tell us where it happened."

"You'll feel better, Bonner. Tell us now." Cliff said almost simultaneously.

"No."

"And 'no' is the right answer."

A new voice sounded from the doorway. Cliff spun around and suppressed a groan. Mike wasn't so subtle and muttered a quick "Dammit!" before composing his face.

"Is that any way to greet a lady?" The newcomer, a wiry middle-aged woman dressed in a lime green pants suit with short blonde hair straight out of a bottle, marched into the room and rested her briefcase on the floor next to Bonner, who sagged back into his chair with relief.

"Hello, Marjorie." Cliff said, dredging up some semblance of composure.

Marjorie Duckworth smiled back. "Always a pleasure, Trooper Codey. And your partner...?"

"Trooper Mike Eldrich, working ISB for the last year and a half."

"Fresh blood. How nice. Now if you both will excuse me, I need some time with my client. I assume the coffee in this place hasn't increased in either price or quality?"

Cliff gestured toward the coffee maker at the end of the room. "Still free and as lousy as ever."

"Excellent. I approve of getting exactly what I pay for. It's nice to see continuity in government service. Now shoo."

Seeing the expression on Mike's face, Cliff cleared his throat sharply and jerked his head toward the door. With a look of half revulsion and half incredulity, Mike followed.

"We'll be in our office when you need us," Cliff said, herding Mike from the room. "You know where it is."

Marjorie's only reply was a quick hand wave as she bent over her briefcase.

Cliff closed the door and sighed. "Her timing is always perfect." Looking at Mike's outraged expression, Cliff gestured toward their office. "C'mon. While we wait I'll try to explain 'Hurricane Marjorie' to you."

****

"Marjorie Duckworth inherited a ton of land, and a ton of money to go with it. She also inherited the family brains and a burning desire to do good. That was fine when she limited herself to the school board and the conservation commission, but about ten years ago she got the bright idea to go to law school." Cliff looked over to make sure their door was firmly shut, but lowered his voice anyway.

"She got her degree in some kind of distance learning course, then passed the bar exam on the first shot. Since then she's made a career out of defending the losers in the area. The money the state saves on public defenders is easily cancelled out by the nothing cases that she drags out forever in court."

Mike also glanced at the door as he leaned across his desk. "Has she always looked like that?"

Cliff snorted. "Today is a calm day. Have you ever heard of that poem about getting old and wearing purple?"

Mike shook his head.

"You're too young. I think Marjorie has made that her own personal creed. You should see her when she's in court! Makes today's lime green get-up seem tame."

Cliff stretched out a hand for the telephone, replacing his glasses as he skimmed his list of phone contacts. "Might as well use the down time to call Brenda with our question about whether we can stretch the time of death out to early October." He dialed, idly drawing a series of concentric squares on his desk calendar. "Hi Brenda, this is Cliff Codey...Yes I do have another question. Could the death have taken place as early as the beginning of October?.....I remember what you told us, but I wanted to be sure....Okay, thanks for your.... Goodbye to you too."

He threw his pencil down on the desk. "Well that didn't win me any friends."

At Mike's inquiring look, he explained. "Seems she took my request for clarification as questioning her professional knowledge and judgment. I'm going to get a chilly reception the next time I see her. Something to look forward to."

"But she confirmed October as a possible time of death?"

"Yup, she didn't like it and dressed it up in a lot of phrases like 'local cold spots' and 'reasonable temperature fluctuations', but in the end she agreed it was possible. So that's one more check against Bonner. We can throw that at Marjorie when she's done talking to him." Cliff glanced at his watch and decided three-thirty was too late for a second lunch. "I'm headed down to the vending machine. You want anything?"

"I'll come with you," Mike said, scrambling to his feet. "What's the lime-green hornet's record like in court?"

Cliff paused with his hand on the door. "Damn good, unfortunately. I have not enjoyed facing her when I'm in the witness box. She makes a bulldozer look gentle." He pushed open the door, then caught it as it bounced back.

"How did she know Bonner was here?"

"Jungle drums. ESP. Nothing would surprise me." Cliff stopped in front of the vending machine, fed in some coins and punched the buttons for Peanut M&Ms. Marjorie's presence cancelled out any notion of sticking to a diet.

Watching Mike waver between cheese doodles and cheesy chex mix, Cliff ripped open the candy. "My guess is that Bonner called her as soon as we left his place this morning. That might mean he knows something and wants some protection." He chomped through the M&Ms, crumpled the wrapper and turned away from the machine once Mike made his selection. "Let's go back and look over what we have so far, make sure it all checks out. I don't want to lose this on some procedural snafu. Those are Margie's specialty."

****

Twenty minutes later a brisk knock sounded and the office door was flung open without waiting for a reply. "Hello gentlemen, no, don't get up. Have you both been waiting just for me? Marvelous. My tax dollars at work."

Cliff made a conscious effort not to grind his teeth. "Cut the crap, Marjorie, and let's get down to business so we can all get home sometime before midnight."

"Charming as always, Cliff. And are those new specs? My, my, they do add a scholarly air." Cliff whipped his glasses off with a glower and Marjorie turned to Mike, who was struggling to keep his expression neutral. "And what excuse do you have for hauling my law-abiding client down here like a common felon, diminishing his upstanding reputation in the community and besmirching his good name?"

Mike smiled sweetly. "Which, of course, he earned by threatening the tax assessor at gun point multiple times."

That stopped Marjorie briefly. "My, my, an *enfant terrible*. What sharp fangs are hidden behind that pretty face. And he only threatened the guy twice."

"If you want to start in about appearances..." Mike began, before Cliff cut across the conversation.

"Like I said, let's get down to business." He gave Mike a warning glance and turned back to Marjorie. "Well?"

"My client has no knowledge of the whereabouts of the young woman in question following late November of last year. He regrets that he can't help you with your investigation and wishes you luck in finding her killer." Marjorie beamed at both men. "There! That's settled! Now I'd like to see him released so that you boys can go back to looking for the real killer." Her expression changed again, and she laid one hand across her chest and the back of the other across her brow. "I don't like the idea of a murderer walking around free in our little community."

"Neither do we," Mike said. "That's why your client is behind bars."

Marjorie took a deep breath, her chest rising dramatically, but Cliff jumped in before her next round of improv.

"Look Margie, you know the drill. Save the next performance for the judge."

"Okay, Cliffie." Marjorie smirked as Cliff winced. "I'll do that." She turned and marched toward the door, opening it with a flourish. "I do mean it about continuing the investigation." Her eyes swept over the two men. "Bonner's a loud-mouthed contrary prick, but he's no killer. Your guy is still out there. So get going and find him." She nodded once, and slammed the door behind her.

Cliff sighed and ran a hand over his face. Mike looked over in concern. "What?"

"That damn woman is as loud and as abrasive as her client. The problem is, ninety percent of the time she's right."

CHAPTER TWENTY

By late Monday afternoon, Nelson's confidence was starting to wane. Slumping in front of his computer, he entered his third combination of words into the search engines he was using. So far he had tried every combination of words that might connect to Jane Doe and read so many sad stories from families of missing girls that he felt the anguish beginning to seep under his hard and polished professional shell. He always made a point of not getting emotionally involved in any of his reporting, but these cases challenged his resolve. Unfortunately, none of the girls matched his Jane Doe in the necessary combination of looks, age and how long they'd been missing.

A small noise brought his attention to his doorway. Jerry stood there, studying him without expression. Nelson quickly rearranged his features into a neutral position, but he knew the damage had already been done.

"Tough time?" Jerry asked, with deceptive mildness.

Nelson wasn't fooled. "Nah, just a long day in front of the screen. You know how it is; first day back and all of that." He made of show of gathering up the materials on his desk. "Best thing to do is pack it in for the day and hit it fresh in the morning."

"What will you have for me?" Again, Jerry's question and the tone were gentle.

Nelson began to get seriously worried. "I'm picking back up on some of the things I had going before vacation. There's the piece on the deteriorating condition of the city's infrastructure, another one on traffic control and limiting cars in Manhattan, and then there's that U.N. thing."

Seeing Jerry's blank look, Nelson elaborated, striving for a casual tone. "I'm looking into an idea about examining how hosting the U.N. affects the city and whether the prestige and income truly offsets the expenses of providing the security needed. Not to mention the revenue lost from tying up prime waterfront real estate in a tax free complex."

Jerry grunted and studied the interior of his coffee cup as though it contained the meaning of life. He finally lifted his head and grimaced – the closest simulation of a smile he ever gave. "Good. Like the U.N. idea." He straightened and waved his cup vaguely toward the window. "And you do understand where I'm coming from about the Jane Doe piece? We need to stay cutting edge and current and I rely on you to give that to me." Saluting Nelson once more with his coffee cup, he turned and sauntered off down the hallway.

Nelson exhaled and slid down in his chair. Jerry yelling and breathing fire was bad, but Jerry talking softly and reasonably was truly terrifying. What was it about the missing girl that set Jerry against it? Usually he trusted Nelson's nose and gave him *carte blanche* to pursue whatever smelled right.

Swiveling his chair, he turned and looked out the window. Jerry's opposition not only hardened Nelson's determination to follow the story, but started him wondering about Jerry in a way he never had before. Maybe there was a story there as well.

****

"I don't think you should go there." Alyssa pushed her drink away and leaned closer to Nelson. "Jerry isn't a tolerant or forgiving guy. And, even though I haven't been in this job very long, I've heard he won't stand for any intrusion into his personal life."

They'd just finished dinner in one of their favorite restaurants, a small place on the Upper East Side that specialized in Asian Fusion. Nelson reveled in the return to civilization – enjoying being greeted by name and the flattering deference from the waiters.

Alyssa paused while they were handed menus. "Wasn't there some woman who tried to get on Jerry's good side by digging up info about where he grew up and giving him some kind of gift related to it?" She dropped her voice and leaned even closer. "I heard she was escorted out of the building and didn't even get to clean out her desk, and Jerry black balled her all up and down the east coast until she had to move out west to find work."

"Jerry doesn't have a good side and that woman was an idiot not to realize it." Nelson took a strand of Alyssa's hair and rubbed it between his fingers, pleased with her concern. "Let's forget about him and celebrate our second night back home."

****

"So this case is a bad one?"

Cliff took off his glasses and put down the file as his wife slid onto the couch next to him, curled her legs underneath her and leaned one elbow on the back of the couch to study him. "We have so little to go on and that asshole Bonner knows something and is playing games with us instead of helping. Now he's got Marjorie Duckworth involved and ...." Cliff stopped as Anna's lips twitched and she put a hand across them to hide the smile. "A murdered runaway is funny?"

Her expression changed immediately. "Of course not, Cliff, you know better than that. For God's sake, we have daughters of our own!" She held up a hand to forestall his comment. "And yes, I am keeping a very tight rein on them until this case is solved and whatever creep that did it is locked away. But...." And the twitch came back. "I just can't help it. I love Marjorie."

Cliff studied his wife's face for a minute, then relaxed. "I know. She can be a hoot. You should have seen Mike's reaction to her – priceless." He described their verbal sparring match then fell silent once again.

Anna laid a hand across his shoulders. "What else is it? There have been other cases that were nastier, but you didn't bring them home like you are with this one."

Cliff looked down at his glasses and flipped the sidepieces up and down a few times. "The idiot who found the body was staying at Kurt's place in Lincoln, so we've had to go down there a couple of times."

"Ah." It was only one syllable, but Anna infused a whole paragraph's worth of meaning into it.

"We kept the conversation professional," Cliff began defensively, but at Anna's raised eyebrow he gave in and continued, "Until we were leaving. He asked me to stop by some Sunday to see him and some of the boys." He waited, but Anna didn't say anything.

"Of course I didn't go..."

"And you feel a bit guilty about that." Anna finished for him.

Cliff leaned forward and tossed his file and glasses onto the coffee table. "I don't know what to think," he started, and then immediately contradicted himself. "I just don't like feeling guilted into doing something." He stopped and shot a quick glance at Anna. "And I know you don't like me hanging around with him – and with good reason." He added before she could do it for him.

Anna paused a moment to think. "You hanging around with Kurt now, as a seasoned officer with a solid record behind you, is a very different thing to you hanging around him as a first year hire and making a name for yourself as a wild-ass wise guy. But second, and more important, why is he making you feel guilty?"

Now it was Cliff's turn to hesitate. Finally he sighed and shook his head. "I guess it's a holdover from when I was a kid and all Kurt had to do was say 'go' and we went without a question or hesitation. And now he's asking me to come over.....and old habits die hard."

Anna waited a bit, then reached over to take his hand. "So why not go see him? Get it out of your system and his. Talk about old times with an old man who was kind to you when you were young. Okay?" She smiled and gave his hand a squeeze. "I'm heading upstairs. Will you be up soon?"

Cliff squeezed back and nodded, then watched Anna leave the room before dropping his chin to his chest. If only talking to Kurt was as simple as Anna made it sound. She didn't know the weight of dread that conversation carried with it.

He looked around their living room, made comfortable by Anna's skill at crafting and repurposing furniture and materials culled from multiple weekend yard-sale expeditions with the girls. In his mind, he pictured his daughters, Debra and Sara, sleeping safely upstairs. Those three were what mattered most in his world, and he'd do anything to protect them and their view of him as a loving husband and father. Would this case threaten that?

Did Kurt want to reopen the subject that they all swore they'd never mention again? Was this new body stirring up memories in everyone else who was involved, too? And even more, what would Anna think if she found out? Excusing his association with Kurt was easy when all she thought it consisted of was a few drunken weekends. What would her reaction be if she knew the truth?

CHAPTER TWENTY-ONE

Tuesday morning was one of those bright and sunny days that could make even the rougher areas of New York City look passable, while downtown literally sparkled. Bright sun, low humidity and a gentle breeze had even seasoned New Yorkers moving with their heads up and a spring in their step. Nelson and Alyssa had slipped out of the office just after nine, and were traveling up the west side of Manhattan.

"Where did you say the queen of baby food lives? We're up into Harlem." Nelson squinted out the window watching the West Side Drive slip by. "We're going to run out of Manhattan soon."

"She lives in Riverdale, in the Bronx." Alyssa said, and tightened her grip on the steering wheel.

"The Bronx! You didn't tell me that. I would have brought my riot gear along. Are you sure you want to bring your own car up there?" He peered through the windshield with a shudder. "I know Riverdale is supposed to be a good neighborhood, but everything is relative. If it looks bad, we're turning right around."

Alyssa shot him an amused look. "Have you ever been there?"

Nelson shook his head. "Not Riverdale. But I've seen enough of the rest of this borough and it's not a nice place. What's a millionaire want to live there for?"

"She grew up in the Bronx. I guess she wants to stay close to her roots. That's one of the things I'll ask her." Alyssa moved over to the right hand lane. "Look for the Riverdale Avenue exit; I think we're getting close now."

Ten minutes later, Nelson was revising his opinions. Broad, tree-lined streets with long curving driveways angled off in all directions. He rolled down his window, took a deep breath and listened to the distant sound of a lawn mower mixed with song birds.

"Damn! This is why I love New York. I've lived in and explored this city all my life, and never suspected this was here."

Alyssa leaned forward and peered at the curb. "Does that look like 4357 to you? The paint is faded."

"I think so." Nelson rolled down the window and leaned out. "Let's go on up. If it's not the baby food queen, they'll be able to tell us where she is."

Alyssa turned into the driveway and pulled up to a well land-scaped house with elaborate flower beds surrounding the front door.

"She must pay a mint for gardening services," Nelson said, unfolding himself from the front seat. "The place looks deserted. Are you sure this is the right day and time?"

Alyssa stepped up to the door. Looking in vain for a doorbell, she finally grabbed the polished brass knocker and gave it several healthy raps. "I'm sure about the day and time, but like I told you, she's a lit-tle eccentric so who knows if she'll keep the appointment."

"Eccentric. That's a PC way of saying she needs a keeper and a padded cell." Nelson stuck his hands in his pockets and rocked back on his heels. "Get ready to enter the Twilight Zone."

Alyssa made a shushing noise, then swung quickly back to face the door as it opened. A small, slightly built woman looked inquiringly out at them. She wore jeans and a peasant blouse, and her graying blonde hair was swept back into a long thick braid.

Nelson kept his face impassive. Maybe the baby food wasn't such a gold mine after all, if this was an example of the hired help Amanda Baxter could afford. Alyssa had risen to the occasion and was asking for the Baxter residence.

"This is it," the woman answered. "Are you here for the inter-view?"

"Yes, is Mrs. Baxter at home?" Alyssa gave her most winning

smile. Nelson barely had time to wonder why she was wasting it on the maid, when the woman opened the door wider and gestured to come in.

"I'm Mrs. Baxter. But please call me Mandy."

****

An hour later Nelson looked impatiently at yet another flower. This one was large and red. The last one had been small and white. And the ten or twelve before that had been different shapes and colors also. None of them were that special. And none was worth the forty-five minutes of exposition and explanation that accompanied them. Why Alyssa had ever commented on them was beyond him. Oh sure, a casual compliment, but to ask for a tour? The only positive he could see was the lack of bugs.

"I will look for that catalogue," Alyssa was saying. "I never knew so many plants could be grown in an apartment as well as outside."

The older woman smiled, but Nelson noticed it didn't reach her eyes. It had been the same throughout the entire visit. Whatever Mandy Baxter spoke about, from the history of her business to her garden, her eyes maintained that opaque appearance that made Nelson wonder if she really even saw them. He was turning over possible causes – drugs and/or mental illness came to mind – when the garden tour mercifully concluded with an invitation into the house for a glass of iced tea before they had to leave.

Alyssa raised her eyebrows to him as they followed Mandy into the house, but Nelson didn't have anything to add. They both knew there was something peculiar going on with their hostess, but Nelson was as clueless as Alyssa, and he didn't like it. Entering the house, the two women went directly into the kitchen. Nelson watched them go, following slowly and peering into rooms along the way.

The feeling of oddness grew with each room he surveyed. Not only did they look unused, but they were a weird mix of classic and ....what? Nelson fumbled for a definition of what he was seeing. Finally he settled for the word childish, although that didn't encompass it completely. The furniture looked like something a child might have chosen, but a child with a lot of money who shopped in very expensive places. And then got bored halfway through the choosing and just dropped everything and left where it fell.

"Nelson?" Alyssa's voice floated down the hall toward him. "Would you like some iced tea?"

"Be right with you," he called, glad to see the visit coming to an end. This woman might have made her fortune in baby food, but her house and personality leaned more toward wacky than wealthy.

CHAPTER TWENTY-TWO

Tuesday morning dawned equally fine in New Hampshire, but neither Cliff nor Mike noticed or cared. The day started with another trip out to Bonner's property to ask further questions about the disappearance of the young woman from his property. After the thirty minute drive, Bonner had refused to speak to them, other than to say he would sic his dog on them unless they left his property.

Cliff and Mike returned to the office fuming, and were discussing what their next move would be when Bonner's lawyer Marjorie – resplendent in pink and orange – swept in to their office for a second sparring match. Any feeling of tolerance Cliff might have carried over from his conversation with Anna the evening before vanished as soon as she walked through their door.

"What is the matter with you people?" her opening salvo began. And it got worse from there. "Why is my client still being harassed? You've already heard he knows nothing of this young woman after she left his house in October. And that she was alive and healthy when she left under her own free will."

"Who could blame her for leaving that dump?" Mike muttered before Cliff could shush him.

Unfortunately, Marjorie had excellent hearing.

"Oh is that how it is around here?" she asked, rounding on Mike.

"Do I detect a prejudice in your attitude that means my client isn't getting impartial treatment in this department? Do I need to apply to have him moved to another jurisdiction to ensure he gets a fair and equitable hearing that isn't skewed by your preconceived notions of who he is?" She finally paused to inhale and Cliff grabbed the opportunity.

"Cut the crap, Marjorie. I seem to recall the assessment you gave us yesterday of your client's personality ran roughly along the same lines as Mike's. Now can we keep the histrionics out of this and come to some kind of agreement?" Throwing a quick scowl at Mike to keep his mouth shut, Cliff leaned against the desk and folded his arms.

Marjorie glowered briefly, and then switched to a sunny smile. "Histrionics! I do so love it when a man uses big words. Soooo much better that the caveman approach. And as long as you can keep a muzzle on junior over there, I'm willing to talk."

Mike opened his mouth to protest, but earned a second scowl from Cliff and subsided back into his chair, having to content himself with glowering from afar. Marjorie smiled and fluttered her eyelashes at him, then turned back to Cliff; who was biting the inside of his cheek to suppress a smile. His good humor restored, he pushed off from the desk and headed to the coffee maker. "Treat you to a cup?" he asked Marjorie in passing.

"Ha, so now you're trying to poison me," but the words had no sting. They collected their coffee and settled down at the conference table.

"Okay, cards on the table. What will it take to get you to leave my client in peace?"

Cliff nodded once in appreciation of her change of direction. "It's really very simple. We want to know what he knows about the young woman who was living with him last year, tentatively known as Melissa. Where did she come from, why was she in this area, and where she might have gone afterwards."

"Excellent! I can tell you all of that right now. If I do so, will you cease pestering him?"

Shaking his head, Cliff leaned back in his chair. "You know that's not good enough, Marjorie. C'mon now, I thought you were ready to get serious. We need to hear it from him."

Marjorie gave a small shrug. "A girl's got to try!" Leaning forward, she dropped the bantering tone. "Here's the deal. We all know my client is a strong willed individual with passionate opinions on a variety of subjects, a fierce resentment of being forced into anything against his will and a deep-seated distrust of all forms of government. Now you, as a representative of that government, trespassed on his property yesterday, then forced him to leave said property and questioned him against his will. All of which have deeply angered him and fed into his sense of persecution. How much cooperation do you realistically expect to get from him?"

"Marjorie, I have a murdered girl with no formal identification and Bonner is the only solid link to her. You know as well as I do that I have the right to question individuals who might have knowledge of the crime. I need to find out what he knows and I can't leave him alone until I am convinced that he has nothing to do with her death. While I am aware of your client's beliefs and prejudices, the bottom line is that until he tells us what we need to know, we're going to keep asking."

Marjorie pursed her lips and stared at the remains of her coffee for a few minutes. "Fair enough. I hear what you're saying and I will urge my client to tell you whatever he knows in order to exonerate himself. But I need your promise that once he does that he can go about his business and you won't hassle him anymore."

"You know I can't promise that at this stage. We have to go where the investigation leads us. Even if we get what we need from Bonner today, there's no guarantee that we won't have to talk to him again if we pick up new evidence that involves him. You have to make him understand that this is much more serious than slogans and tax assessors. This is a murder case and it's not going to go away."

Marjorie stood up and gathered up her purse and file folder. "He knows that, Cliff. He's not treating this as a trifle or a joke. To him, this situation strikes at the essence, the bedrock, of what he believes in, and he's not going to compromise his belief system for you or anyone else."

"Just do what you can, Marjorie. He trusts you."

"Only as long as I don't take part in anything he considers a betrayal. But I'll try."

Mike waited several minutes after she left to be sure he couldn't be overheard, then rounded on Cliff. "So that's it? We're going to let that asshole jerk us around with his stupid quotes and smart mouth and hold up the entire investigation?"

"Calm down. We're only on day two of having him as our main suspect. We may just have to wait while he decides which he hates more – sharing information or losing his privacy. From what I've heard of him, the latter might outweigh the former pretty quickly. Also, don't underestimate Marjorie. She knows it's in his best interest to talk to us, and she can be pretty damn persuasive when she needs to be. She'll spell it out to him and I wouldn't be surprised if she gets it into his ornery head before the day is out."

"I hope so," Mike shoved his hands into his pockets and kicked his chair back under the table. "We've finally got a possible lead and we just have to sit around till that joker decides to spill. Doesn't seem right."

Cliff carefully set his chair back in place and sighed. "Welcome to law enforcement. In the meantime, what we can do is try for a search warrant and check Bonner's property for any signs of the girl."

"Great! If we could find...." Mike's initial eagerness faded to apprehension as he thought about that. "Jeezum Crow, that could take us weeks to wade through all the crap he's got on that property."

"Yep. But at least we won't be sitting around."

****

Alyssa gave Mandy Baxter a final wave good-bye then started the car and moved slowly down the driveway. Once they were out of sight of the house, she slowed to a stop and turned to Nelson. "That was a waste of time, wasn't it."

It was more a statement than question, but Nelson answered anyway. "Yes, unless you want to write some kind of bland, milk-toast article that focuses on flowers. You might sell it to a gardening magazine, but Jerry's not going to like it."

Alyssa sighed and leaned forward to rest her head on the steering wheel. "What should I do? What would you do?"

"For starters, I wouldn't give up. You need another angle on Ms. Mandy Baxter. Where would you go to get that?"

"I don't know..." Alyssa stopped and sighed. "She never mentioned any friends or family and when I asked her specifically about them she never really answered either question."

"Okaaay...." Nelson deliberately drew the word out to show he was being patient. "So what does that leave you with?" Getting no immediate response, he tried again. "Look around you, what do you see?"

Alyssa obediently looked to the left and right, but Nelson could see by her puzzled expression that she wasn't following him.

"Neighbors!" He smacked the dashboard for emphasis, making Alyssa jump. "They are always your best source of information, whether it's a tenement or a high class neighborhood like this. And sometimes," he lowered his voice and leaned closer, even though there was no one to hear, "the higher the class the bitchier they are. Let's see if we can find some bored stay at home housewife willing to dish about her anti-social neighbor."

They struck out at the first two houses they tried – no one home in house number one and the maid in house number two had a tenuous grasp of English and appeared afraid to try it on them. "Bet she thinks we're actually Immigration officials," Nelson muttered as they left. "Hope we didn't scare her out of that job."

Having exhausted the neighbors to the right and left, they crossed the street next. A pleasant looking woman in a pink 'for the cure' jogging suit and inch-long nails opened the door immediately after they rang the bell.

"I wondered when you'd get around to me. I'm Jeanine Lockwood." She leaned a hip against the door jam and looked them both over. "What do you want? You don't have any paperwork or products so I know you're not selling anything, you're dressed too stylishly to be Jehovah's Witnesses, and census time doesn't come around for a few more years. So what's up?"

Nelson mentally rubbed his palms together – jackpot! This woman was smart and observant, the best type of source for information. Time to lay on the charm. "You're right, miss. We are none of those things. We are actually reporters who would like to do a human interest feature on your neighbor, Mrs. Baxter. We have spoken to her and toured her lovely gardens and would just like a bit of background info on her, you know what I mean – what type of neighbor she is, how involved in local events and organizations, to give some finishing touches to make a complete picture." Nelson managed to make it sound like the success of the project hinged on anything Ms. Lockwood could tell them.

The extra effort proved unnecessary. Their new friend invited them to call her Jeanine and come on in almost before Nelson finished talking.

"That poor woman," she began, leading them to a comfortable sun room, furnished with blue and white gingham chairs and white whicker tables. "And obviously I don't mean poor in the material sense, but in every other way she is completely bankrupt."

"Really?" Nelson encouraged, but she swept on before he finished the second syllable.

"Oh my yes! I mean, couldn't you see it when you talked to her? She is just a lost soul. When I think of what she used to be like – all fire and energy and determination – it just breaks my heart to see her now. She has completely withdrawn from life and given up." Jeanine settled herself into one of the gingham chairs and gestured for Nelson and Alyssa to follow suit.

"What happened? When did she move here and what changed her?" Nelson asked, trying to get her focused to give a coherent story with a linear time line rather than a rambling emotional soliloquy.

"Well," Jeanine leaned forward so Nelson and Alyssa followed suit, "she moved here about ten years ago, that was just after her baby food had gone into national distribution. She didn't talk about it much, but I gathered they had lived pretty rough up until then, with any money they had going to build up the business rather than spent on them. And they were so happy to buy that house! Kept saying it was like a dream come true."

Nelson hated to interrupt the flow of information, but he had to clarify. "Jeanine, you keep saying 'they'. Who else was there? Was she married?"

"Oh no, she wasn't married. Maybe she was once but if so, that was all over and done by the time they got here. No, Mandy moved up with her daughter, Melissa. Cute little thing, must have been about seven or eight when they got here. Called her Missy. That's how they introduced themselves to the neighborhood – Mandy and Missy." Jeanine fell unexpectedly silent, studying her fingernails.

Nelson nodded to Alyssa, feeling a woman's touch might be better here. "What happened to Missy?" Alyssa asked gently.

"It's not easy, running a company all by yourself." Jeanine began the story on a tangent. "And Mandy was so very invested in the quality of the food. She used to talk all the time about how she had struggled to find healthy food for Missy when she was a baby and how much time it took to make it. Mandy also worried about sustaining that quality as the company grew into mass production. She was used to overseeing everything herself, you see, and she found it hard to delegate."

"And Missy...?" Alyssa prompted.

"At first Missy was so happy to be in the new house and a nicer school that she accepted everything – all the travel and the meetings – without any complaints. But after a while.....￼" Jeanine stopped and twisted the rings on her right hand, then began again, speaking slowly. "It's tough to be a teenager no matter what the circumstances. And after a while, Missy began to get resentful and think Mandy cared more for the business than for her. And that's not how it was, Mandy would have gladly cut off her right arm for the girl, but she just didn't see that Missy wanted a share of her passion directed her way until it was too late."

Jeanine sat with her head bowed for a moment. This time it was Nelson who asked the question. "Suicide?"

"Oh no!" Jeanine's head snapped up, her eyes wide. "Nothing like that! She ran away. Just left last summer, one day when her mother was away. Mandy came home and found a note saying she was leaving and not to try to find her."

Jeanine shook her head. "Mandy did, of course. But she didn't want any publicity, so she didn't go to the police. Instead, she hired a firm of private investigators who promised to keep it out of the papers. I don't think that was the best idea, but you couldn't talk to her about it at all."

This time Jeanine twisted the nails on her left hand. "I tried, of course. I wanted to help, be supportive, be a friend or whatever she needed. So did the people in her company – they all came up to try to talk to her. First about Missy, then about the business and what needed to be done."

Jeanine got up and started pacing. "Mandy just shut everyone out. Stopped answering the door, took the phone off the hook and ignored her business and her employees. She just closed herself away in that big old house and cut off all contact with everyone. Let the business run itself and spent all her time in the garden. So sad."

Jeanine stopped in front of them. "I worry about Missy. She was so, I don't know how to put it, not backward but kind of like a throwback, you know? Like she belonged in a different time. Instead of going to the mall like other girls, she dressed just like her mother. They shared clothes, all the type of stuff Mandy liked that went out of style back in the sixties. They even wore their hair the same way – in that long braid. Sometimes, from the back, you couldn't tell who was who."

Nelson sat up straight in his chair and swallowed. He looked over and saw the same thought mirrored in Alyssa's widening eyes. His movement attracted Jeanine's attention and she looked from one to the other. "What?" she asked picking up on their excitement.

"Would you look at a picture for us?" Nelson slipped Jane Doe's photo out of his inside jacket pocket. He leaned over and passed the picture to Jeanine, eyes tight on her face. She accepted it with a frown, glanced down and gasped.

"That's Missy! Or....is it? It looks a lot like her but there's something..." She put a hand across her mouth. "Oh Lord, is she dead? Is that why she looks so.....Oh dear God what happened to her?" She dropped the picture as if it burned, covered her face in her hands and burst into tears.

It took an hour and several cups of tea laced with brandy to calm Jeanine down and convince her that running right over to tell Mandy was not a good idea. Alyssa was instrumental in this, telling her they needed to be very sure they had the right person before potentially breaking Mandy's heart. After assuring Jeanine that they would let Mandy know the minute they knew something definite and promising they'd keep Jeanine in the loop as well, they escaped to Alyssa's car and pulled over a block away to discuss the next step.

"I can't believe we found out who she is."

Nelson held up a hand. "Who she might be."

"But that woman identified her!"

"She thought she recognized her but remember, we'd just been talking about this girl and then we pull out a picture that looks similar. Even she said she wasn't sure after her initial reaction."

"That's because it's a photo of a reconstruction. I think her first instinct was correct."

"Maybe so. But I want something more to tie this picture to Missy

Baxter before we go in and put our theory out to the woman who might be her mother and further ruin her life."

Alyssa reached out and covered Nelson's hand with her own. "I like to see this caring side of you."

"I care. And I also don't care – to be sued for causing undue stress over a false identification."

Alyssa squeezed once, then removed her hand and got back to business. "So what's our next step?"

"We leave for New Hampshire tomorrow morning early. Now we have a name to throw at those arrogant two-bit troopers. We can use it to barter for more information to try and make a positive identification." Nelson took the picture out and looked at it again. "We can do another internet search tonight, now that we have a name, to see if anything else turns up that might be useful – either for identification, or as a bargaining tool."

CHAPTER TWENTY-THREE

Tuesday afternoon found Cliff and Mike in a bargaining stalemate with Bonner and Marjorie. Marjorie had convinced Bonner to come back in to the station for the conversation, arguing that this would prevent further trespass upon his property. Bonner had come – but insisted he would give no information until he was given a promise he wouldn't be badgered again. Cliff insisted equally that he couldn't make any promises but had to follow where the investigation led, while Marjorie and Mike supported their respective partners.

By four o'clock everyone was tired and cranky and even Marjorie's famous good humor was wearing thin. Telling Bonner she needed to answer nature's call, Marjorie left the room, looking hard at Cliff as she did so. "And don't you coerce my client while I'm out of the room. Maybe I should just call for a chamber pot so I can keep an eye on you!"

Cliff took the hint. Holding up both hands in a surrender motion, he said. "To be honest, I could do with the same. Why don't we both leave the room and Mike here will guard the door until we get back. Will that satisfy you?"

Marjorie looked over at Bonner, who gave a brief nod, then turned to Mike. "Scout's honor that you'll stay outside and behave yourself while we're gone, junior?"

Mike glowered at both lawyer and client but, after catching a stern frown from Cliff, agreed.

Cliff held the door for Marjorie and followed her a few steps down the hallway toward the restrooms. Once there, Cliff stopped and signaled for Mike to join them, placing a finger to his lips for quiet. "Good work," he whispered, turning to Marjorie, "Now what did you want to say?"

Marjorie glanced down the hallway and kept her voice low. "Look. We've been going round and round all day and we're all sick of it. You can't keep my client here indefinitely solely for interrogation and he's not going to say a damn thing until he hears a promise you won't make. We are gridlocked. So either charge him or release him or I'm going to go find a judge."

Cliff sighed, removed his glasses and rubbed his eyes with his thumb and index finger. "Don't you understand, Marjorie? I'm trying my best to keep a murder charge off Bonner's record. Once you're associated with something like that, even if charges are dismissed or you are acquitted, you never quite shake it and a whole bunch of doors are closed to you forever."

"You think I don't know that?" Marjorie hissed back. "But I am bound to follow my client's instructions and his are that he won't talk until he is assured this is the last time he has to."

They glared at each other until Cliff stepped back and looked up at the ceiling. "Look, I get that you're trying to do your job the best way you can, and I think you know I'm trying to do the same. How about we do it this way. We tell Bonner he's got one more night to think it all over before we charge him. In the meantime, we are expecting a signed warrant to search his house and grounds within the next hour. We will complete the search as soon as we get it. If we find nothing there that connects him with this crime, we will reconsider our approach to him. If we find something incriminating, he gets charged. Fair enough?"

Marjorie exhaled sharply. "Don't think I don't see through this. You are using this search to pressure my client into talking. You know the thought of law enforcement personnel on his property and looking through his possessions will drive him up the wall and right back down again. Fair? It sounds much more like bureaucratic bullying to me."

Cliff shrugged and spread his hands. "That's all I've got."

Drumming her fingers against her cheek, Marjorie stared at a spot above Cliff's head. Finally she sighed. "All right. I will try and sell this to my client. But it's not going to be easy and I'm going to take a butt-load of crap by even bringing this up to him, much less supporting it. So you better realize you owe me for even trying this on. And I truly hope you're not screwing me over on this one, or I will find a way to get you by the short hairs and pull them till you scream!"

Cliff raised an eyebrow. "You do realize that technically it's illegal to threaten an officer's short hairs."

There was a short silence, then Marjorie barked with laughter. "That's why I love you, Cliffie. If I were twenty years younger you really would be crying for mercy." She straightened up and fluffed her hair. "Ah well, there's no rest for the witty. Now it's time to sweet talk my client into the lame-est deal of the century. But first, I will use your facilities just so I won't be guilty of lying to my client!"

"Good idea – I'll do the same."

They met back in the interrogation room and Cliff and Mike stepped out to give Marjorie time for a private consultation with her client. Fifteen minutes and several raised voices later she opened the door. Giving a discreet wink she told them. "My client agrees to allow you access to his property as long as he and I both accompany you. Once he is satisfied you haven't damaged or removed anything of value, he agrees to speak to you – briefly – on the subject of the possible whereabouts of the young woman Melissa who was his guest for a brief period last fall." She turned back to Bonner. "Let's head on back to your place." Following her client down the hallway, she threw a quick wave over her shoulder. "Ta ta boys, don't bother to see us out!"

Both Cliff and Mike sat savoring the silence for a few minutes and then Mike got to his feet and came over and offered his hand to Cliff.

Cliff stared at the hand, then up at Mike. "What the hell is this for?"

Mike dropped his hand and snapped a salute instead.

"Have you been drinking or sniffing something you shouldn't?" Cliff asked, "Or have you just completely lost your mind?"

"I've got to hand it to you, Cliff. I couldn't have done what you just did. How you kept your cool in the face of what that woman was dishing out to you...." Mike paused and rubbed a hand over the top of his crew cut. "And the way she changed direction every couple of minutes, and it didn't even shake you."

"You forget, I live in a house full of women. And now that the girls have hit puberty it's just one hair-raising hormonal scene after another. So this? Just a little hiccup, comparatively speaking. At least Marjorie doesn't throw things."

"But how did you know she wanted to talk to you in private? And why go through all that bathroom bull?"

Cliff grinned. "Experience. I've seen that woman perform in the courtroom for hours at a time without any need for a break. So when she started talking about not being able to last, I knew there was something else going on. And, I also know we couldn't have had that conversation in front of Bonner. He would have fired her immediately if he thought she was cooperating with us in any way. And I couldn't talk that honestly about my thoughts in front of him either – he has to believe there's a serious danger he'll be charged with murder or he'll keep playing twenty quotations with us."

The telephone's ring cut off any comment Mike might have made. "Maybe that's our search warrant," Cliff said, and reached the phone in three hefty steps. "Hello?"

Mike watched with growing puzzlement as Cliff's expression changed from expectancy to disbelief and finally exasperation. He made a 'what gives' motion and Cliff covered the mouthpiece to tell him, "You're not going to believe this. It's that idiot Brainerd calling to offer his 'services' in helping us find the killer. Jeezum, can this day get any more bizarre?"

He took his hand off the mouthpiece and, after several false starts, finally interrupted the free flow of Kenny's ideas. "Mr. Brainerd, while I appreciate your sincere wish to be helpful and it seems you have some fascinating and remarkable theories about the crime, I must stress that this investigation is being handled by trained law enforcement personnel *only* – do I make myself perfectly clear?" There was a brief pause while Cliff held the phone slightly away from his ear and rolled his eyes, then he finished, "Please keep in mind what I said before, Mr. Brainerd. And if you have any other theories to share with us, please feel free to put them in writing and send them on. Good-bye."

This time Mike actually applauded. "I wish I could have caught that on tape. That's the smoothest brush-off I've ever seen. Actually makes this whole day worthwhile!"

Cliff shook his head and grinned back. "The trick is to be off the phone before they realize they've been rejected."

The phone rang again and Cliff took a mock step back. "Oh no, Kenny the kook has come up with a couple more theories for us!" Gingerly he picked up the phone. "Hello?" His shoulders relaxed as he heard the voice on the other end. "Oh hi, Marjorie. Uh, huh. Yup. Okay, good. I understand. Yeah, we can do that. You too."

Mike nodded toward the phone. "And?"

"Marjorie managed to convince Bonner that talking to us really is a lesser evil than having a murder charge on his record. So he has decided he will consent to meet with us tomorrow, but not too early because he's not a morning person."

"Big of him, isn't it – like he's granting us and audience."

"And further, he has decided it's just fine if we want to search his property – since he has nothing to hide, he has nothing to fear. That was a quote, Marjorie said."

"Oh, for the love of...."

"Look Mike, she managed to get us everything we asked for without having to hear any more abuse from that bozo. I'm good with that."

"Me too. So we can toss his place early tomorrow morning when the light is good, and then see if we can get some answers, right?"

"Sounds like a plan. As long as that warrant comes through."

"Why don't I head down to the courthouse and just wait there till it's ready?" Mike said. "I don't mind and it's one less thing to worry about."

"If you're sure you don't mind..."

"Not a problem." Mike sketched a mock salute and headed out the door.

Cliff sat back to his desk to make a few notes on how he wanted to approach the interview tomorrow. He was interrupted by the phone once again. Thinking it was just the call saying the warrant was ready, he answered the phone without hesitation.

"Cliff? That you?"

"Kurt." Cliff sat back in his chair and suppressed a sigh. "What can I do for you?"

"Didn't see you this past Sunday."

So that's what this was, Cliff thought, another dose of guilt. But remembering his wife's advice, Cliff tried to put some warmth into his voice. "Sorry to have missed you, but Debra's tournament ran long."

"Mmmm... I was really hoping you'd stop by... Got a couple of things I wanted to run by you... Get your professional opinion, you might say."

Listening to the long pauses between the sentences, Cliff felt a prickle of unease. There was something going on here – something out of the ordinary. And Cliff wasn't sure he wanted to know what it was. If Kurt or one of his Crew had gotten themselves in some kind of mess, he didn't want to get involved. Especially if it turned into the same sort of problem he'd been involved in twenty four years ago. And it seemed likely – why else would Kurt suddenly start calling like this?

"Is it anything you can talk about now? Over the phone?"

Another long pause. "Naw, not over the phone. Look, it's probably nothing, my imagination getting the better of me. Must be getting old. Just wanted to see what your nose told you about something."

Cliff closed his eyes. That phrase – see what your nose told you – took him back. Kurt had always been big on following your nose. He told them not to follow their gut because their gut could be queasy with fear or burning with rage and would lead them astray. But their following their nose would point them toward the next sensible thing. And nine times out of ten, he'd tell them, in an emergency, keeping calm and following their nose was the best course of action. But to hear Kurt talking about imagining things and getting old; that just wasn't like him.

"Look Kurt, let me see what I can do tomorrow evening once I'm done here, ok? I'll try my best to swing by and we can talk. How does that sound?"

"Fair enough. I should be around and have a few minutes to spare."

That sounded more like the old Kurt. "Okay, tomorrow evening. Hope to see you then." Cliff hung up and sat staring at the phone. Something was definitely going on and now he needed to find out what.

He eased back away from the door, moving soundlessly, the way he'd taught himself, disturbed by what he'd just heard. So the old man wanted to talk to the cop again, did he? He wondered if it might have anything to do with the way the old man had been acting over the last few days.

It was pure bad luck that Kurt had seen him return from his trip to Lafayette. The old guy must've noticed the mud on his boots and the vegetation stuck in his pack and started asking questions, trying to make it sound casual. Other people at the Inn had taken a day for themselves here and there and hadn't gotten the third degree. And he knew no questions were casual, each one was an invasion and an invitation to disaster, so he'd tried to shut the old man down. But Kurt had been watching him ever since; he could feel it. And he was sure the old man had been in his room, looking through his stuff. Luckily he'd kept everything that needed hiding safely hidden, out at his special place.

He was sure that was still a secret.

But now the old geezer wanted to bring one of the cops in for a chat. That was bad news. It was a betrayal as well. He'd been promised a sanctuary, but the old man was changing the rules. Now he'd have to change some rules as well – take action. Protect himself. Eliminate the danger.

CHAPTER TWENTY-FOUR

Wednesday morning, Cliff nosed the cruiser slowly into the clearing in the center of Bonner's property, thankful that the Tahoe had good ground clearance and that Bonner had made arrangements to board his dog for the day. He squinted into the early morning sun that slanted through the leaves and glinted off various windshields and piles of scrap metal, highlighting the dew glistening on the vegetation and bringing the myriad spider webs into sharp visibility. Stepping out of the car, Mike sniffed the air cautiously. "It may look like a dump, but at least it doesn't smell like one." He turned in a complete circle, surveying the collection of buildings surrounding their parking spot. "How do we decide which one we should search first? Flip a coin?"

Cliff joined Mike in surveying the scene. "Good question. Which do you think is his 'house'?"

There were a total of six buildings in a rough circle around the car, including a ramshackle old barn with a suspicious sag in the middle of the roof, a long low building with no windows and a series of mismatched doors along the front, two old single wide trailers, each sporting additional roofing materials in a mixture of plastic and metal sheeting – each trailer had also been provided with a roughly enclosed porch stacked with old barrels, gas cans, garbage cans and wooden crates – a small cabin made of rough hewn logs roofed with tarp covered particle board, and a ramshackle house, where the outer walls had asbestos shingles competing with silver Tyvek wall casing. A moss covered roof completed the picture.

"I'd say it's a toss-up between the house and the cabin for possibly usable living space. But I wouldn't put money on either." Mike said. "I'm glad I wore boots and I'm keeping my hat on in whatever space we go into."

Cliff grunted in agreement and gestured toward the house. "That's the biggest building. Let's start there."

Mike nodded and as they turned toward the house, the front door opened and Bonner stepped out, followed a moment later by Marjorie. "Good morning!" she called. My client and I will wait here on the porch while you gentlemen look around inside. Be advised that my client will inspect his house once you are done so work carefully."

With a muttered "Oh brother" from Mike, they stepped inside, donning gloves as they went. The house appeared basically clean and furnished with well-worn and mismatched pieces that gave the impression of comfortable quality. There were bookcases in every room, filled to overflowing, with additional stacks on the floor in corners and next to chairs. Cliff stepped up and donned his glasses to scan some of the titles. "John Paine, Voltaire, Jefferson, Adams, Thoreau....I think this is where all the books from my high school civics class ended up."

"There's more modern stuff in here," Mike called from the next room. "Still mostly philosophy and everything seems second hand or just plain old."

Cliff crossed the hallway to the other side of the house and whistled. "This one is all magazines."

"Porn?"

"Not that I can see. The shelves are labeled – Mother Earth News, Countryside, The Smithsonian, and I think every National Geographic that's ever been printed."

Mike joined him. "Nothing of interest on this wall, no hunting or guns, but here's a whole shelf of Popular Mechanics."

"No browsing, we've got work to do."

Mike shot him a 'like I would' look and both men moved to the back of the house where it looked like the walls of several rooms had been removed to form a large kitchen with a table in front of a wood-stove at one end and the standard kitchen components of sink, stove, cabinets and refrigerator at the other. Cliff gave a small "huh" of surprise as he surveyed the equipment. "This stuff is just like what my Grandmother had in her house – this porcelain sink top with the built in draining board, pine cabinets and lots of chrome with rounded corners on the stove."

Mike tried the faucet on the sink. "He's got running water and the plumbing works – at least for this sink."

A quick scan of all the cabinets revealed an assortment of mismatched plates, glasses and mugs, a variety of pots and pans hung on one wall with cast iron additions stored inside the stove. The refrigerator held an array of Mason jars of differing sizes holding what appeared to be milk, mustards and salsa. Eggs were stored in a wire basket and blocks of cheese were wrapped in newspaper. "Nothing interesting in here" Mike announced. "Let's head upstairs."

They found a out-size closet and two bedrooms, but only the larger one showed signs of use. "This is where we take a closer look. If there's any sign of a woman in the house, it's usually here." Cliff said. During the next half hour they looked through drawers and closets, under beds and rugs, and behind cabinets and bookcases.

"Nothing." Mike said in disgust, whipping his forehead with the back of his sleeve. "If the girl was living here, she left no trace."

"We still have several structures to search," Cliff reminded him. "And I didn't think we'd find anything in the main house. Bonner's too smart for that."

For the next hour they trampled through the barn – holding piles of old equipment and a flock of militant chickens – the two single-wides – containing more books and magazines in one, piles of clothing and house wares in the other – the low building with multiple doors – sporting a surprisingly sophisticated sugaring operation and more mason jars presumably filled with maple syrup – while Bonner and Marjorie waited placidly on the porch of the main house. Finally they came to the log cabin.

"This is our last chance to find something, I hope it works." Mike said, as both men stepped inside.

"Well I'll be damned." Cliff finally said, walking a few paces into the room. "Bingo! Who'd've thought ol' Bonner had it in him?"

The cabin had no interior walls, and the back part of the roof consisted of four large skylights. An easel took pride of place under the skylights and the upper walls were hung with paintings, while stacked canvasses leaned against the lower walls, awaiting their turn for paint. Cliff stepped up to the easel and bent down to sniff a jar holding several sized brushes soaking their bristles in some kind of liquid.

"Must be watercolor, doesn't smell like turpentine or solvent."

Mike completed a stroll around the room to examine the pictures and started flipping through the canvasses on the floor. Cliff tackled the one table in the room, where paint tubes, additional brushes and rags competed for space with a jumble of paper in an assortment of sizes – all covered with pencil sketches, and obviously rough drafts for the paintings. He paged quickly through the drawings, finding nothing of interest, then slid the table away from the wall to check behind it. He bent to pick up a small scrap jammed under the leg and gave a low whistle. "Jackpot!"

The sketch showed a young woman with a long braid looking out a window with a dreamy expression on her face. Cliff took the picture of their victim out of his pocket and held it up next to the sketch. The resemblance was undeniable.

Mike hurried over, inspected the paper and smiled. "Gotcha, you bastard."

"Not quite. We have evidence she was here, at least long enough for Bonner to have sketched her. We're still quite a ways from linking him to her murder. But we do have a few more talking points to use with him today." Cliff looked again at the paper in his hand. "You know, he's really pretty good. I get a much better sense of what this girl was like from this sketch, than from the computer generated picture."

"Fine, but let's not get all soft and gooey over it. He's still the last one to see her alive that we know of and that keeps him at the top of the hit parade of suspects."

Cliff nodded. "I'd say we're done here, let's go try and pry some answers out of Bonner Van Gogh."

****

Marjorie was waiting at the door as they emerged from the cabin to tell them Bonner finally agreed to 'grant them an audience' as Mike put it. "What changed his mind and made him decide to talk?" Cliff asked Marjorie as they walked back to the main house.

Marjorie shrugged. "Because it's Wednesday? Who knows? Although," she paused at the door, "it might have something to do with knowing that girl is dead. I thought I heard him make a comment about doing something for her, but I might have been mistaken. And even if I was right, he'd probably deny it, 'cause that's just the kind of guy he is. So remember, don't poke that snake with any kind of stick!"

The foursome re-adjourned to the kitchen and settled around the table, Mike and Cliff facing Marjorie and Bonner, with a tape recorder acting as referee in the center of the table.

Once everyone was seated, Cliff turned the recorder on and dove right in. "We are meeting to take a preliminary statement from Bonwit Felton, also known as Bonner, regarding his knowledge of and information about a young woman known as Missy who shared his home for an unspecified period of time last fall, ending in October." He looked across the table. "Agreed?"

Marjorie looked at her client and raised her eyebrows.

Bonner shook his head. "Sounds like a god-damn inquisition."

Mike sighed and rolled his eyes while Cliff looked pointedly at Marjorie, who turned to Bonner. "I thought we decided..."

Bonner held up his hands, "Okay, okay, I'm talking. Go ahead and ask your questions. I just want everyone to know I don't like any of this."

"So noted," Cliff said smoothly. "Now, can you tell us what you know about the young woman known as ....."

"Missy. Yeah, I heard it all the first time." Bonner slumped down in his chair and rubbed his eyes. "Let me think. It was Labor Day weekend when I first met her. I was down at a farmer's market in the Lake's Region, in Weirs Beach, and she was getting rousted by a couple of assholes."

"Rousted? Could you clarify that?"

"Hassled. Bothered. Harrassed. Crowded. Addressed in uncomplimentary terms with foul language. Is that sufficiently clarified?"

Cliff gave a tight smile. "Admirably so. Please continue."

"As I said, she was getting rousted so I approached the two buffoons and told them to get lost. We exchanged words but I have a few friends that regularly sell at that market, and we combined forces to suggest the two young men should take their business elsewhere and they did so. Missy...the young woman thanked me and introduced herself and I did the same and we started talking. She stayed with me as I made my rounds and she seemed to know a bit about antiques. That led to further conversations that lasted until the market shut down for the day. I asked her if I could give her a lift home and she declined but something didn't sound right. After a few more questions, I found out why. She didn't have a home and she'd been sleeping in an empty boathouse down along the lake. I offered to let her stay with me and she agreed."

"Just like that." Mike commented, earning a frown from both Cliff and Marjorie.

Bonner sighed, and addressed Mike directly. "Yes, just like that. I was worried about the Neanderthals that were bothering her earlier. I was afraid they might still be around and also...Missy seemed younger than her age, or at least, younger than twenty-one, the age she gave me. The way she talked and the way she dressed all seemed extremely unsophisticated. I'm not generally an altruistic person, but in this case I made an exception."

"Can you describe how she was dressed?"

"Some kind of smock or jumper with a t-shirt underneath. She had a small back pack that had a few more clothes, none of them very stylish, but good quality so I thought she might come from money."

"Did she say anything about her background or her family or where she grew up?"

Bonner shook his head. "I dropped a few hints and finally asked her straight out, but she never gave a direct answer. She'd change the subject or make a joke or invent something."

"Can you give us an example of an invention? Sometimes runaways give away more than they realize."

"Most of the answers were related to children's books, things like 'I came up the rabbit hole with Alice' or 'Charlotte wove me in her web'."

"And when the answers weren't literary?"

"She'd say things like 'the wind blew me in' or 'I'm a stray mermaid washed ashore.' After awhile I just stopped asking."

Cliff nodded. "So to return to the timeline, the young woman known as Missy came to stay with you in the beginning of September. How long did she stay?"

"Almost two months. At first she seemed very content, explored the property, made friends with the chickens, did some reading, and helped out with the cooking. She enjoyed going around to the markets with me and she started doing some weaving, bartering plants she dug up from around the property for yarn. Then after Columbus Day she started getting restless. Of course, the days are getting shorter and colder then, so there was less to do outside, but I think it was more than that. She started spending a lot of time out near the road. I don't know if she was meeting someone out there or what."

Cliff and Mike exchanged glances. "We had a report from the Dalton road crew that one of their members had a couple of conversations with her."

Bonner stared down at the table, and then nodded his head once. "Makes sense in one way, but not in another. I know those boys and I can't imagine any of them as a killer. Did she go off with one of them?"

Cliff and Mike completed another glance of partner speak. "No, though one of the crew did give her the name of a couple of bars in the area."

"And she went to one and made the wrong connection." Bonner finished for him.

"That is our theory at the moment. Do you remember what day she left?"

"The twenty-ninth. I'd gone over to Monroe to look at some furniture, and when I came back, she and her backpack were gone."

"Did she leave a note of any kind?"

"Not written. She did leave two of her weavings that I had admired. I interpreted that as a thank you."

Cliff hesitated and then cleared his throat. "Mr. Felton, you understand I have to ask you this. What was the extent of your relationship with the deceased?"

"I never touched her."

He looked over at Marjorie, who immediately pushed back from the table and stood up. "Gentlemen, this interview is over. I think my

142

CATHY STRASSER

client has fulfilled his part of the bargain and now it is time for you to do the same. I'm confident you will be removing him from your list of suspects, effective immediately."

"Give us a few minutes to do the paperwork Marjorie and we're done for the day."

"I'll give you ten."

****

Neither Cliff or Mike waved goodbye as they drove out of Bonner's driveway. The two men were quiet on the way back to the station, busy with their own thoughts and agreeing to wait to talk until they'd returned.

"Let's go grab some lunch," Mike said as they walked into their office, "I need something to take the bad taste out of my mouth."

"I'm with you on lunch, but I thought the interview went pretty well, all things considered."

"I guess, compared to our first couple of go rounds with him." Mike flopped down at his desk and pulled out his cooler. "I noticed you didn't show him that picture we found." He opened the cooler and started unloading sandwiches, chips, granola bars and cookies into a heap in front of him.

Cliff carefully unpacked his sandwich and apple and tried not to openly salivate at the feast spread out on his partner's desk. "I wanted to keep something back as a bargaining chip in case we need anything more from Mr. Bonner."

"Good idea," Mike mumbled around a mouthful. "It's always good to stay a step ahead. Where to next?"

"I want to stop in at the two bars the kid on the road crew mentioned, the Mooseland Grill and the Dewdrop Inn, show our pictures around and see if we get any reactions." Cliff finished the rest of his sandwich and looked dispiritedly at his apple. "You going to be done with that mountain of food any time soon?"

Mike grinned, his spirits rising along with his blood sugar level. "Just give me five to finish my dessert and I'll be ready to roll."

Cliff muttered something about gluttony and went to work on his apple, making a point of ignoring Mike's wrapper rustling in the corner.

CHAPTER TWENTY-FIVE

Nelson looked at his watch in satisfaction. Just after noon, they'd made good time on their trip north. Alyssa's little sports car had a lot of spunk, and the traffic free roads had given her the opportunity to use it. They'd decided to stay in Littleton this time, in a hotel that had less charm but more mod cons – not to mention being half the price. Either way, Nelson was happy to exchange mood furnishings for more modern plumbing. And Littleton seemed more central to the places they needed to visit, specifically the Investigative Services Bureau for the area.

"Let's grab some lunch and head out to visit our friendly neighborhood troopers." Nelson said, once they'd deposited their bags in their room. "This conversation should go a bit differently than my last one."

Alyssa turned away from the window where she'd been disappointedly gazing at the lack of view, but brightening at the thought of pursuing the story. "Great! I want to hear everything there is to know!"

Nelson and Alyssa arrived at the ISB in Twin Mountain just after one thirty. Nelson noted with satisfaction that the parking lot held the same license plates he had seen on his last visit. That meant the troopers were in.

He stopped Alyssa just before the front door. "I've met these guys before and they are pretty typical small town cops. They have all the power in the area and they like to keep a tight hold it. They're used to throwing their weight around with people who don't know any better, but that's not us. We have something they want pretty badly and that's going to make them play nice and share."

Alyssa nodded. "What can I do to help?"

Nelson smiled and squeezed her elbow. "Nothing much today, sweetie. You took the point in things yesterday; today it's up to me. Just keep your eyes and ears open!"

Alyssa nodded again and followed Nelson as he swept into the building and marched straight up to the counter. "Hello Patti! It's so nice to see you again!"

Patti looked up and gave an audible groan. "You're back."

"Yes I am," Nelson grinned. "And this time I don't want to get information from this office, I want to give it." He waited a moment for that to register, but seeing no noticeable change of expression, he plowed on. "So why don't you get right on your nice little intercom and let the troopers know that I'm here and why. Because you know," he leaned forward and dropped his voice, "I won't leave till you do."

Patti stared at him without expression, then stood without a word and walked through a door at the back of her office, leaving Nelson standing in front of an empty desk.

Thrown by her action, Nelson retreated two steps to where Alyssa waited. "What's going on?" she whispered.

"Either she went for reinforcements or she's hiding in the washroom. Whichever it is, all we have to do is wait and they will eventually come to us.

Cliff and Mike were gathering up car keys and disposing of the last remnants of lunch when Patti entered the office. One look at the grim expression on her normally smiling face told both men something was amiss.

"What's up?" Cliff asked, mentally running through former calamities: a therapy dog that defecated in the middle of the office, the woman who showed up each month demanding a different (and better) picture for her driver's license, and the occasional patron who failed the eye exam and blamed Patti rather than their vision.

"He's back." Patti said, which didn't really help clarify things.

"Who? Bonner?"

Now it was Patti's turn to look confused. "No, him I can handle. It's that jack-ass reporter who was here last week threatening not to leave until he got information. But this time he says he has information for you – about that girl's murder."

Cliff sighed. "Just what we need. But if his last visit was any indication, he won't leave until we talk to him." He jammed his hat on his head and signaled to Mike. "Let's do this. I don't have time for games today."

****

Nelson smothered a smile as the troopers filed into the room. "Thank you for such prompt attention ...."

Cliff cut right across the pleasantries. "I thought I made myself clear the last time we met. We don't share information about an ongoing investigation. You need to listen to the rules and stop pestering our office staff or you will find yourself looking at a hefty fine for disturbing the peace, obstructing justice, and whatever else I can think of to throw at you. Now you have two minutes to take yourselves out of this building and make sure you don't come back again."

Nelson's eyes gleamed. "For shame, officer! Is that any way to treat someone who is coming to offer you," he raised his voice as Mike and Cliff stepped toward him, "the last name and home address of your victim Melissa, usually known as Missy? Now why don't we go back into your office and pool our information."

Cliff paced back and forth in front of the conference table while Mike leaned against the wall, glowering at their guests. Nelson sat with his chair tilted back against the wall and smiling at the troopers, with Alyssa next to him, trying her best to imitate his casual manner.

"Mr. Simon, I am getting tired of repeating myself. You have placed yourself in the middle of a murder investigation and are now in the position of withholding evidence. Either you give us your information or I will charge you with obstructing justice and you will find yourself in jail."

Nelson nodded. "I understand what you're saying Officer Codey, and I'm sure you mean it. However, I think once you weigh the importance of my information to your investigation, you'll conclude that it will suit you much better to have those facts in your hand today, instead of going through all those time consuming court battles, and just agree to a simple quid pro quo of data sharing."

"Your sharing sounds an awful lot like blackmail – another prose-cutable offence." Mike said, coming to stand shoulder to shoulder with Cliff.

"I fail to see what the problem is. I give you what I know, and you give me what you know. Simple."

"Not simple," Cliff answered. "This all may seem like a joke to you, but this is still a murder investigation and there is still a killer out there who may be preparing to strike again, and I don't want your greed over selling a story to tip him off and prevent us from finding him and locking him away where he belongs."

Nelson studied the man in front of him and slowly brought his chair legs flat on the floor. "I see I haven't made myself clear. The last thing I want to do is jeopardize your investigation. The arrest and trial will be a vital part of my story. But none of that story will be published until you've caught the killer, for exactly the reasons you've stated. But I still want information stating what you know be-cause that means I can continue to help you. I have resources you don't and a wide network of information sharing." He leaned forward across the table. "Look, I've brought you your victim's name and ad-dress when all I had was her doctored picture. Imagine what I could do with more information?"

****

Nelson maintained his earnest demeanor until they pulled out of the ISB parking lot and on to Route 302. Then he let out a whoop that almost made Alyssa swerve off the road.

"Look at this!" He held up the folder containing the file on the in-vestigation to date. "We hit the mother lode on this one, and all we gave them in return is Missy's last name and her address. And we still have all the juicy details we got from that chatty neighbor Jeanine if we need to go back to the bargaining table. That is how it's done, my dear; that is how it's done!"

"I thought you handled the cops really well," Alyssa said, trying to divide her gaze between the road and Nelson's face, "but I'm con-fused. Are we going to try to help them with the investigation or aren't we?"

"Excellent question, my dear." Nelson was feeling expansive after his victory and happy to provide additional information on his plans. "We are going to continue to investigate, just as we were before. And our main goal is still to write a hell of a story, something with Pulitzer potential. Beyond that, if we want to share more of what we uncover, we will....providing of course, that they are willing to keep sharing too."

Alyssa nodded and smiled, letting Nelson talk on about what their next stop should be, but in her mind she was back in the garden with Mandy Baxter, a woman only half alive since her daughter's disappearance. Would finding the killer and seeing him brought to justice bring some animation back to those empty eyes? Driving toward the small town that had last seen Missy alive, Alyssa acknowledged that she shared it as a personal goal.

****

Mike kept his head down as they prepared to make their belated start to the two bars where Missy might have been seen last. He answered Cliff's questions and comments with monosyllables and avoided his partner's eyes.

Finally, Cliff had enough. "All right, out with it. Something's obviously on your mind, so let's hear it."

Mike took a deep breath, opened his mouth; then closed it. He tapped the table twice and turned to point at Cliff, then waved him away. Cliff watched the performance, raising first one, then both eyebrows. "In a minute I'm going to hold you down and give you the Heimlich Maneuver. Now out with it!"

Mike threw both his hands in the air. "I just can't believe you caved to that nasty piece of New York trash! I mean, I know it helps to have that name, but giving in to his demands just burns my butt."

"Oh ye of little faith. Do you really think I would meekly hand over all our hard work just like that? While you had him fill out the release of information form, I did a quick paper-ectomy on the contents of that folder. Then I made a big show of taking it to the copy machine, making sure I dragged my feet the whole time, copied everything I'd left in the folder, and handed it over. He doesn't have a clue that it's only half of the information, but he's happy as a worm in a compost pile with what he's got."

Mike's lips had started to twitch as Cliff talked, and by the time he was finished, he sported a full grown grin. "I stand corrected. I should never have doubted you. So what did you actually give him?"

Cliff's grin matched his partner's. "Just the interview from Kenny Brainerd and Bonner's name and address. My only regret is that we won't be there to see the meeting between him and either of those two."

CHAPTER TWENTY-SIX

Cliff and Mike's late start in heading to the bars actually worked in their favor. Cliff took the cruiser and Mike took his personal car so they could each head home after the interviews. They started with the Mooseland Grill because it was closest, just down 302 from the station.

The Mooseland Grill was one quarter of large building that also housed a Laundromat, convenience store and gas station, each business claiming its own side of the building. The interior represented comfort and familiarity, like a well worn baseball glove – maybe a bit shabby but doing the job with ease and experience. Like any bar in any town, it had its cast of regulars. And by the time the troopers reached the Mooseland, most of the regulars had already arrived and claimed their seats.

Cliff started by signaling to the bartender that he wanted a word in private. Leaving Mike to stand by the bar with crossed arms looking grim and serious, Cliff followed the owner/bartender, Hank, into his office. Looking at the cascading piles of paper on every surface, including the two guest chairs, Cliff elected to stand.

Hank stood too, trying to figure out what to do with his hands and darting his gaze around the room as if the papers could tell him what the troopers wanted.

"Relax Hank. You haven't done anything wrong. We just want some information. Think back to the end of last October, just before Halloween. Do you remember this girl coming in to the bar? She might have been wearing these clothes and carrying a back pack." Cliff took the two pictures out and held them up for Hank to see, then added in a copy of Bonner's sketch.

"Was she underage? Oh Jeez Cliff, you know I card everyone, but if they have a fake ID, I don't always catch them. I try to read all the bulletins you guys send, but there's so much paperwork..."

"It's nothing to do with carding people. We're just trying to track down this girl and we think she might have stopped here. Take a look."

Hank took the two snapshots first and started to shake his head until Cliff handed him the sketch. He stopped and took it over to hold under the lamp on his desk. He looked up and pointed to it. "This... this looks familiar. I feel like I've seen her before but I can't remember any details. We should take it out and show it to a couple of the regulars. I swear they know more about what goes on in this place than I do. They see everything and spend every night talking about what they've seen. If anyone would know, they would."

Cliff took the pictures back. "Sure Hank, just point me toward who to talk to."

****

Cliff looked at the three men crowded into an end booth for privacy. He checked his notebook for their names – Roger, Bert and Jake – though he was still a little fuzzy about who was who. It didn't seem to matter because they all seemed to blend together when they told a story, interrupting and finishing each other's sentences in no particular pattern.

"I remember that girl," Jake began, "she came in here just as it was getting dark one night last fall."

"It was the week before Halloween, I remember 'cause Hank got himself all in a tizzy about putting up the decorations," Bert interjected.

"That's right," Roger chimed in. "It was a cold night and she came in almost frost bit 'cause she didn't have a coat, just a sweater and some kind of shawl."

"It was a poncho. Don't you know anything?"

"Not about fruity ponchos I don't."

"Gentlemen," Cliff tried to bring them back on track. "You were saying, the girl came in..."

Jake leaned forward and reclaimed the floor. "Like I was saying, she come in, practically blue with cold, and just kinda stood in the doorway, looking around."

"That's right. Harold practically had to push her over to get past her when he came in."

"And the look he gave her...."

Mercifully, Jake overrode both his friends. "She finally come all the way in, slides into one of the chairs by the fire and tries to get as close as she can to it."

"'Cause she was freezing."

"We told him that already! You going senile or something?"

"Anyway, she sits there for a bit, looking over at the door every time it opens..."

"Like she was expecting someone."

"Right. But after a bit this guy about her age gets up and goes over to talk to her."

"He'd been sitting back in a corner; I didn't see him come in."

"Me neither. Matter of fact I don't think I'd ever seen him here before."

"That didn't make any difference to her because before you know it they're chattering away like nobody's business and she loses that blue frozen look and starts smiling."

"Looked like a whole different girl than from when she came in."

"Finally they both stand up, and she puts her shawl thing..."

"Poncho!"

"...back on and they go out together, with him carrying her back-pack."

"And we've never seen either of them back here since!"

Cliff jumped into the break in the act. "What did this guy look like?"

Jake sniffed. "Nothing much. Tall, skinny, kinda stooped when he walked.

"That's right, long tall drink of water. Dark hair, walked kinda funny, like he was stepping on tacks."

"Didn't see much of his face, it was dark in that back corner where he was sitting earlier, and he sat with his back to us when he went to join the girl, and then he kept his head down when they were leaving."

"That's 'cause he was looking down at her, and she was way shorter than him."

Sensing a break, Cliff interjected another question. "Which table did he start out at?"

"That one back in the corner."

"The one with all them boxes piled on it."

"There's always stuff piled on that table."

"True. Strange that he picked that one...."

"Cuz no one ever sits there."

Cliff tried to follow the conversation with his eyes, coming back to Jake at the end. "Have you ever seen him in here before that night?"

"Naw, that was the only time."

"Unless he sat back there before and we didn't see him."

"Couldn't be, cuz no one ever sits there!"

"Well, thank you, gentlemen, you've been very helpful," Cliff began, deciding they could keep talking in circles like this all evening, but Bert kept talking as if there'd been no interruption.

"And then, not fifteen minutes after they left, that other kid comes in, looking for a girl with a long blonde braid."

"Had to be her, what're the odds we would've had two like that in here on one night?"

"He was real disappointed to find she'd already left."

"Now he was a nice looking boy, had red hair and a good face."

"He might have been a Hanrahan, from up around Dalton. They're all redheads."

"Not all, some got hair so light they're its almost pink – what to do they call that?"

"Strawberry blonde. You really are going senile...."

Cliff excused himself and left them happily squabbling about family genetics to rejoin Mike. "She was here. They ID'd her and said she left with a tall, skinny guy with dark hair about her own age. No one has seen either one here since that night."

"That's all they could tell you? Nothing more about the guy?"

"That's it, and believe me, it took forever to even get that much!"

"Damn, we need more than just that vague description." He looked over at Cliff, then asked, "What?"

"Here's the kicker. Fifteen minutes after our girl leaves with mystery man, Jimmy from the road crew shows up. They must have arranged to meet..."

"...and either he was late or she was early, and that sealed her fate."

Cliff gave him a funny look. "Don't do that."

"Do what?"

"Interrupt and finish my sentences. It's kind of creepy."

Mike took a step back and raised his hands in a gesture of surrender. "Okaaaay....whatever you say, big guy."

"Just don't, all right? Now let's head over to the Dew Drop and show our pictures around there. See if Missy and the tall guy ever stopped in there."

****

The Dewdrop in was louder and sported a younger, rowdier crowd. Mike earned a few catcalls when he entered in uniform, quickly squelched by the bartender and the more sober patrons who didn't want any trouble.

Since Mike was on familiar ground, he showed the pictures around while Cliff talked to the bartender. The pictures of Missy came up empty as far as her ever having visited the bar, but they generated a lot of interest as the girl who'd been found up on Lafayette. Then Mike asked about the admittedly vague description of the tall skinny stranger, with a slightly more positive result.

"There has been this guy comes in here occasionally who sounds a little like that. Tall skinny dude, doesn't say much, takes a beer and sits by himself most nights. But that description could match a whole bunch of different guys – you don't give us much to go on."

"When did you see him last?"

The bartender frowned and looked down at the floor for inspiration. "Two-three weeks ago?"

"You asking me or telling me?" Mike said, a little of his exasperation showing.

"Hell, Mike, I don't know. Like I said, it might not even have been the guy you're looking for!"

"What did the guy do while he was here?"

"Hung around over in the corner then spent some time talking to a redhead at a table by the door. Then her date came back to the table and I didn't see the guy again so I'm guessing he left."

Mike and Cliff agreed it was all the information they were going to get but convinced them to call if the stranger ever showed up again, and they had to be satisfied with that.

He had a close call tonight; the troopers were at the Dewdrop Inn, Mike and his partner, in uniform. Must be on official business. That had never happened before. Mike seemed to be a semi-regular but never in uniform. Could it be something to do with Missy? He didn't see how, but things had been happening since her body had been found, people starting to ask questions and look for answers. Luckily, Missy had never been to this bar. Missy never went to any bars after that first night, when he'd met her and brought her away with him. No, he'd explained to her what was and wasn't proper, and she had listened and learned.

Still, he didn't like troopers and decided to skip the bar for the night. It was always better to stay invisible. And now that he knew Mike's off duty car, it would be easy to avoid him at any time. Maybe he should stop coming altogether. That would be hard – this was one of the few places he might meet a girl, and he needed to do that soon.

Conclusion: proceed with his plan, but use extra caution.

****

Cliff settled down on the couch with a sigh. It had been a long day, and tonight's dinner with the girls couldn't be termed relaxing. The topic of discussion had been music groups. He loved when the girls defended their opinions ardently, but unfortunately that often meant stridently as well. They'd gone upstairs to do homework, each supported –loudly- by their favorite band, so he'd retreated to the relative peace of the den. Anna joined him after a few minutes and settled down on the couch next to him.

"As long as the noise level remains consistent, we're ok," She warned. "If it grows out of control or stops suddenly, we'll have to intercede. Tough day?"

"Crazy." He filled her in on some of the highlights: Bonner's house and studio, the information he provided, the deal with Nelson, and the three interchangeable conversationalists at the Mooseland Grill.

By the time he'd finished, Anna was shaking her head. "You just have all the fun, don't you?" Turning serious, she laid her head on his shoulder. "This case is getting tougher, isn't it."

"Mmmm." He nodded against her hair. "There are just too many oddballs involved. First Bonner, then that idiot reporter, and now some mystery man that only three extremely unreliable witnesses have ever seen." He put his feet up on the coffee table and settled further down into the cushions. "It's enough to make me wish I was on Highway Patrol again."

Anna chuckled. "I know you don't mean that and by morning you'll know it too. You just need a little time away to get it in perspective."

"The thing I feel really bad about is that I ran out of time to pop down to Lincoln to see Kurt."

"Was it a specific invitation for tonight?"

"No, but I pretty much promised I'd be coming today."

"Well, he knows what your job is, and he should know your time isn't always your own. He'll understand."

Cliff wasn't so sure about that but he didn't want to get into it so he answered with one of those indeterminate noises that acknowledge a comment without giving an answer either way. He leaned his head back and tuned into the noises of his house – his wife's soft breathing, the distant rhythmic drumbeat of the girls' music, and even the intermittent barking of the neighbor's yappy puppy seemed reassuring, and helped to push away the thoughts of the two bodies. The current official one and the older, hidden one that seems to be intruding into the present case more and more.

CHAPTER TWENTY-SEVEN

"What's our plan for today?" Alyssa asked Nelson, making a final check of her make-up in the mirror. Meeting the dead girl's mother on Tuesday had made this story personal for her and left her totally invested in providing some closure for Mandy Baxter by finding Missy's killer. Nelson could go for the by-line and the glory, she wanted vengeance.

Nelson stepped out of the bathroom and into his shoes. "First on the agenda, find a decent breakfast. I'm not a fan whatever reconstituted food they might try to pass off in the 'complimentary buffet' downstairs. There must be a decent diner somewhere in this town!"

"I think there is. I asked the front desk about food choices yesterday when we checked in and they mentioned a place right here in town that had been recommended in a local magazine or travel guide or something. We can stop in the lobby for directions on our way out."

"Sure." Nelson grabbed his jacket and the file folder from the ISB office and joined Alyssa at the door. "Shouldn't be too hard to find as long as it's in town!" They headed down the hallway toward the elevator. "And then we go and tackle," he flipped the folder open and scanned the top page, "Bonwit Felton, who answers to the unfortunate name of 'Bonner'. Apparently the girl lived with him for a while before she disappeared."

"Sounds good. I'll take some pictures of the place."

"Excellent idea. Might add some nice background to the story. See if you can get one of this guy, Bonner. If he looks as weird as his name, it might be a good angle to play up. You know, 'innocent runaway flees from demented to deadly', something along those lines."

Alyssa nodded as they stepped into the elevator, but secretly she hoped for a few private moments with Mr. Felton. Missy had lived there almost two months and those might have been her last period of safety and contentment before her death. Alyssa wanted to get that story to bring to the poor girl's mother. Or, as it was now, the girl's poor mother.

****

Cliff sat at his desk, staring at the paper in his hand.

Mike walked over and clapped one hand on his shoulder. "It's not going to change, no matter how long you look at it." When Cliff didn't reply, he placed both hands on the desk and bent down to catch Cliff's eye. "Do you want me to do this one? I know I never have, but I've listened to you....." His voice trailed off as Cliff shook his head and put the paper down.

"Thanks for the offer Mike, but I'll handle it. Not that I don't trust you to do a good job, but this is a tough one to start with." He sighed and smoothed the paper out on the desk. "Calling victims' families is the worst part of the job."

Mike nodded and retreated to his desk when Cliff picked up the phone to dial. He always sat at attention when he made these calls, Mike noticed; as though he was trying to provide one more layer of respect.

"Hello, could I please speak to Amanda Baxter?...My name is Clifford Codey and I'm an officer with New Hampshire Investigative Services Bureau...that's right, New Hampshire. I understand you have a daughter that has been missing....I might have some news....No, I'm afraid it's not good. Do you have a friend or relative?...I see. I need some information about your daughter to determine....we can't be completely sure of our identification until I get some details. To your knowledge, has your daughter ever had any dental work or cosmetic surgery...? I see, yes of course. I will need to have those records faxed or emailed up to me before I officially.... I can't say definitely until we've given this information to our medical examiner and gotten her report....Ma'am? Ma'am? Are you certain there isn't anyone you can call?.... Do you want me to contact those two offices for you and just have them call you for consent? That might be easiest for you...yes of course, the minute I know anything....I understand, of course you do. If you could give me the names and phone numbers of the surgeon and the dentist....no that's okay, take your time..." he quickly jotted down the information "yes, I have it now. I'll be in contact as soon as....I'm sorry, I don't really have a time estimate....yes of course, please take care of yourself....thank you. Good-bye." Cliff hung up the phone and sat with his shoulders slumped, staring at his notes.

Mike gave him a minute then cleared his throat. "What did she say?"

"That her daughter had her teeth capped and breast reduction surgery, just like our Jane Doe. I'll call each of the doctors to send up the records, but I think it's just a formality."

"So now we have a name." Mike got up and walked over to look at the pictures Cliff had spread out across the top of his desk. "Looks like our Jane Doe is actually Melissa Baxter."

****

"I am not driving my car into that." Alyssa stared at the ruts in Bonner's driveway and gripped her steering wheel protectively. "It would ripe the guts right out of it. I'll pull it off the road, but we walk from here!"

Nelson briefly considered trying to find a rental with better ground clearance, but rejected the idea due to time considerations. His editor, Jerry, had given them leave to pursue what Nelson assured him was a great lead, but they had to be back by Monday and they had a lot to do before then. "All right, we walk. I just hope the ground is dry in there."

Alyssa weighed the value of their matching Italian leather shoes against the muffler, oil pan and who knew what else under her car and decided the shoes were easier to replace if needed. "Me too. And a short driveway. I didn't bring any cookie crumbs to drop in case we get lost."

They advanced down the driveway, looking askance at the hand lettered signs, the number and variety of abandoned vehicles and the overgrown weeds partially hiding piles of who knew what. Neither of them cared enough to venture off the driveway to find out. Finally they rounded a curve and confronted a circle of ramshackle buildings with two pick-up trucks, looking like before and after versions of themselves, parked in the center. Stopping to consider their next step, they could hear a dog barking somewhere close by.

"Does anyone know we planned to come down here?" Alyssa asked. "I mean, if we were just to disappear, who would know?"

"Nonsense, no one's going to do any disappearing." Nelson began, then caught himself, remembering Missy. "And anyway," he amended, "those cops gave us this guy's name. If we go missing, this is one of the first places they'd look."

Alyssa took a deep breath and recalling her earlier resolution, mentally shook herself. She wanted information about Missy and this guy had it. "Which....structure should we try first?"

Nelson was spared the need to answer as the door to what looked like the oldest building in the group opened and two people stepped out. The man was above average height and sported a worn flannel shirt, jeans and longish hair. In complete contrast, the woman blazed in an almost day-glow orange pantsuit with rhinestone details on the cuffs and collar. "Holy shit." Nelson murmured, then collected himself. "Let the games begin!" he told Alyssa and walked forward, lifting a hand and calling out "Hello there! We're looking for a Mr. Bonwit Felton? Can you help us with that?"

"I'm Bonner, who the hell wants to know?" the man called back, "And what are you doing on my goddamn property?"

Shaking her head, Alyssa followed Nelson forward. This didn't seem like the beginning of a beautiful friendship.

****

Twenty minutes later they were inside the house, but with no appreciable thaw in Bonner's attitude. He'd threatened to sic his dog on them when he'd heard they were reporters, accused them of being 'blood sucking vermin' among other things, and introduced the day-glow suit as his lawyer, and threatened to sue them for trespassing and harassment. He finally calmed down enough to allow them inside when Alyssa stepped in and mentioned their visit to Missy's mother. "I'd like to be able to bring back anything that might comfort poor Mrs. Baxter. She's going to hear some horrible things in the next few weeks, if we could just bring her something to counterbalance that, I think it would help."

"So what do you want to know?" Bonner asked. He didn't invite them to sit down. "I want you to realize that Marjorie here is listening to everything, to provide legal protection if I need it."

"Of course," Nelson replied smoothly, "although I'm sure that won't be necessary."

"Don't bet on it, honey." Marjorie jumped in. "I've seen sharks like you before, all sweetness one minute and all self-centered greed the next. Gutted more than a few in my time too."

"*Advertisements contain the only truths to be relied on in a newspaper.*" Thomas Jefferson," Bonner added.

"*Our liberty depends on freedom of the press, and that cannot be limited without being lost.*" – alsoThomas Jefferson."

They all looked at Nelson in surprise, but he stared back at Bonner, chin-up and a small smile playing around his lips.

"*A nation may lose its liberties in a day and not miss them in a century.*" – Montesquieu."

Nelson nodded in acknowledgement. "*The death of a democracy is not likely to be an assassination by ambush. It will be a slow extinction from apathy, indifference and undernourishment.*"

"*Those who profess to favor freedom, and yet depreciate agitation, are men who want rain without thunder and lightning,*" Bonner shot back.

"What the hell is going on?" Marjorie said, *sotto voce*, to Alyssa, who just shook her head in bewilderment.

"*Those who deny freedom to others deserve it not for themselves.*" Nelson continued.

"*Liberty means responsibility. That is why most men dread it.*" Bonner replied

Finally Nelson held both hands up. "Pax! Shall we call it a draw?"

Bonner nodded. "Not bad, I don't usually meet anyone who can manage more than two."

"Civics class. I had a professor who started each class with a quotation and beat it to death by the time class ended." Nelson explained. "I'm always surprised how many of them pop back into my head at the strangest times."

"Careful there, we were doing so well." Both men grinned, flushed with accomplishment.

"Well knock me over with a powder puff," Marjorie said. "Up until five minutes ago I would've bet good money that it would be all I could do to keep Bonner from sending you both on your way with a load of buckshot in your britches, but instead, here he is, practically purring. Stranger things keep happening every day."

They stayed another hour, while Nelson and Alyssa took turns interviewing Bonner under Marjorie's watchful eye. He provided a fairly detailed report of Missy's activities while she stayed with him, agreed to pictures of his house and one of himself, but flatly refused to provide any information or speculation about what might have happened once she left his property.

Nelson had a tough time with this. "C'mon. Are you really telling us that once she left your property you didn't go after her, try to find out where she went, or make sure she was safe? You just wiped her out of your life like she'd never been here?"

"I had no claim on her. She wasn't related to me and I'm not in the business of tying people down. I just figured she'd moved on because it was time."

"Even though you knew what poor survival skills she had – since she'd been living in an abandoned boathouse when you found her!"

Bonner's face flushed. "It's easy for you to judge after the fact. I knew she had the money she'd earned with her weaving and I knew she was looking for people her own age to mix with."

Nelson pounced. "How did you know that? Did you see her talking with someone? Did she start asking questions about anyone?"

Bonner stood up and went to the door. "This interview is over. You've gotten what you came for – at least, what you say you came for – and now you need to leave."

Marjorie followed them out on to the porch. "Pushed your luck too far, Nelson. You won't get anything else out of him. And remember, I was there for every word so if I read anything – and I mean *anything* – attributed to my client that didn't come from his mouth; I will slap a suit on you faster than you think you can talk. I bet that magazine of yours has some pretty deep pockets. I'd love to spread some of that New York money around up here."

She turned next to Alyssa. "You seem like a nice girl, don't let this joker gobble you up and turn into a clone. Remember, fancy quotes aside, you were the one who got Bonner to let you through the door."

"I hate to leave him so angry. And Nelson's question really was a logical one. Do you know why he didn't go after her?"

Marjorie snorted. "Didn't get in the front door so now you're going around to the side? Nice try honey. And if you can figure out that it's such a logical question, I'm sure you can come up with a logical answer." She walked them to the edge of the porch. "Now scat or Bonner really will sic his dog on you."

Both Nelson and Alyssa were silent and busy with their own thoughts during the long tramp back to the car. Once they were safely inside, Nelson turned a speculative look at Alyssa. "So what would your logical answer be about why Bonner didn't go after Missy?"

Alyssa signaled and pulled out onto the road before answering. "She hurt his feelings. That's why he didn't go after her and that's why he got so angry when you asked about it."

"Hurt his feelings? Because she was looking for someone younger than him? Or because after all he'd done, she was leaving?"

"No, simpler than that. She didn't say good-bye."

****

Cliff and Mike sat in Brenda's office that afternoon, waiting while the medical examiner compared the surgical and dental records of Melissa Baxter that had been faxed up from New York to the body of the Jane Doe found on Mount Lafayette.

It had been a tedious morning, filled with phone calls, completing and faxing official paperwork, requests for information, and finally receiving permission that granted access to medical records. While Cliff and Mike were pleased that they were close to identifying the body, putting a name and a history on her made the investigation more personal. It had changed from an abstract trail of evidence and facts to a connection with a grieving mother – making them more determined than ever to find the killer.

Brenda entered the office, carrying a file and bringing the faint odor of formaldehyde with her. Mike backed unobtrusively away from the smell, but Cliff remained totally focused on the file. "Is it her?"

Brenda allowed herself one nod, then stated formally for the record. "I have completed the examination on Jane Doe and found that her dental and medical records concur and form a match with those areas of the body in question, leaving me to identify her as Melissa Baxter, age nineteen at the time of death, former resident of New York."

Brenda stopped and handed the file to Cliff. "Poor girl," she added as a final benediction.

"Poor girl is right." Cliff said, accepting the file and standing up. "Thanks Brenda. We'll take it from here – notify the mother and add your identification to the record."

"Tell her mother I'll keep her safe until the trial is over and she can bring her home."

"She'll appreciate that." Cliff sketched a wave and followed Mike out the door. Back in the cruiser, Mike turned to Cliff. "Are you going to call the mother tonight?"

"No, let's give her one more night with a sliver of hope. She'll have the rest of her life to live with the emptiness."

****

Nelson and Alyssa picked up a couple of sandwiches to bring back to the hotel and then spent most of the afternoon on their computers. Nelson was eager to get his impressions of the morning down in writing while they were still fresh. He sat hunched over the keyboard, fingers flying. The story was really starting to come together – the background provided by Missy's mother and their chatty neighbor, Bonner's story of finding Missy and how she spent her time with him, and finally his impression that she went off searching for people her own age. Now if he could just get a line on her killer...it might be time for another trip to talk to the troopers, he decided.

Alyssa's story followed a similar timeline. She was working to put together a summary of Missy's time with Bonner too – but from a very different angle. She wanted to give Mandy some comfort; some sense that her daughter's life had some positives before the end. Alyssa made sure she included the information about Melissa's weaving and work with plants and emphasized the platonic affection Bonner had shown the girl from her rescue onward. She worked to fit the pictures of Bonner's property into the narrative, glad they'd picked a sunny day to visit. Alyssa wasn't sure how or when she would give this story to Mandy, but that didn't affect the compulsion she felt to write it.

By five o'clock, both Nelson and Alyssa had reached the end of what they could do with the information they possessed. Alyssa stood and stretched, then went to the window. "Nelson, last week when we were up here, you went to a few places on your own while I was hiking. Do you think we could drive around and you could show me some of those areas? The hiking was wonderful, but I'm ready to see more of where the people are."

Nelson jumped up, obviously pleased at the suggestion. "Excellent idea. I can be you tour guide extraordinaire! I think we still have time to catch my good friend Muriel the librarian. She provides a hefty dose of local color in one small dynamic package. She might even have some recommendations as to where Missy would have gone to meet people who were closer to her own age. Maybe we can pick up the next piece of the puzzle from her and get a suggestion for a dinner place with lots of regional ambiance."

Alyssa laughed and linked her arm through the elbow he offered. "Lead on!"

She's back, the girl with the little red sports car, the one I talked to at the bar, the one I connected to – the one who will be my next Missy. I saw the car at a sandwich shop downtown. She won't be as soft or compliant, but that doesn't matter because I've grown. I'm stronger now, and much more confident of what I want. What I need. I'm ready for the challenges she will bring.

She's not staying at the same hotel, but no matter. A car like that will stand out in any parking lot. Once I find her I will make her come to me, alone, and I will prepare the seduction. And she will come. The fact that she has returned shows how my power over her is growing. I have thought of little else since I talked to her, and now she's here, answering my call, feeling the pull.

I need to go and prepare the cabin. But I need to do it in a way that will keep the old man from getting suspicious. Does he remember that I know about it? It was late one night when one of his dog-faced Crew brought it up. They all yammered on about it until the old man brought up a name. Then they shut up pretty fast. And a couple of them looked scared. I've asked around but everyone pretends not to know what I'm talking about.

It didn't take too long to find the cabin once I had a general idea of where to look. And the dim-witted Crew are right about one thing at least – it's the perfect hideout. Far enough away from any major trails to be private but close enough to provision without too much difficulty.

The place was a mess when I first brought Missy there. I'd done some basic maintenance – eliminated the mice and the worst of the spider webs – but it still had a ways to go to be habitable. It needed a woman's touch. And Missy gave it that. She loved that cabin and worked hard to fix it up. We were a team, hiding from the world. She talked about wishing she had some weavings she'd done to hang on the walls so I went and got them for her. That was the first time she argued with me, and the first time I had to educate her.

I don't know what else happened in that cabin with that brainless Crew, but I will. I'm not stupid and I wasn't drunk that night. I will find out. And they might regret not having told me when they had the chance.

CHAPTER TWENTY-EIGHT

Friday morning Cliff called Mandy Baxter to tell her that the girl found on the mountain had been identified as her daughter. Cliff tried to talk to her about what the next steps would be and to pass on Brenda's message, but it was a very unsatisfactory conversation. Cliff had the feeling Mandy really wasn't taking in anything that he told her. He repeated several times that all the information would be sent to her in an official statement, but even that sparked no interest.

"Shock or drugs." Mike said when Cliff filled him in on the conversation. Having recently completed an advanced first aid course, Mike considered himself a minor authority on all things medical. Cliff tried not to let it get on his nerves.

"Right." He agreed, then, hoping to distract Mike from moving into full lecture mode, he asked him to call around to the local restaurants, hotels and shops to compile a list of tall, thin, male seasonal workers hired within the last nine months.

Mike accepted the task cheerfully enough, adding, "I'll also call my Aunt Muriel. She's pretty good at keeping tabs on who's new in the area."

Cliff nodded. "Knock yourself out. If you think the Mounties might help, call them in too."

Mike's "Bloyer" helped Cliff refocus on the task at hand. He needed a map of the Franconia Notch State Park. He wanted to re-fresh his memory on what type of terrain could be found surrounding the spot where the body was found. He found a topo map - one that included the topographic details of elevation changes with a series of concentric circles, the closer the circles were to each other, the steeper the terrain. Cliff wanted a workable theory of how the killer brought his victim to that spot. He seemed to remember the land around that spot changed elevation sharply in all directions.

He had just placed an X where the body had been found, when the intercom buzzed. "Someone to see you, Cliff. Thinks he has some helpful information about your case."

If Cliff hadn't been so engrossed in his task, he would have heard the undertone of irony in Patti's voice. But he missed it, absentmind-edly telling her "Send them in" as he penciled in a circle representing a half mile radius around his X. In an area composed of small towns, it wasn't that unusual to receive information in this manner.

The door opened and Cliff looked up and just managed to stifle a groan as Kenny Brainerd bounced into the room.

"Hi guys! Good to see you again! So this is where you work, huh? Great office. Lots of space."

"What are you doing here, Mr. Brainerd?" Cliff asked, once he found his voice.

"Didn't you hear the lady at the desk? I've come to help with your investigation. I took a personal day today and got up real early to drive up here. I've been thinking about the case all week and doing some research into this type of murder and I have some great ideas about how we might find the killer. And didn't I tell you guys to call me Kenny?"

"Mr. Brainerd, didn't we tell you last week that this investigation was going to be handled solely by professionals? So I'm afraid you've driven up here for nothing." Cliff tried to keep his tone polite, but his guest cut right across his measured tones.

"No listen, these are great ideas. Why don't we find a girl that looks like the victim and have her hang around the place where I found the body, that might draw the killer in and we could catch him in the act. Or we could put a bunch of posters about the murder all around town and keep a watch on the busses and trains out of the area for anyone acting suspicious and grab him. Or we could hire a psychic to touch the girl's clothing and see if she receives a picture of what the killer looks like or where the murder took place. Or...."

"Mr. Brainerd!" The volume and tone of Cliff's interruption cut Kenny off in mid-flow. "Thank you for your ideas. If we need your help we will contact you. I assume you are staying at the Mountain Glen Inn again?"

"No, Kurt told me they were full up, which is kind of strange, since the parking lot looked really empty when I drove by, so I'm down at the Mountain View cottages..."

"I know them well," Cliff said, gently shepherding Kenny toward the door, "but let me repeat, this investigation is for professionals only. Go on back home." He all but shoved Kenny out the door and wiped his forehead as he returned to his desk. "Patti's going to pay for that one."

Mike grinned and shook his head. "What a load of crap! What did he do, memorize the script for every B murder movie ever made? I wonder why he didn't add the alien abduction theory to all that garbage. It would have fit right in!"

Cliff muttered something about wanting to commit a murder of his own, namely Kenny, and returned to his map. Mike returned to his phone calls and peace reigned for about thirty minutes. Cliff had just about concluded that the murderer couldn't have carried a body to the spot where it was found due to the steepness of the surrounding terrain and was toying with the idea of an accomplice when Patti buzzed the office again.

"Mr. Nelson Simon to see you. He says it's urgent."

"For Christ's sake!" Cliff threw his pencil down on the desk. "Is there some sign on the door saying 'lunatics welcome'?"

Mike glanced over. "We better see him or we'll never get rid of him. Want me to take it?"

"Thanks, but let's do it together. That way we can tag team him out the door as quickly as possible." Cliff punched the button on the intercom. "Send him in."

He'd barely finished speaking when Nelson sauntered into the room. "Good morning, officers. Just checking in to see how the investigation is going and see if you have anything new – keeping our information sharing agreement in mind." He raised his eyebrows and looked from Mike to Cliff and back again.

"Actually I do, Mr. Simon. I'm glad you stopped in because that saves me a phone call." Cliff said, stepping quickly in front of Mike to screen the quizzical expression on his face. "I wanted to let you in on a stroke of luck. Kenneth Brainerd, you remember his name from the file I gave you? He's the gentleman who originally found the body, and I've just learned he's back here in town for the weekend. He called to say he had some interesting ideas about the case and I thought you might like to interview him for your article and then the two of you could get together and compare notes."

Nelson listened with growing interest. "I'd like that very much. Thank you for the help, Officer Codey. I must admit, I've been mistaken about you. I didn't think you were really going to honor our little bargain."

"Not at all, Mr. Simon. I always try to honor an agreement. You'll find Mr. Brainerd at the Mountain View Cottages in Lincoln. If you head right down there you should catch him."

Cliff kept the pleasantly helpful expression on his face until Nelson left the room and they heard a car start outside. Then he sat back in his chair and let out a grin of pure satisfaction.

Mike shook with laughter. "You are a truly an evil person. I've had my suspicions but now I know it's true."

"I have my moments of brilliance," Cliff agreed. "I just wish I could see that reporter's face after five minutes in Brainerd's company. It would be priceless."

"They deserve each other."

They both resumed working with a sense that balance had been restored in the universe.

****

It took less than the allotted five minutes for Nelson to recognize that Kenny Brainerd had nothing of value to say and probably never would. He also realized that Officer Codey had put one over on him, and – settling back to listen with half and ear as Kenny droned on – he contemplated ways to even the score.

Suddenly, he heard Kenny mention Codey by name. "Wait a minute, Kenny. What was that again?"

Kenny, thrilled to be interviewed by two professional reporters and blissfully imagining that his picture on the cover of a magazine would lead to appearances on talk shows, was happy to oblige. "I was talking about the owner of the Mountain Glen Inn, Kurt. He's big in the hiking fraternity up here, although personally I think he's a little past it now – he didn't tell me anything I didn't already know. I heard someone saying that he and Officer Codey go way back together, though I'm not sure doing what because Kurt was certainly never in law enforcement. I considered going into law enforcement myself once, but I found my talents were better used elsewhere. I still try to keep my hand in though, through magazines and websites....."

Nelson tuned Kenny out again, thinking about the connection between Codey and this hotel owner. This might give him the ammunition he needed to even the score a bit. It would be worth going down to interview the man and see if he could shake any old skeletons loose. Sounded like this Kurt wasn't so sharp anymore, the perfect type of subject to let slip some incriminating information.

Kenny continued to prattle on about Kurt, now playing up to Alyssa. "And of course he's got no patience for women. All the hikers that hang out with him are men, and almost all his employees are guys too and a couple of them are kinda creepy looking but they do the work well so I guess it's really no big deal." He hitched his chair closer to Alyssa and leaned toward her. "Now let me tell you about the day I found the body..."

"Let me get out a notebook" Alyssa said, managing to inch her chair away from Kenny as she did so, and sending a 'get me the hell out of this' look at her partner.

Nelson cleared his throat and hastily cut in. "You know, Kenny, this is really good stuff, but you can't give us too much at once or we'll lose some of the details. Tell you what, we need to go back to our hotel and transcribe all our notes, and then we'll be ready to hear about finding the body. Are you going to be here for the rest of the day?"

"Well, I....."

"Great!" Nelson beamed and jumped out of his chair. "Here's what I'm going to do. You sit tight and we'll give you a call when we've got all your info on the computer so we can set up a time to get the next installment, okay?"

"I guess so..."

"Super! Gotta dash and get working while it's all still fresh in our heads." He turned toward Alyssa, but she was up and moving toward the door. "Thanks Kenny! We'll be calling you!"

They piled into Alyssa's car and pulled swiftly out of the parking lot, ducking their heads to hide their snickers. "Did you really say 'super'?" Alyssa asked, once she caught her breath.

"I would have said almost anything to get us away from that windbag," Nelson told her, "and you should be grateful. He was getting ready to put the moves on you."

"Oh please, don't put that picture in my head." Alyssa shuddered. "How on earth did Officer Codey think we were going to learn anything from such a pompous blowhard?"

"He didn't." Nelson's smile took on a grimmer edge. "He set us up for this one on purpose. He knew all about what our good friend Kenny is like, he had to interview him after he found that body."

"Why on purpose? We haven't done anything but help them."

"He's trying to keep all the information and the glory for himself. This was his way of telling me to get lost. He's gotten what he wanted from us and it's his way of saying he doesn't want to see us again."

Frowning, Alyssa opened her mouth and then slowly closed it. She didn't want to argue with Nelson – especially in this mood. She didn't agree with his assessment of Officer Codey, he seemed like a decent man trying to do a tough job to her. And Nelson had definitely rubbed him the wrong way about sharing Missy's name. He'd started off the same way with Bonner, but luckily the whole quotations thing saved that interview.

Alyssa was beginning to see that Nelson's tough New York approach could sometimes work against him. It made her more determined to follow through with her plan to meet her mystery source. The note she'd found on her car that morning had been very clear about wanting to talk to her alone. It might be someone they'd already talked to who objected to Nelson's in-your-face interview style. Alyssa controlled a small fission of excitement. The note mentioned a possible connection to Missy. This could be her big break; a chance to obtain information that no one else had. She just needed to find an excuse to go off on her own.

Nelson stared out the window, trying to think of a graceful way to discourage Alyssa from accompanying him on his interview of Kurt at the Mountain Inn. He wanted the freedom to shade certain questions to get the answers he needed to teach Officer Codey a lesson and he had the distinct feeling that Alyssa would not be on board with that plan. A few of her recent comments had revealed what sounded suspiciously like disloyalty. Having only one car between them further complicated matters. So, figuring out how to convince her to drive him to the hotel and then go off and do something else during the interview posed quite a challenge.

****

It turned out to be much easier than he imagined. He put out a feeler to test the waters during lunch by asking her opinion on what the next step should be.

"I don't know what your plans are, but I'd love a chance to repeat the drive we did yesterday evening but taking the time to stop and take pictures of some of the buildings and scenery. There are some lovely architectural details I'd like to capture as well as some local plant specimens." She sighed. "But I know that would be terribly boring for you."

Nelson pursed his lips and pretended to ponder the issue. "One way we could make it work...suppose you drop me off at that hotel with the funny owner Kenny was talking about – Kurt or Clem or whatever his name was. I could interview him while you take your pictures." He gave her a quick glance to see her reaction. "I'd bring you along except it sounds like the old guy is a real woman hater and I wouldn't want to expose you to that."

"How long would you be there?"

"About an hour."

"I think that will work," Alyssa said with a big smile. "It's a plan!"

He was waiting at the rendezvous. He'd left the note on her car last night, after cruising the hotel parking lots in Lincoln, Franconia and Littleton until he found her car.

He'd put a lot of thought into the note, wanting to strike just the right tone to make it irresistible. He'd started by reminding her of their conversation at the Dewdrop, and emphasized how he'd felt a connection. Now he said he needed her help, he didn't know who else to turn to, she was the only one he could trust. That he had information about the murdered girl and he needed to tell someone.

And he would share that information. Before he was finished, she would know everything about Missy and what happened to her.

He'd asked her to meet him at the Skookumchuck Trail Head, a place with little traffic and a parking lot that couldn't be seen from the road. And most important, it was close to the cabin.

He'd gone there last night, after leaving the note, to prepare. He'd had a moment of hesitation. The cabin was Missy's, would it be a mistake to bring someone else there? Looking around the room, he decided that he should. Missy would approve, she might even enjoy the company. The thought of comparing the two revved him up and made it difficult to sleep even the few hours he knew he needed.

The supplies he'd brought in would be enough to do what he needed to do and then get across the border into Canada. With all the attention focused on Missy, it was time to disappear again. After this one, he'd head north and get ready to start again. Even in these days of heightened security there were places to cross unseen – if you knew how to travel in the woods and where to look.

So he settled down to wait, willing her to come, wanting, needing her to come. So he could begin. Again.

CHAPTER TWENTY-NINE

Nelson and Alyssa left Littleton and headed south on I 93. They entered the Franconia Notch, passing the deep blue oval of Echo Lake on the right, where the ski slopes of Cannon Mountain seemed to run right down into the water. Next came Profile Lake, surrounded by woods and hosting two to three fisherman on its rocky shore. On the left, Mount Lafayette's cliffs rose to four thousand feet, towering over three thousand foot Cannon. Alyssa never looked that way anymore. Since she'd gotten caught up in Missy's story the mountain's wooded slopes and rocky outcrops seemed more sinister than beautiful or majestic.

As the Notch widened, they passed one of the entrances to Cannon Mountain Ski Area and the base lodge for the two Trams to the top of the mountain, one yellow, one red, that the locals called Ketchup and Mustard. Further down the notch were turnoffs for hiking trails, camping areas, and the visitor's display showing where the famous Old Man of the Mountains used to be, before it crumbled and fell just after midnight one cold May morning in 2003. Briefly, Alyssa thought back to when she'd first seen and enjoyed the scenery of these mountains, when it still looked innocently beautiful, before she had any knowledge of Missy.

Emerging at the south end of the Notch, they pulled off the highway into the town of Lincoln, locating the Mountain Glenn Inn on a busy side street, its porch crowded with hiking equipment and hikers, preparing for the weekend ahead. Alyssa pulled over in the first empty spot she found and turned to face Nelson, suddenly nervous.

"I'll be back in about an hour, give or take."

"I'd say call me on your cell phone but reception is so spotty up here." Nelson handed Alyssa a piece of hotel stationary. "That has the number of the hotel here. Try to borrow a land line if you need to contact me. Otherwise, see you in an hour." He slid out of the car, already focused on the next interview.

Alyssa watched him go then pulled away from the corner. She had a lead who wanted to talk just to her. If she wanted to break into the big leagues, she'd have to get used acting on her own. This is what it took to do the job and she'd have to prove she could handle it.

****

The directions the hotel clerk had given her were clear and easy to follow. Heading north on 93 to exit thirty-five, Alyssa pulled into the Skookumchuck parking lot and looked around for her contact. She half-remembered him from their conversation at the Dewdrop Inn and hoped he looked a little less creepy in the daylight. Stifling the thought of how much easier it would have been to have gotten his information that night; she got out of her car and scanned the parking lot.

He was standing by a large wooden sign with a small shingled roof, displaying two thirds map and one third regulations. Alyssa was relieved to see that he looked younger and less threatening than he had in the bar. She studied him as she approached. He was tall and gawky, with oversized hands and feet. He had shaggy dark hair that looked like it hadn't been cut recently. He stood with his head hanging so it was difficult to see his eyes. Shy, she thought, relaxing slightly, and maybe a bit intimidated.

That impression vanished immediately when he reached out and grabbed her arm.

"I knew you'd come." He stared into her eyes, tightening his grip on her arm. "I have so much to tell you."

He held her arm, savoring the feeling of power. He'd gotten her here. His will, his planning, his knowledge had brought her to him.

Her amazing blue eyes widened. She could feel it, his mastery of her. She was in awe of him. It was beginning.

Alyssa tried to pull back, alarmed by the change in him and realizing creepy didn't do him justice. He was downright scary. The parking lot was empty except for her car, which was too far away to be helpful. Cursing herself for not taking additional safety precautions, Alyssa made an effort to relax. First she'd try to talk her way out.

He could feel her fear and it added to his exhilaration, but he held himself in check. He still needed to get her to the cabin; and walking would be far easier than dragging or carrying. Slowly, he told himself. There was no need to rush things. In fact, it would be better drawn out and savored.

Alyssa felt him loosen his grip on her arm – not enough to break loose, but enough to ease the tension. He ducked his head and mumbled what sounded like 'sorry', adding "I got too wound up."

"What's your name?" Alyssa asked. She'd read somewhere that finding out an assailant's name was the first and most important part of negotiating. Not that this situation would come to that, she assured herself.

"I'm Neil, and I need to show you where the girl stayed, the one that was killed. She lived in a cabin near here. I want you to see it. Someone should know."

Alyssa's breathing steadied as she shifted from terror to anticipation. What a scoop! To be lead right to the spot....and she had thought to bring her camera too. This could be exactly the break she needed. But what about this guy Neil? He definitely creeped her out.

He'd picked the most unthreatening name he could think of, and put on the helpless act. It was getting harder to hide his true self with his growing sense of power. Soon, he told himself. And he had been taught patience. Long hard lessons that were finally bearing fruit.

Alyssa studied Neil, thrown by his apparent change in personality. Her feeling of alarm was fading and curiosity taking its place. Could

Missy have lived in a cabin up here before she was killed? If so, why did she leave Bonner's cabin for one even more isolated? And for how long?

Pushing those questions aside, Alyssa knew she didn't want to go to see any cabin today, alone with this guy. Now that she knew where to start, she could come back with a professional guide and find it without having to depend on this creep who had no idea of personal space boundaries. Time to ease gracefully out of this situation before it got any worse. "Wow, Neil, I'd love to see that cabin, but I'm not wearing the right shoes for hiking. But I have better ones in the car. Just give me a minute to go change and we can head right out."

Watching her covertly through his screen of hair, he could see exactly when she decided to reject him. He wouldn't allow that. It had been a mistake to try to treat her like Missy. She was too different. Where Missy was soft and sweet and eager to please, this one was hard and demanding and bossy. It was time to let her know how things were going to work from now on.

He reached into his pocket and brought out his knife.

Alyssa felt light-headed at the sight of the knife. Frantically she tried to remember any instructions from the numerous self-defense classes she'd attended, but the cold silver shine of the blade filled her eyes and froze her brain as though she was hypnotized. Feeling short of breath she tried to retreat a step, but he held her firmly in place. "Oh please" she tried to say, but it came out as the thinnest whisper that even she could barely hear.

"Here's how it's going to be," he said, and she struggled to pay attention to something other than the thick, brutal looking blade. "You are going to walk with me to the cabin. Once we get there we will talk. If you fight me, I'll cut you. If you try to escape, I'll kill you. Are we clear?"

Alyssa nodded, trying to take comfort from the fact that he'd mentioned talking as his main goal, and cutting only as a consequence of resistance. Her job, she decided was to stay alive as long as she could. And if that meant playing along with this guy for now, then that's what she would do. She allowed him to lead her past the sign and on to the trail, stumbling a bit as she left the pavement.

"Slow down a bit – please." She tried for a smile. "I really wasn't kidding about the shoes." Neil did slow down, but her small feeling of accomplishment disappeared when he turned to smile at her. His eyes burned with a fanatical light, and she wondered helplessly how soon Nelson could be expected to miss her.

****

Nelson sat facing Kurt across the desk in his office. The walls were lined with pictures – groups of men in progressively more modern winter clothing, newspaper articles of dramatic rescues, and several raised maps of what must be local mountains. Nelson nodded toward what looked like the most recent group of men. "Is that your famous Crew?"

"Yup."

Nelson waited, but Kurt didn't add anything, so he tried again.

"Looks like you've all done some great work with all those rescues."

"Yup."

This was getting old fast, Nelson decided. Time to cut to the chase. "I don't see Officer Codey in any of these pictures. I thought he was one of the Crew when he was younger."

"Who said that?"

Success! Three words! "Kenny Brainerd, the guy who found the body on Lafayette."

"And you believed a fool like him? Some investigator." Contempt dripped from the words.

Nelson flushed. This wasn't going at all how he had planned. Kenny's assessment of Kurt's mental prowess was obviously as flawed as the rest of his theories. "I'm just trying to gather some background material on the officers investigating this case."

"Right."

Great, back to single words. Nelson decided he was wasting his time. "Well, Kurt, since you obviously don't want to talk to me, I'll be on my way." Nelson pushed back his chair and headed for the door, but this failed to drown out Kurt's final comment.

"'Bout time."

Filing the whole interview under 'things to forget as soon as possible' Nelson checked his watch. Not even fifteen minutes since Alyssa dropped him off. If he couldn't reach her he'd have a significant amount of time to kill. Taking out his cell phone he tried calling her, but went right to voicemail. Obviously, she was someplace without service. Mountains played hell with cell signals. He'd keep trying every ten minutes or so to see if he could get her as she moved around.

****

Kenny checked his watch again. It had been over two hours since the reporters drove away and he was getting restless. They'd said they were coming back, but he didn't intend to waste his whole day waiting for them. He wanted another dose of the glory and attention he'd had so briefly after finding that girl's body and he had some ideas of how he might get it.

First stop would be the Mountain Glenn Inn. Even though the Inn was full, he was sure Kurt would be glad to see him again. He'd just walk in through the back entrance and surprise him in his office. Grabbing his backpack to show Kurt that he never went anywhere unprepared anymore, Kenny headed out to the car for the short drive up to the mountain Glenn Inn.

Arriving at the Inn, Kenny noticed it seemed amazingly quiet for a place that had no vacancies. He walked in through the back door and soft-footed cautiously up the hallway to Kurt's office. He paused outside the door to prepare for the surprise and caught a few words of a discussion taking place inside. "..... he's missed both of his last two shifts and no one has seen him for over twenty-four hours. Where does he go? Does he have a girl on the side somewhere?"

"Hardly." That was Kurt's voice. "He goes up to that cabin up on Skookumchuck. Someone made the mistake of mentioning it to him once and now he's obsessed."

"That place? It gives me the creeps. I can't think of it without seeing that body lying there."

"Shut it. We agreed, remember?"

Kenny hadn't registered any of the conversation after the phrase 'body lying there.' If he could locate another body....what a story that would make! He could see the headline now – Kenny Brainerd: the body finder. He backed slowly down the hallway and out the door. In the privacy of his car, he looked up Skookumchuck in his trail map.

Seemed pretty simple to get to. He just had to head up I 93 and get off at the first exit after leaving the Notch. The trail was just a few hundred yards off the exit. The book had an aerial photo of the trail as well. Taking out his magnifying glass Kenny found what he thought might be a small cabin, surrounded by trees. That had to be the place. He'd head right out there and see what he could find.

****

Nelson had run through a whole rainbow of emotions as he waited for Alyssa to return, ranging from the cool blue of gloom (how could he have been so foolish as to listen to Kenny's opinion on anything), to the red glow of anger (where the hell was Alyssa and how could she keep him waiting like this) to the white hot stab of anxiety (Alyssa was never late, what if something had happened to her?). To make matters worse, he'd tried calling Alyssa so many times his battery had died. He needed to find a land line he could use to find out if she'd been back to their hotel and if she hadn't, to call the police and report her missing.

Nelson decided to go back to the Mountain Glenn Inn for the phone. It was the only place he had any kind of connection to in this area, even if it was a negative one. Once he explained his errand, Kurt was surprisingly civil, giving him access to the phone on the front desk and finding the phone number for his hotel for him.

Waiting on hold while the front desk sent someone out to check the parking lot for Alyssa's car, Nelson tuned in to a quiet conversation between Kurt and one of his employees in the office behind him.

"I know he's been gone almost twenty-four hours Paul. But he's done this before and come back after." Kurt looked out the window. "With the weather getting nicer, it's hard to blame him."

"Yeah, well I searched his room." Paul – whoever he was – told Kurt. "And most of his stuff is gone. I think he might've cleared out for good. Not that I'll miss him, I'm just tired of having holes in our coverage schedule because he's unreliable."

"He took everything?"

"The only thing I found was this old sheet of paper jammed behind the dresser with a bunch of crazy things written on it – stuff like 'travel food' 'note' and 'red TT hardtop.'"

Nelson leaped to his feet, scattering phone, pen and notepad as he pushed his way into the office. "Did you say a red TT hardtop? That's what Alyssa drives! There can't be too many of those around. Whose paper is that? Is he missing too?"

Paul looked at Kurt. "Who is this guy? Why is he here? And who the hell is Alyssa? And what does her car have to do with our missing busboy?"

Kurt looked from Nelson, to the notebook, to Paul, and back at Nelson. He bent over, picked up the phone and dialed a number. "Hello? I need to talk to Cliff Codey. Tell him it's Kurt and we've got another girl gone missing."

CHAPTER THIRTY

Cliff looked over the group in the conference room and raised his voice to be heard over the babble of voices. "All right, let's get focused here people. I want to hear all your information so we can put together a plan, instead of everyone dashing off in different directions without thinking things through." This last bit was directed at Nelson, who'd had to be forcibly restrained from rushing off on his own.

Conversation gradually died out and everyone turned to face Cliff. "Nelson, let's start with you. Give us a summary of the events leading up to the finding of Alyssa's car."

Nelson gave an abbreviated version of his day, touching on the interview with Kenny, their separate plans for the afternoon, his increasing anxiety about Alyssa's failure to return, and the tie between the busboy and Alyssa's car.

"So on the way here, Kurt pulled into this parking area, just off I 93, and we found her car. I have no idea how he knew where to look because he won't tell me anything." He turned to glare at Kurt. "I wanted to go look for her right away, but this yahoo over here wouldn't let me. He just kept saying we had to come and talk to you." Nelson turned his scowl on the rest of the room. "And I don't understand why we're all just sitting here. She could be lying out in the woods, hurt or unconscious and we're wasting time. We've got to do something!"

"I agree," Cliff said, "but we have to be sure of what we're getting in to. Your description of Alyssa's plans to photograph local architecture doesn't match up with finding her car parked at the start of an isolated, little used hiking trail."

Nelson's eyes widened. "You don't think she's been abducted...."

"I don't think anything until I have all the facts." Cliff said, then turned to Kurt. "Tell us about this missing employee of yours."

The two men exchanged a look, and then Kurt gave a decisive nod. "Right. He showed up around the end of last summer, looking for work, he said; but I think it was more looking for a handout. He looked scruffy and underfed – like maybe he'd been living rough – and didn't want to give a name or much history when I asked. I wasn't too concerned; as you know, I've had strays show up at my door before and I can usually get 'em straightened up and turned around."

The last sentence was directed at Cliff, who merely nodded and let it pass, trying to ignore the feeling that this sounded all too familiar. "Did he give a name?"

"He told us to call him Neo after some foolish movie character. Most of us changed it to Neil - wouldn't do for our customers to get caught up in his nonsense."

"Can we please move this along a little bit?" Nelson interjected. "It's getting late and I think we should start searching before the light is gone."

"Nelson, please! I understand your concern but we have a system here and if you can't control yourself and work with us, I'm going to have to ask you to leave the room." Cliff turned back to Kurt. "How'd he do as an employee?"

"Fair. He did the work, but not fast and never anything extra. He kept himself to himself in between times. The only thing that interested him was the rescue work. Not so much to save anyone, but to master the outdoor skills. He had some knowledge in that area and took every chance he could get to improve them."

Cliff exchanged a glance with Mike – this didn't sound good – and worked to keep his increasing sense of unease off his face. "So you never got any more information about him? Not even a social security number so you could pay him?"

The older man dropped his gaze to the floor. "Paid him in cash. Off the books."

Sighing, Cliff refrained from commenting. There'd be another time for that particular lecture. "So when did this guy disappear?"

"He's been doing it on and off since he started with me. Usually he tells me, says he 'needs some space' or 'has to clear his head' and goes off for a day or two."

"Any pattern to his absences?"

Kurt brought out his employee log books and thumbed through them. "Goes in cycles. He started last fall, end of September through November, then nothing much in December through March – guess the weather was too cold for him – and started up again with a couple times in April and May, but really heavy these last couple of weeks."

Cliff looked at Mike again, each thinking about a possible time connection to the murder they'd been focusing on. "And what was his behavior like for the last two weeks when he was at work?"

"At first, he seemed even less social and angrier, almost snapped Paul's head off when he was trying to make up the work schedule. But the last few days it's been different. He's been kind of worked up, like a simmering pot that could boil over any minute."

This sounded worse and worse, Cliff thought. "Do you have any ideas about where he goes when he takes off?"

Kurt's shoulders sagged and he lowered his head. "Might be the cabin. He knows about it. Got the information from Duane one night when he'd had too much."

Cliff sighed. That would be almost every night. He knew Duane from back in his days with the Crew, and that had been an issue even then. And for him to bring up the cabin – after they had all promised...

Mike's voice brought him back to the present with a jerk. "What cabin are we talking about?"

"Abandoned place off the Skookumchuck Trail."

"Does this Neil character have any access to weapons?"

"He has a big Ka-Bar knife that's his prize possession. And one of my hunting rifles is missing."

"Which one?"

"The thirty aught six with the scope."

Anyone who hadn't grasped the implications up to that point; finally got it.

Cliff cleared his throat. "Gentlemen, I am declaring this a probable abduction. Mike, get on the phone to the SWAT team and get them up here with a hostage negotiator, a couple of extra sharp shooters and a K9 unit as soon as possible. We only have about five hours of daylight left and I want to use as much of it as we can. Kurt and Nelson, consider yourselves formally notified that this is now a police matter and will be run by official personnel. Thank you for your information, but we will be handling things from here."

Both men protested immediately.

"You can't just push us aside like that!"

"I have a right to know what's going on!"

"I know the mountains better than anyone."

"I can offer this guy national coverage for whatever he wants to say in return for Alyssa's safe return."

"I'm the only one who around who has any kind of positive relationship with your kidnaper."

The last statement from Kurt got Cliff's attention. "True enough. All right, you can come along when we set up our command station. But you take instructions from me or my team and make sure you follow them. This is not the time for any wild-assed heroics; are we clear?"

"Gotcha." Kurt nodded once and squared his shoulders. "But I want Nelson there with me."

Cliff narrowed his eyes and studied the older man. "Why?"

"I know the kidnaper, but he knows the victim. He might give me information that could help me convince him to release her." Kurt held Cliff's eye for a moment and then continued, "I'm the one that's been giving this lunatic a base to operate from. I want to make sure I do everything in my power to fix things."

"Fine. But I meant what I said about following instructions. I don't want either one of you to make a sound unless someone gives you permission." Cliff looked hard from Kurt to Nelson and back again. "Got that?"

Both men nodded.

"Good. Now sit tight until we're ready to leave. And don't get in anyone's way or interrupt with questions." Cliff said and left them in conference room.

After a small silence, Nelson turned to Kurt. "Thanks for convincing him to bring me along. I'd have gone nuts, waiting and not knowing what's going on."

Kurt looked over, nodded once, and went back to studying the table in front of him.

Nelson waited a minute, but when Kurt didn't add anything, he tried again. "Why did you do it? I know you don't like me."

Kurt replied without interrupting his study of the table. "Don't press your luck." And Nelson had to be content with that.

****

Alyssa sat motionless in the chair and tried to keep from screaming. The immobility wasn't her choice, the man who told her to call him Neo had duct taped her arms and ankles to the arms and legs of the chair. He'd told her that as long as she was quiet he wouldn't duct tape her mouth shut. After that he went around the cabin kicking everything away from her chair and then went out through the only door, leaving her alone. In order to distract herself, she looked around the cabin, trying to concentrate on what she was seeing rather than what she was feeling.

The cabin itself was small, only about fourteen feet square, made of logs with what looked like moss or dirt jammed in between them. It only had two small windows – one next to the front door and one on the wall opposite. Both windows provided indirect light from the late afternoon sun that cast the two side walls in shadow. One windowless wall featured a small loft that held a mixture of bundles and cardboard boxes. Underneath the loft, a low platform was piled with a back-pack, a few more bundles, and some blankets. The other windowless wall contained a rough made stone fireplace and two old plastic crates with LottaRock Dairy stenciled in faded letters on the side and filled with logs and sticks.

Alyssa's chair was between the fireplace and the back window, positioned so that she couldn't see directly out either window or through the door. A large round wooden table stood nearest to her – it looked like an oversized wire spool with canned goods stacked on one side, and gallon containers of water on the other. The size of the canned goods pile seemed to indicate plans for a long stay, and Alyssa felt the desire to scream growing again.

The door opened and Neil reappeared, carrying a long gun with some kind of telescope on top of it, and a lantern. He met her eyes and smiled, sending a jolt of panic down through her stomach. She stared at the wall opposite her chair, and worked to distract herself by trying to decide why a pair of women's shoes were nailed to the wall. She squinted, hoping to decipher the name. Possibly either Dansko or Birkenstock, brands she'd never bought. Out of the corner of her eye, she watched Neil return outside without speaking.

He hadn't said much after they left the parking lot. He made Alyssa walk ahead of him, pointing out which way to go whenever she looked back. She'd tried talking to him at first – everything she'd read always stressed the importance of making a connection with an abductor – but Neil ignored everything she said. His only response was that creepy smile he'd greeted her with at the trailhead. As the trail got rougher Alyssa stopped trying to talk and put all her energy to keeping her balance on the uneven rocky trail.

Once they'd reached the cabin, he'd said just two words, 'in' and 'sit', before giving her the instructions not to scream. Alyssa decided when he came back, she would try once more to get him talking, find out what he wanted, and see if an offer of money would convince him to let her go. Maybe he was just one of those kooks who hate the world and want everyone to know it. She could offer him a chance to publish his story. Fighting to keep calm, she closed her eyes and practiced some deep breathing exercises.

He made another circuit around the cabin, satisfied with his arrangements. After watching the Crew prepare for their search and rescues and hearing about others, he knew it would take some time for all the different first responder teams to get moving. And then it would take time to decide where to search. The mountains that made up the state and national parks in this area covered a vast territory and there was nothing to point them in this direction. The woman's distinctive car wasn't visible from the road and since no one knew of his connection with her, nothing should point the searchers his way for hours, if not days. He thought he could safely count on at least twelve hours before anyone disturbed them and that was all he needed.

He'd made his plans last night. Missy had been a personal connection, so it had been fitting that he'd used his bare hands for her.

This woman wasn't personal, so he'd decided to use tools for her. He would finish by the time darkness fell and be gone. And since he didn't plan to ever be found, much less return to this area, he didn't need to concern himself with how he left the place. He only needed to concentrate on his mission.

He squinted up at the sun. It was time to begin.

Alyssa opened her eyes when she heard the door open. Time to put her plan into action. "Neil, what is this place? Did you build it?" First tactic, flatter him.

No response. She swallowed and tried again. "Do you live here full time?"

This time she got a snort of derision. At least it was a response. Heartened, she tried again. "Did you know I'm a reporter? For a big New York paper. I can help you get what you want."

Another snort. That showed he was listening. "The thing is, you have to tell me what it is. Money? Celebrity status? I could do an exclusive story about you and make you famous."

He turned and opened his mouth to speak, then closed his mouth and turned away. Alyssa decided she was on the right track. "I know people would be interested to hear your story. I could tell it and make sure people get to read it."

That finally got him. "My story? MY STORY? You have no idea what you're dealing with. And you don't realize you are going to be part of it!"

He was shouting now, coming closer and closer, screaming as he went, until he could rest his hands on her arms. Alyssa could feel the heat through the duct tape and strained back away from his hate-distorted face.

She dared to presume she could take him and smear his life across her pretentious magazine to be defiled by millions of cheap thrill seekers? Did she think that kind of shallow thrill was what he was after? He welcomed the anger her inane questions brought. It added heat to his fire. He'd found himself delaying the start, feeling intimidated by her looks and polish. He must not let those feelings desecrate this spot and his memories. She was nothing compared to his Missy, and he'd make sure she understood this before he was through!

Alyssa slid down in the chair, straining against the duct tape, trying to escape his furious face and burning eyes, wondering what had triggered the change from disdainful detachment to enraged aggression. His hysterical voice filled her ears and she closed her eyes and turned her head away, but he grabbed her hair and dragged her back to face him.

"You stupid bitch! You don't understand anything about me! You think you can reduce me to a few words on a page? You think you can begin to understand Missy and me and how it was between us? Do you think you can comprehend the reasons she had to die and the beauty it brought to her and the peace it brought to me?"

The name Missy and the word die slammed into Alyssa's brain. Could there be two dead girls named Missy in this area? No, someone would have mentioned that. And what did he say about she had to die? Could he be the one responsible? She opened her eyes and looked with terror at the man in front of her. An avalanche of fear, horror, anger and despair started in her gut and came roaring up through her chest. "YOU! YOU KILLED MISSY? YOU MISERABLE WORM! HOW DARE YOU!"

Neil reeled back, shocked by Alyssa's reaction. She tried to hold on to her advantage. "Missy was a sweet, warm, loving person. How could you kill her? HOW COULD YOU?"

"You...you knew her?"

Alyssa's mind raced. How could she turn this to her advantage? Take the truth and twist it just a little. "Of course I did. I know her mother. I've been to her house." Alyssa paused, Neil was standing with his back to her, hands covering his ears – she wasn't sure where to go next. Her gut said keep him off balance so she changed tactics, lowered her voice and asked urgently, "Tell me Neil, tell me how it happened."

"She wanted to leave...she wouldn't stay" he said slowly. "I had everything all set for us and she didn't want it..."

The silence stretched between them and Alyssa tried to connect again. "Why Neil, why wouldn't she stay?" There was no answer. She'd pushed too far. He'd retreated into himself and his silence screamed her failure.

He turned away trying to collect his scattered thoughts. This woman was Missy's friend? Had been to her house? Could it be? Or were these just more lies? No, it was all lies. When she'd first come here, Missy had talked – about her life, her lack of friends, how lonely she was – so this woman was definitely lying. It was all a trick. And she deserved punishment for tricking him. That meant he could still follow his plan, still finish his job and reach his goal. He felt for his knife in its sheath. It was time.

Alyssa watched him lift his head, slowly lower his hands and reach in toward his waist. When his hand reappeared holding his knife, she knew she had lost. Suddenly voiceless, she struggled frantically against the duct tape as he walked slowly toward her. He stopped in front of her and smiled, slowly stroking the knife. She looked away from the gloating expression on his face to see the door, slowly easing open. Something in her expression must have alerted him, and he spun away from her, lunging for the gun leaning against the wall.

CHAPTER THIRTY-ONE

Cliff had decided to use the parking area at the Skookumchuck trail head as his command center. He and Mike arrived there, with Nelson and Kurt in tow, and completed a fast reconnoiter of the scene.

Alyssa's car remained undisturbed but now it had company, a blue sedan with rental plates. Kurt turned to Mike. "Run the plate and find out who signed it out. I don't want any civilians caught up in this, or if this guy has an accomplice, I want to know that too."

Mike checked his watch. "It's after five, might take some time to track down the rental info."

"Call in some local talent to rattle the cage. We can't wait around."

The first cars were starting to pull into the parking area, lights flashing but sirens off, as troopers, fish and game patrol, conservation officers, and police from the surrounding towns arrived to give support. They clustered around Cliff as he took out his topo map and spread it out on the hood of his cruiser. He placed one finger on the parking area and one on the general location of the cabin.

"Here's our goal. It's a fourteen by fourteen log cabin with one point of egress, a single wide solid wood door facing in the direction of the trail and two glass windows, one next to the door and the other on the opposite wall. Both are to the left of the cabin as you look at it.

The cabin sits in a small clearing surrounded by tall pines." Cliff paused a minute and looked over his shoulder, working to keep focused on the current case. He hadn't been back to the cabin since that night almost thirty years ago....and having it feature in this current case strained his sense of focus.

Kurt and Nelson were standing on the outer fringe of the group, far enough away to avoid seeming part of it, bur close enough to hear what Cliff was saying. Cliff nodded at Kurt. "You have anything to add to that?"

"Couple trees have fallen around the clearing in that big windstorm last year, but didn't touch the cabin. Windows are still intact, they're typical double hung type and could open last I knew."

Kurt stepped back as Cliff continued. "We've got a missing person situation. Female reporter named Alyssa was last seen around one o'clock this afternoon in Lincoln, driving off from the Mountain Glenn Inn. Her stated plan was to travel around town, photographing local landmarks for an hour and then return to the Inn and pick up her companion, another reporter named Nelson."

Kurt nodded over toward Nelson, and heads swiveled toward him and back again. "She never showed. Her companion brought his concerns about her to us. At the same time, Kurt reported a missing employee and a missing rifle – a thirty aught six." There were a few low whistles and shifting feet. Everyone's attention intensified.

"This missing employee knows of the cabin in question and has been using it sporadically to camp out in."

A hand rose in the middle of the group. "Does this employee have any kind of record or history of violence?"

Cliff kept his voice as neutral as possible. "We know nothing of this employee's background, not even his name." Another murmur greeted this information and a few head shakes; Kurt's hiring practices were well known in the area. "However," Cliff continued, speaking over the comments, "He's worked for Kurt for eight months without any signs of trouble."

Cliff paused to collect his thoughts. "Right now we're not completely sure what we're looking at. Could be as simple as an inexperienced hiker – the woman – lost in the woods and the employee coincidentally took off with Kurt's rifle at the same time, but I don't like coincidences, so we're going to treat this as abduction by an armed and potentially dangerous young man until we know different. That means everyone should be geared up. Local people – I want vests on everyone."

"The plan is to move in and surround the cabin as quietly as possible...."

****

Nelson stood on the fringes of the group, listening as Cliff started making individual assignments. He was reluctantly impressed with Cliff's handling of the situation; having worried that Cliff would dismiss his concerns out of hand based on their former verbal clashes. But, to his credit, once Cliff understood that Alyssa was missing and the circumstances surrounding her disappearance, he'd become completely and reassuringly professional.

As his attention wandered, he began alternately looking at Alyssa's car and then up toward the start of the trail. It was tough to stay focused on what Cliff was saying; disturbing pictures of Alyssa in a variety of possibly dangerous situations kept intruding. And he felt a bit disoriented. He'd been in on plenty of stake-outs and hostage command posts during his newspaper career and had even won awards for his reporting detailing the emotions of the waiting family members. Now he realized he'd never even come close to understanding their true feelings.

Kurt leaned over toward him. "Steady son. We've got a good team here and with Cliff heading it the chances are good they'll bring your lady back unharmed."

Nelson swallowed and nodded, thinking of how much Kurt's attitude had changed once he realized Alyssa was caught up in his employee's disappearance. It was both comforting and alarming – Nelson worried his kindness was due solely to his anticipation of a tragic outcome. And he couldn't bear to consider that.

The group in front of him was breaking apart, and people were heading out in to the woods in different directions. Nelson took and instinctive step forward, but froze when Kurt's hand fell lightly on his shoulder. "Stand back and let them do their work. You'd be an obstacle if you were out there – one more thing for them to worry about."

"Are they all going out to that cabin?"

"Some. The largest group, that's the sharp shooters and most experienced members of the SWAT team. They're going to bushwhack through to the cabin and surround it, hopefully undetected. The smaller groups leaving after them are with Fish and Game. They're going to fan out through the woods to make sure your lady didn't just stray off the path and get hurt somehow and unable to get back to her car." Nelson flushed and wiped the sheen of sweat off his upper lip. He didn't want to think of Alyssa being hurt or how that might happen with an armed mystery man apparently roaming the countryside.

"Tell me about this employee that's missing." Nelson wanted to keep Kurt talking, now that he appeared to be in the mood. Anything distraction would help.

Kurt shrugged. "You heard what I told Cliff and Mike."

"What's he look like?"

"Tall, skinny, kind of stoops when he stands. Dark hair and eyes. Stares at people a lot. Looks gawky and uncoordinated, but he's not."

"Wait a minute, we might have met him. In one of the bars around here, the Dewdrop Inn. I was getting a couple drinks from the bar and when I came back he was talking to Alyssa. He was wearing a long ratty black leather coat. I didn't like the look of him so I chased him off and never gave it another thought."

Kurt's shoulders sagged slightly. "That was him. That black coat is all he ever wears. C'mon, we better go over and tell Cliff."

Cliff listened in silence to the update. "I'll send the info on as a heads up to everyone." He switched his phone to text mode, then reached irritably into the squad car for his glasses case. Propping them on his nose, he typed out a quick message.

Nelson had to ask. "Any news yet?"

Cliff shook his head and turned away. Nelson rubbed the back of his hand across his mouth to disguise a sudden tremble.

Kurt led him back to the second squad car. "No news could be good. Means they haven't found any bodies."

Nelson stared – was the man trying to be cruel? But under Kurt's level stare, realized he was just telling the truth. He took a deep breath to ask him how many bodies he'd found in his rescue career when the radio in Cliff's squad car crackled to life.

Both Nelson and Kurt watched Cliff bend down and pick up the handset. It looked like he was arguing with whoever was on the other end, looking over at the other car in the parking lot as he did so. He finally hung up and stood looking from the car to Nelson and back for a moment and then started across the parking lot toward him.

"Nelson, what did you and Alyssa do after you left my office this morning?"

"Went to interview the guy who found the body last week. I meant to thank you for that, one of the worst time wastes in my entire journalistic career." His annoyance at the hoax reverberated in his voice even in this situation. "Why?"

"Did Alyssa come with you?"

"Of course she did." Nelson snapped. He couldn't understand why Cliff would be bringing this up now; surely there were more important issues to deal with?

"And how did she get along with Brainerd?"

Nelson threw up his hands. "What the hell does this have to do with anything?"

"Just answer the question."

Giving an exaggerated sigh, Nelson said, "She didn't say much during the first part of the interview. Once it became clear that he had absolutely nothing useful to tell us, I sat back to figure out how to get us away from that blabbermouth and he turned his attention to Alyssa. I remember I even teased her about it on the way to lunch."

"And what was her reaction to him?"

"She thought he was a big bag of wind and was happy to get away from him."

"Did either of you have any contact with him after that?"

"Of course not. We wanted to use our time productively, not waste it, like you are doing with all these ridiculous questions. What is going on?"

Cliff took a deep breath of air and blew it out through his lips. "Because that rental car over there is registered to Kenny Brainerd and I'm trying to figure out what the hell it's doing here and if there's any connection between him and our two missing persons."

Cliff turned to Kurt next. "Did you notice any contact between the two men when Brainerd stayed at your hotel?"

"No. All the staff avoided Brainerd as much as they could for the same reasons Nelson here mentioned. And our missing guy Neil or Neo, or whoever he turns out to be had less contact with the guests than most."

"Why was that?"

"Poor social skills or just plain pigheadedness. He wouldn't talk to people or even answer direct questions. We got complaints. So we moved him to dishwasher and after hour's jobs like setting the tables for breakfast and cleaning the bar." Kurt stopped and shook his head. "Saying all this now, it seems so obvious that he was a lost cause who needed to be cut loose. I don't know why I didn't see the danger sooner."

Cliff turned away, thinking this might be the second case where blood indirectly stained the old man's hands. He hoped Kurt's habit of not seeing his "strays" as they really were and allowing them too much freedom hadn't paved the way for another body – or two.

CHAPTER THIRTY-TWO

Kenny's adventure had started off so well. The Skookumchuck Trail parking area had been easy to find and uncrowded, with only one other car in the parking area. It was a cute little red car that Kenny felt he might have seen somewhere before, but dismissed the idea in order to concentrate on the task at hand.

The trail leading into the woods was fairly level – something Kenny was thankful for after the grueling climb on Lafayette the week before – and he occupied his walking time imagining the glory that finding a second body would bring. He'd just gotten to the part where the President was awarding him a medal with the entire ceremony televised, when he reached a turn off on the right of the trail. It matched the description of the side trail he'd overheard Kurt talking about, so he blithely turned off onto the side track. Trying hard to recall what his survival manuals said, he scanned the trail and vegetation around him. Finding nothing that looked remotely like evidence, he settled for following the trail until he found some kind of cabin.

Stopping in the shade of some pines to cool down a bit, he thought he heard a man shouting off to the right of the trail. Holding his breath to listen, he thought he heard a woman shouting as well. Immediately deciding to switch roles from body finder to rescuer,

Kenny pushed his way through the evergreens toward the sound of the voices. They'd stopped now, but he could see the outline of a house ahead through the trees.

Stepping past the last of the bushes he looked doubtfully at the structure in front of him. It looked old and grimy and deserted, in fact it matched Kurt's description of the perfect place to find a body. Finding the reality a lot less appealing than the imagining, Kenny crept up, eased the cabin door open with two fingers and peered inside. It took a minute for his eyes to adjust to the darkness and they crossed once they did, focusing on the long barrel of a very big gun pointed right at his nose. Kenny froze, trying to grasp the fact that instead of finding a body in the cabin, he might become one. The thought left him speechless. But not for long.

"Are you alone?" the man with the gun growled at Kenny, then repeated the question in a shout when Kenny didn't answer immediately. "ARE YOU ALONE?"

"Y...yes," Kenny stuttered, and the man backed two steps away from him and demanded "Get in here." When Kenny hesitated, finally starting to realize that whatever was going on here, it wasn't good, the man screamed "GET IN HERE!" again and poked the gun forward at him. Kenny got the hint and scuttled inside.

The man with the gun kicked the door closed and said, "Over there!" swinging the gun from Kenny's face to a chair next to a round table and back again. Kenny looked over and finally noticed there was a woman in the room as well. It looked like...it was! The pretty woman from the interview earlier!

"Oh hi! I waited for you before but you never came back." He exclaimed, with an involuntary smile, which faded under the twin effects of seeing her duct taped to her chair and having the man with the gun scream at him "SHUT UP!" He froze, unsure what to do next, but the man solved that dilemma, telling him to sit in the only remaining chair and not to move. Kenny followed the instruction, but decided it was important to tell the gunman that this was all a terrible mistake and he didn't mean any harm, he'd just been misinformed. Taking a deep breath, he said, "Let me explain..."

He stood looking at the fat fool in the chair next to the woman and tried to revise his plan to include this sudden interruption. He needed to know how this chubby idiot found them, if he was alone, and how he knew the woman. He narrowed his eyes as he looked at them. Were they in this together? Had fatty told anyone else about his plans? All these questions were harder to think through because the guy hadn't shut up almost since he'd walked through the door.

The easiest thing to do would be to shoot them both now, and get as far away from the area as possible. The problem was, he'd rehearsed what he wanted to do to the woman in his mind so often and anticipated how it would feel so completely that he didn't want to let it go. Killing Missy had been so fast, he'd grabbed her throat and it had been over in under a minute. He'd wanted to savor killing this woman, but he couldn't do that with this idiot blabbering away next to her. He needed to create the mood and have a chance to enjoy it.

Alyssa thought she'd lost her increasingly tenuous grip on reality when Kenny walked through the door. Her mind tried to grapple with the implications. How did he know they were here? Was he part of the rescue team? No, worse than ridiculous. Could he be in league with the gunman? Was the whole interview they did with him earlier and elaborate hoax? And why couldn't he just shut up for five minutes so she could think?

****

Kenny's story had gotten to the point of explaining why he'd decided to go see Kurt before the man reacted. "Shut up!" he hissed at Kenny, advancing a step with the gun rising from Kenny's nose to a spot on his forehead. "Shut up a minute for God's sake or I'll shoot you right now!"

Kenny nodded earnestly. "Sure, I'll shut up, I'm glad to shut up because I know sometimes it's hard to concentrate when there's a lot of noise. When I'm at work I wear noise-cancelling headphones a lot because....."

****

Cliff had placed a late arriving trooper at the communication post in his squad car and headed rapidly up the trail, letting the team know he was on his way with new information. They'd radioed back that they were in position around the cabin and the path in was clear. Mike came part way back to meet him.

"Status?" Cliff asked, trying to control his breathing after the race-walk up the trail.

"Voices inside, more than one speaker but hard to tell what they're saying with the door and window closed. We hear an occasional angry shout, however no shots or screams."

"Can you tell if there are more than two voices?"

Mike's eyebrows climbed up his forehead. "You think there's a third person involved?"

Cliff told him about Kenny Brainerd's car in the parking area.

"Holy shit," Mike murmured. "We just can't get rid of this guy!" He thought a moment. "Do you want to try to talk to whoever is in there?"

"I want to know who's in there before we do anything else. I need to know if Alyssa is there, still alive, and where Brainerd fits into this whole scene. For all we know Brainerd's a homicidal maniac who's working with this creep from the Inn."

Mike nodded. "The back of the cabin is a north east exposure so it's deep in shadow now. They lit some kind of lamp about ten minutes ago, I'm going to sneak around back and look inside. Unless someone's standing right at that window, I'll be able to see in without anyone seeing me."

"Okay, just be careful. I don't want any heroes."

"Bloyer," Mike said and crept around the back of the cabin. He returned in under five minutes and Cliff signaled two squad leaders over to listen to the report. "Here's what we've got. The reporter, Alyssa, and the guy from the rental car, Kenny, are immobilized on two chairs with duct tape, the gunman's standing in front of them with his gun on Kenny, looking pissed while Kenny rambles on."

"How far is the gunman from the two hostages?"

"About six feet."

"How's the angle for a shot?"

"Good."

"Fine, get one of the sharp shooters back there. Once he's in position, I'll try to talk the gunman out. But if he threatens our hostages, take him down."

"Gotcha," Mike said, and melted back into the trees.

Five minutes later, Cliff's radio clicked twice to let him know everything was in place. Clicking back once in reply, he took a deep breath and brought the megaphone to his lips.

As he depressed the button to talk, and earsplitting shout broke out from inside the cabin, incoherent at first then resolving into two words repeated over and over. "Shut Up, SHUT UP, **SHUT UP, SHUT UP!!"** follow by a sustained piercing scream. Cliff whipped the radio to his mouth and shouted "GO!" into it.

A single shot rang out and in the silence afterwards, they heard a woman's voice crying "Oh God, Oh God, Oh God" on a rising crescendo.

Cliff's radio crackled and Mike's voice shouted, "Clear!" and two troopers ran to the door and kicked it open, taking stances on either side of the door with weapons drawn. Cliff followed close behind and at a nod from one of the officers, stepped through the door. The gunman lay on the floor unmoving. The sharpshooter had done his work well. Alyssa sobbed quietly in one chair, while Kenny sat completely silent, having fainted dead away.

CHAPTER THIRTY-THREE

Afterwards – when all the other officers had returned to their respective jurisdictions, when the crime scene people had done their job, when Dr. Harris arrived to declare the shooter and make appropriate arrangements to transport the body back to her office, and when Kenny had been transported to the local hospital to be treated for shock all the while telling his story in excruciating detail to the EMT's – Cliff, Mike, Nelson, Alyssa, and Kurt sat down in the conference room to debrief.

Alyssa sat curled inside the curve of Nelson's arm and reviewed her side of the story, from finding the gunman's letter wedged in her car door, until he snapped while listening to Kenny's unceasing chatter.

"He pointed the gun right at Kenny's forehead and told him to shut up and Kenny kept right on going!" Alyssa shuddered and Nelson stroked her arm. "So he started telling Kenny to shut up, and each time he said it he stepped closer and closer and got louder and louder and his face got redder and redder and then there was a loud bang and when I looked over they both were slumped over in a heap. At first I didn't even know who'd been shot!"

"I can almost feel sorry for the guy," Mike said. "To be trapped in a cabin with Kenny talking and talking and no end in sight? I might snap too."

"Kenny saved my life." Alyssa said flatly. "That madman was about to come at me with his knife when Kenny opened the door." Nelson gave her shoulders a brief squeeze while they all thought about the other possible ending to the day's events. "Will we ever find out who that guy was and why he wanted to kill me?"

"We know he killed Missy Baxter," Cliff told them. "Her shoes were hanging on the wall of the cabin, like a trophy."

"I know," Alyssa covered her face with her hands. "I saw then there and wondered. And then later he started screaming at me about 'Missy' and I made the connection." Nelson gave her another squeeze and she finally lowered her hands. "Do we know what happened? Why he did what he did....?"

Cliff shook his head. "We'll never know for certain now. My guess is this: After talking to Jimmy on the Dalton road crew, Missy decided to go meet him at the Mooseland Grill. This guy calling himself Neo or Neil or whatever seems to have already been at the Grill and hooked up with her instead, convincing her to leave with him. Jimmy showed up fifteen minutes later, but at that point they were long gone."

Alyssa sighed. "If only it had been the other way....she might be safely married by now. Instead...?"

"I'd guess he took her to the cabin that night. She may have lived there happily for a few weeks or even months. Maybe this creep fed her some kind of story that kept her happy – some 'back to the land we don't need anyone but us' philosophy or something like that."

"Amazing that a nice smart young woman would buy into that," Mike said. "You'd think she'd meet him and immediately run the other way."

Alyssa shuddered. "He had a weird mesmerizing way of sucking you in." They all turned to look at her and she flushed. "If I could feel in the ten minutes we talked at the Dewdrop Inn, imagine how it would affect a younger girl without much worldly experience."

"My guess is that eventually she got tired of the cold and the isolation..."

"And the lack of indoor plumbing" Alyssa muttered.

"....and she tried to leave. He grabbed her with his large hands around her small neck," Cliff paused. "I'm sure it was over quickly."

After a small silence, Alyssa asked. "Then why did he have the knife out for me?"

Cliff sighed and pushed his glasses around on his desk. "An escalating desire to kill in a more dramatic way. Lack of personal connection. An accelerating descent into mental illness. A power trip. Take your pick. It could be any of the above or a combination of a few different ones." He stopped and picked up Bonner's sketch of Missy. "Like I said, we'll never really know."

Taking a deep breath and squaring his shoulders, Cliff shifted to professional mode and looked at the others in the room. "We'll be taking official statements that we'll have typed up and ask you to sign. Then you'll be free to leave."

He looked over at Nelson. "And now you have your story, with all the details you could possibly desire."

Nelson shook his head. "Too high a price. I'm going back to reporting something safer – like mobsters or drug cartels."

"But I'll write the story," Alyssa said, to surprised looks from everyone, Nelson most of all. "Two stories, actually. One about Missy, tracing the last year of her life and outlining all the dangers a runaway can face. And the other one," she gave the start of a smile, "about Kenny. Give him the moment in the spotlight he so desperately wants." The smile faded away. "It's the least I can do to thank him for saving me."

Nelson and Alyssa said their goodbyes and headed back to their motel.

After they left, Cliff caught Mike's eye then looked over at Kurt and back again. Mike got the hint immediately.

"I'll see you in the AM, then, and we'll start on the paperwork for this mess."

"Sounds good. We can call the hospital in the morning to get a status report on Brainerd. See if he's up to making a statement."

Mike looked at the ceiling. "Something to look forward to."

"We can tell him to keep it brief and save his strength for Alyssa's interview and newspaper story..."

"Brilliant idea. Maybe that way we can get out of there in under two hours." Sketching a wave cum salute, Mike left, closing the door softly behind him.

Cliff finally turned to Kurt, who'd sat silent and preoccupied during the whole discussion. "And we can find you at the Inn if we need you?"

Kurt nodded. "For now."

Cliff studied the older man. "Meaning?"

"Meaning it's time for me to retire. I kept that boy there at the Inn, made excuses for him, ignored his bizarre behaviors and didn't see any of this coming. My judgment obviously isn't what it used to be and it's time to pack it in." He paused as if waiting for Cliff to disagree, but continued, shoulders sagging, when he didn't. "I'll put the place up for sale. I've got a sister downstate who keeps asking me to come and stay with her. I might take her up on that."

He stood to leave and Cliff asked, "You need a ride?"

Kurt hesitated, and then squared his shoulders and shook his head. "I said I'm retiring, not going senile or dying."

Cliff watched the older man leave then picked up the sketch of Missy, put it in his bottom drawer, turned out his desk lamp and headed home.

CHAPTER THIRTY-FOUR

Over a late dinner, Cliff gave his family an abbreviated version of the day, emphasizing and underlining the dangers a young runaway could face without dwelling on the details. Both his daughters listened straight-faced and sober-eyed before heading upstairs for the rest of the evening. Cliff moved on to the couch in the den where Anna joined him.

"This was a rough one for you, wasn't it," she asked, settling sideways on the couch and tucking her feet up under her. "Why this one more than the others? Was it having to deal with Kurt?"

"Not just that." Cliff sat silently for a minute then reached out to place a hand on Anna's knee. "It was the combination of Kurt and that damned cabin."

"What does the cabin have to do with anything?"

"That's not the first body Kurt and I have dealt with out at that cabin." Taking a deep breath, Cliff said, "Let me tell you about a guy we called Phil who used to hang with the Crew back when I was with them. He just drifted in one day and never really left."

"But who was he? Did he have a last name?"

Cliff shook his head. "If he did, he wasn't telling. But remember, we were a group of young punks playing at being macho. We didn't talk much about our history, just bragged about the things we thought we were going to do."

"And you never knew anything else about him?" Anna said, "Just a nickname?"

"Back then things were a lot looser. You could still hitchhike around the country in relative safety, and setting off to 'find yourself' was considered admirable. So Phil hitched a ride up here to the mountains and ended up on Kurt's doorstep, like most of the penniless waifs and strays did. Kurt took him in as an honorary member of the Crew. We didn't know if he would stay that long, but he we enjoyed his company while he was there."

"How did the cabin tie in to everything?"

Cliff sighed. "Another good idea gone bad. It had been built by squatters back in the sixties using trees they had felled by hand, very self-sufficient and pioneer-ish. Then when the park service took over the land, they ejected the squatters and the cabin started to decay. Kurt had the idea – and in theory, it was a good one – to restore the cabin and use it as a kind of home away from home when the Crew was doing a rescue."

"Sounds reasonable," Anna said. "What was the problem?"

"As you know, our group was a bit wilder in those days. We were all young and Kurt encouraged a bit of competition within the group – he called it 'keeping your edge' – and we'd do stupid stuff like see how fast we could hike up steep trails or who could build the best survival shelter and then who could stay in it longest during freezing weather. We'd make bets on who could snow shoe the farthest and the fastest or who was the best skier – downhill and cross country. Basically we'd work on any skills we might need on a rescue."

Anna nodded, "And in the meantime, he used it as a harmless way for you guys to burn off excess energy."

"Exactly. And it worked just fine until Phil joined us. Somehow he changed the dynamic. He was a little bit wilder, a bigger risk taker, and less worried about consequences, just enough to push us past the boundaries of reasonable. He suggested using the cabin as a kind of clubhouse between rescues, a place to get away and blow off steam. We already had all our rescue stuff there: food, lanterns, portable stoves, sleeping bags; he added booze to the mix. It turned out to be a deadly combination."

Cliff shook his head and continued. "We were all up there one night drinking and someone got the bright idea to have a tree climbing contest. In the dark. Without any safety gear. It went against everything Kurt had taught us, but Phil wouldn't let it drop. So we all piled out of the cabin, too drunk to think anything through, and started swarming up the trees around the cabin. Phil wasn't a big guy so he was able to climb higher than all of us. He couldn't beat us that often, so he was really rubbing it in, hanging off the edge of a branch like a goddamn monkey. Until the branch broke and he fell on to some rocks. He hit his head and died instantly."

Anna slid her hand into Cliff's.

"The accident sobered some of us up and made the rest of us hysterical. Me and another guy went tearing into town to get Kurt."

"Not the police?" Anna said.

"No, remember there wasn't any 9-1-1 to call back then and anyway, we'd been conditioned to bring all our problems to Kurt. He came up, looked at us all, wasted and out of our heads and made us drink gallons of coffee. Once we'd calmed down and sobered up a bit, he told us we were going to take a night hike up Lafayette and put Phil's body down a crevice."

"Oh dear Lord. What was he thinking to suggest a thing like that?"

"I'd say it was an equal mix of altruism and self-preservation. He didn't want to put us through the trauma of possible trial, and he also didn't want to damage the good name of his Crew. So we did what he told us to and promised never to mention it again, even among ourselves."

"What a wicked thing to do to a bunch of kids barely out of adolescence!"

"Like I said, back then people didn't know about post-traumatic stress or the long term effects of guilt. Phil's death helped bond some of the Crew closer and it drove others, like me, out and away. The ones that stayed settled down and have done some great work over the years."

"As you have, in your job." Anna put her other hand on top of Cliff's and squeezed. "I'm glad to finally hear the story."

"And I'm glad to have it out in the open so I can get it out of my system." Cliff looked down at their clasped hands. "I just wish we could have arranged something better for him than that dark and lonely place up on Lafayette."

Anna smiled. "It's not too late. You can do something now."

****

Two weeks later, Cliff and Anna stood together with Kurt, Duane and four other members of the original Crew at the conclusion of a memorial service for the man known only as 'Phil'– he'd told everyone to call him that because he came from Philadelphia.

"What's haunted me most for all those years, is wondering if he had any family – parents, brothers, sisters, or even grandparents, aunts, uncles and cousins – who have been wondering and worrying about him all this time." Cliff looked up at Mount Lafayette. "In a way, we were no better than that drifter Neo was. He left Missy Baxter up on Lafayette and we did the same to Phil."

Kurt cleared his throat. "It was wrong. And I knew it almost immediately, but by then it was too late to get his body back. I did the wrong thing, but it was for the right reason. I didn't want any of you boys ruining your futures with a trial and all the publicity that would go along with it. I wanted to protect all of you."

"I know you did your best, Kurt." Duane looked around Kurt's back and nodded at Cliff and the rest of the Crew. "Right?"

Cliff answered for the rest of them. "I know you meant well and I'm sure it seemed right at the time. You did the wrong thing for a good reason and I think we've all come to realize that."

Kurt bowed his head and nodded twice. "I appreciate you organizing this and for taking the point on getting the headstone."

They all looked over at the simple two foot by two foot stone that read "In Memory of Phil – a high climber".

"Rest in peace," Duane said, and the others followed suit and drifted away. Anna followed, leaving Kurt facing Cliff across the stone.

"I found a buyer for the Inn. We should have the deal wrapped up in the next few weeks then I'm headed downstate to my sister's."

"You okay with that?"

Kurt shrugged slightly. "It's time. I've been thinking of going for a while. This" he nodded down at the stone, "makes it easier."

"It makes a lot of things easier." Cliff stopped and looked down toward the parking lot where Anna stood waiting, then back at Kurt. "I thought you might like to come to dinner tomorrow evening. Talk over old times."

Kurt lifted his chin and studied Cliff for a moment. "Sure."

"I'd like you to meet my daughters."

"So you've got girls." Kurt's lip twitched. "You always did do things a bit half-assed."

Cliff bit the inside of his cheek, looked away until he had his expression under control, and then back again. "And you never missed a chance to tell me about it. Now let's go home."

CHAPTER THIRTY-FIVE

Two hundred and fifty miles away, Nelson and Alyssa were also attending a memorial service.

Two weeks before, on their way home from New Hampshire, they'd stopped in Riverdale to see Missy's mother, Mandy Baxter. Mandy had let them in and listened to all they had to tell her about her daughter's life after leaving home, but had been surprisingly quiet, almost indifferent.

"You'd think she'd have more questions," Alyssa muttered as they left the house. "At least a thank you for stopping and solving the mystery would have been nice."

"It's shock." They reached the car and Nelson opened and held the driver's side door for Alyssa. "I've seen this before. People put their grief into a little compartment to make it bearable and wall it away. Then we come along and break the compartment open with a jack hammer."

"I tried to say it all as gently as I could and emphasize the positive points." Alyssa waited as Nelson went around to the other side of the car and slid in beside her. "I thought it would help to hear the details in person."

"It's too soon. Later she might thank you or want to ask questions, but right now....she's just trying to come to grips with it."

Alyssa frowned up at the house as she started the car. "I hate to think of her all alone up there."

"Remember our talkative friend Jeanine from across the street? I think she'd perform the role of supportive emotional prop for tonight. What do you think?"

Jeanine had been just the right person for the job. She'd bustled right across the street and promised Nelson and Alyssa frequent updates on the trajectory of Mandy's grief. She'd also done all the public work to help Mandy organize the memorial service and fiercely fought to keep all media attention at bay. Except, of course, for Nelson and Alyssa. The subject of who would write what type of article came to a head when Jeanine – speaking for Mandy – asked them to come over and take her through all they knew about Missy's time in New Hampshire.

"....and the young man was killed by the sniper after he'd kidnapped Alyssa." Nelson finished the story, leaned back and waited for questions.

"No one ever knew his name or anything about him?"

Nelson shook his head. "I followed up with Trooper Codey last week. They said they'd run his prints but didn't get any matches. They'd also looked into all the missing persons' databases without any luck. So no one really knows anything more about him than what he told them."

Mandy sat silently for a moment. "Except that he killed my daughter. And I'll never know why."

Alyssa leaned forward. "I don't think he meant to. I think he'd built up a fantasy where they would live together in this cabin and have no contact with the outside world. But Missy didn't want that. And when she told Neil, I think he lost his temper and killed her without meaning too. Afterward, I think the guilt from knowing what he'd done overwhelmed him and broke his final contact with reality."

"Thank you, Alyssa. It's easier to think about it that way." Mandy sighed and looked up at the two reporters. "Is that how you'll write about it in your article?"

Nelson shook his head. "Not me. I'm done glamorizing these animals who prey on young women. But...." He looked over at Alyssa.

"I'm going to write about Missy and only Missy. I want to spell out what can happen to a young woman who thinks she can solve her problems by leaving home for a life on the streets. And how disastrously wrong a decision to do that can be." She looked over at Mandy. "I'd like to use some pictures of your house for background, with your permission."

Mandy nodded and rose to her feet. "Of course. Whatever you think will help."

****

The limited publicity for the memorial service kept the crowd to a minimum, making it easier for Nelson and Alyssa to spot Jerry, their editor, skulking in the back. After paying their final respects to Mandy, Nelson strolled over to join Jerry on the park bench he'd commandeered.

"Didn't expect to see you here, Jerry." Nelson settled down next to his boss and spent a few minutes tugging the creases in his sleeves and pants legs into alignment. "I wasn't sure you could be seen outside in daylight."

"Always the wise-ass." Jerry nodded briefly at Alyssa, who waved and loitered just in earshot, pretending to look at the gravestones. "I came to see what other power people would be at the funeral. Recognized a couple of faces. I assume you'll be playing up that angle? All the money in the world can't keep someone safe – use a little fear to titillate masses."

"Nope"

Jerry waited, but when Nelson didn't continue, he finally asked, "Then what?"

"Then nothing. I'm not writing the article."

"Very funny. If this is your way of asking for a raise, forget it. You should know by now that I don't respond well to threats."

"This is no threat. It's fact. I've changed my mind and I'm not going to write this article. At all."

"C'mon Nelson. You've been salivating over this thing for almost a month. Not to mention all the time you've taken with trips practically up into Canada. You owe me this."

"Then dock my pay. I'm not doing it and there's no point in discussing it further."

"Dock your pay?" Jerry snarled. "How about I cut it off entirely and tell you to take your smart-ass mouth and attitude out of my magazine? In case you've forgotten, this is how it works. I hand out assignments and you do them. Got that?"

Nelson braced his hands on his knees and met Jerry's glare calmly. "Nope, not anymore. I'm through. I'm done working for you and tiptoeing around your moods. I'm tired of taking crap from you."

"You throw a bunch of your own crap around Nelson, and you won't find anyone else around here that's going to take it from you. I can guarantee that."

"I can live with that. I'll be around to clear out my desk in the morning." Nelson stood up, nodded goodbye and went to join Alyssa, leaving Jerry glowering alone on the bench.

"Did you really mean to do that?" Alyssa asked as they reached her car. "You could probably have gotten out of the article by saying Mandy threatened a lawsuit over it. She'd support you if you asked her."

"I didn't go over to Jerry with the intention to quit, but once he started in with his usual garbage, I suddenly felt that I couldn't stand another day of it. So I quit. And no," Nelson said, smiling into Alyssa's worried face, "it has nothing to do with you selling Missy's story to someone else. Although I'd love to see Jerry's face when he learns about that!" Turning serious, he continued, "You know you won't be able to stay either once Jerry finds out."

"I know. But I think I'm ready to try freelance for a bit. What about you?"

"It might be time to try that book I've been thinking about. Who knows? Could be a whole new direction for both of us."

About the Author

Cathy Strasser lives in Sugar Hill, New Hampshire with her husband and two dogs. Her hobbies are hiking, gardening and writing. This is her first crime novel.